The Beauty of the Beast

A CONTEMPORARY FAIRYTALE MM ROMANCE

EVER AFTER SERIES

GABBI GREY

Blurb

DEAN

All my life, I dreamed about making the long trip from Australia to Canada to study forestry amid the old-growth stands of the Pacific Northwest. Now here I am, living the dream. Of course, nothing's perfect. The only housing I can find is renting a room from a grumpy, reclusive guy who doesn't seem to want me around. I should keep out of his way and focus on my studies, but there's something about him that keeps drawing me in. I feel less homesick when I'm with him, and maybe I can make a difference for more than just the trees.

ADAM

Life as I knew it ended with my horrific accident ten years ago. There's no point to my existence now, but I can't seem to stop living, so I hide my battered carcass in my mountain home. There, I can wander from room to room and no one stares, no one laughs, no one even remembers I exist. Until I make the mistake of offering a stranded Aussie a room to rent. It should've been a simple favor—two men with our own spaces, ignoring each other. Instead, he's always close by, and he won't let me wallow, and what's worse, I think I'm starting to like that. But there's no way someone like me can have a future with someone like him. Right?

The Beauty of the Beast is a retelling of Beauty and the Beast, set in the wilds of British Columbia, where an Aussie forester a long way from home falls for the untouchable man he shouldn't want. The novel has moderate angst, a feisty foreigner, and what happens when someone trusts again.

Edits by ELF

Cover by Leanne Clugston

Kaje
Patti
ELF
Renae
Wendy
Tracey
Mirela
Leanne

DEAN

As I walked into the Fifties diner in Mission City, British Columbia, the scent of grease wafted over me.

Just like home.

Reminded me of the Red Rooster back home, in fact. Whenever I visited my mate, Sam, in Sydney, we'd go for a bite. He'd have a burger, and I'd have chicken. With chips, of course.

A slightly harried-looking blonde woman approached me. "For one?"

"Uh, yeah, that would be great, thanks."

She cocked her head.

I'd seen that look before, whenever I opened my mouth on this side of the ocean. "Australian."

"Ah. We don't get many of those. Americans? Sure, because we're so close to the border. Anyway, any of the booths on the left." She glanced into the restaurant. "Oops."

All the booths on the left were full. As were all the larger booths on the right.

Together, we glanced over at the stools by the breakfast counter. All full.

I cocked an eyebrow.

She winced. "Busy day. It's the Raspberry Festival. That's always a little crazy. If you could wait...?" She indicated a corner of the entryway.

"Nah. I can go somewhere else."

"That's got to be an Australian accent." A tanned man with sparkling dark-brown eyes smiled at me. He'd come up behind me, likely having just come in the front door. "My family's from the Philippines, so I know Aussie."

"Great." His accent sounded...very Canadian. Right out of the training materials I'd studied.

"You're visiting? New in town? Did I hear Sarabeth say you need a seat?"

I blinked.

The guy just kept right ongoing. "My name's Ravi. I'm here with my husband, Maddox, and our toddlers. If you're adventurous, you're welcome to join us. Sarabeth just brought our drinks, and I had to run out to the car to grab bibs because, well..." He shrugged sheepishly, holding up two gray rubber bibs.

I blinked again. "Uh, that'd be great. Maddox won't mind?"

Ravi grinned. "My husband is a permanent fixture in Mission City. He's good about welcoming strangers."

I glanced at Sarabeth, who smiled and nodded enthusiastically.

Okay, then. What do I have to lose? "I'd love to join you." My luggage and rucksack were in the rental car, which had to be returned tomorrow.

"Great." Ravi guided me to the last booth in the diner.

As we approached, I spotted the two toddlers with tanned skin and silky black hair, seated on booster seats across from each other. Each sipped from a red cup with a lid. Milk? Juice?

Right, because that's what's really important.

The large man with his back to me had a shock of reddish-gold hair. He turned as Ravi slid into the booth across from him.

Ah, his beard matched his hair.

"Scooch over, kiddo." Ravi pushed the toddler, whom I guessed to be a girl, closer to the wall. Then he patted the spot next to him. "Have a seat. Oh God, I didn't even ask your name."

The man, who had to be Maddox, chuckled. "Picking up strays again, my love?"

As I slid into the booth, Ravi laughed. "Wasn't that the other way around? I was the stranded stranger." He nudged my shoulder. "This guy—"

"Uh, Dean."

"—Dean is from Australia. So a long way from home." Ravi gestured around the restaurant. "He would've had to wait for a table. Or even a stool."

Maddox sipped his coffee. "I'm amazed there isn't a line out the door. What with it being the Raspberry festival and all."

"I know, right?" Ravi caught a cup before his child sent it flying. "No, Violet, we don't throw things." Then he turned to me. "That's Victor—" He pointed to the child next to Maddox. "—and this hellion is Violet."

"Hellion?" I sort of whispered the word. Did she understand?

Maddox chuckled. "Our child very much understands the word—and does everything she can to live up to that name."

"Your genes," Ravi contended.

I was startled. Maddox was as pale as I was, while the children favored Ravi.

"His sister was our surrogate," Maddox quickly supplied. "So they've got her genes as well." He narrowed his eyes. "Namita's far worse than me."

3

"But you could say Meg's tamed her." Ravi again cut me a glance. "Maddox's friend and my sister wound up together. Creating chaos wherever they go."

Maddox snickered. "That's the truth."

"Okay, what can I get everyone?" Sarabeth held a notebook with a pen at the ready.

"An order of chicken fingers and fries to share." Maddox eyed his toddlers. "They've got enough milk."

"More." Violet banged her cup on the table.

Ravi held it as if weighing it. "There's plenty, darling."

She stuck her lower lip out.

He laughed.

"I'll have the Montreal smoked-meat sandwich." Maddox scratched his beard. "Can you make my fries poutine?"

"You bet." Sarabeth turned her attention to Ravi.

"Even though it's early afternoon—" Ravi eyed his husband.

Maddox snickered.

Ravi glared. "I'm going to have a waffle."

"Of course you are."

"Hey, you introduced them to me. I'm feeling nostalgic."

"Strawberries?" Sarabeth held her pen aloft.

"Yep."

"With extra whipped cream," Maddox added.

All three adults laughed.

Okay, then.

She pivoted her attention to me. "And you, hon? Did you get a chance to see the menu?"

"No, but that's okay. You have poutine?"

"For sure. You can have it as a side or as an entire meal."

"That sounds...decadent." I'd yet to try this very traditional Canadian food, but was curious.

"You're better off having it as a side and then getting a

4

good meal." Ravi looked me up and down. "Any allergies or food preferences?"

"Uh...no."

"Well, Fifties does have the best burgers in Mission City."

Victor clapped his hands. Whether in acknowledgement of his father's statement or just because of some weird timing that only a toddler understood, I wasn't certain.

"I love burgers."

"Then I recommend the classic." He handed the menus to Sarabeth.

She nodded. "Two patties, bacon, cheese, sautéed mushrooms, mayo, and special sauce."

"Special sauce?"

"Yeah, like so special we don't share."

We all laughed.

"That's great. Thank you."

"Oh, and something to drink?"

I glanced at Maddox's dark brew that was clearly coffee and Ravi's lighter colored liquid that I guessed was tea.

"Do you like milkshakes?" Maddox's blue eyes sparkled.

"I love them."

"And you're hungry?" Ravi added that question.

"Haven't eaten since I devoured a sandwich over the Pacific."

"Well, then you have to have one." Sarabeth grinned. Then proceeded to list off so many flavors that my head spun.

"Uh..." I tried to grasp what I'd heard. "Did you say Espresso?"

"Yep."

"Well, I could use some pep in my step."

"Oh well, remember you asked for it." She headed back toward the front of the restaurant.

Maddox chuckled. "You're going to be so full."

"I'm looking forward to it. Honestly, I'm starving."

"You flew in just now?"

"Well, to Vancouver International Airport. I picked up my rental car and headed here."

"And remembered to drive on the right side of the road." Ravi winked. "I've visited Australia—that left-side-of-the-road thing drove me nuts."

I wasn't going to be affronted, because I'd had the same reaction here, trying to adapt to the right side. Would take some getting used to.

"Is this your first visit to Canada?" Maddox nudged Victor's milk back at him. "Keep drinking, buddy."

Dark-brown eyes blinked.

Ravi chuckled. "Nice try, kiddo."

I didn't ask. "Uh, first visit overseas. Well, I've been to Tassie—Tasmania—and New Zealand, obviously, but not beyond that."

Maddox whistled. "Well, this is a long way to come for your first trip."

I wasn't going to say that money had always been an issue. "I'm here on a work visa, actually."

Ravi glanced at me. "You don't say."

"Well, he just did." Maddox offered what I'd term a sardonic grin.

"So, you just have to share all." Ravi nudged the cup toward Violet.

Sarabeth arrived before I could speak, saving me from a degree of panic. *Share all? What does that even mean?*

She placed the milkshake before me and headed back.

I unwrapped the paper straw and stuck it into the drink. Playing for time, I took a sip. "Holy crap." The taste exploded on my tongue—rich and delicious.

"Crap. Crap. Crap." Violet giddily parroted my words.

I nearly uttered *shit* in response. Heat crept up my cheeks. "I'm so sorry." I whispered the words.

Ravi nudged my shoulder with his. "You think they haven't heard a million times worse?" He indicated Maddox. "That dude's their dad."

"Hey." Maddox narrowed his gaze.

"What did you call Sofia yesterday?"

"Uh." Maddox reddened. "Well, she was being difficult."

"Is Sofia your daughter?"

Ravi burst out laughing. "No, Princess Sofia is our dog. But Maddox treats her like she's our child as well."

"Hey, you care about her, too. Who was sneaking her bacon the other day, despite Dr. Zephyra saying Sof needs to watch her diet?"

Again, Ravi laughed. "Right, like you didn't give her that slice of cheese—"

"So, I'm a forester." I could foresee this situation devolving, and I wanted no part in it. My fault for asking about the daughter who was, in fact, a dog. "Well, I have a degree in forestry management from the Fenner School of Environment and Science at the Australian National University in Canberra, and that was way more than you needed to know."

Ravi sipped his tea. "No, I'd say that's about the right amount of information. Too much would be me telling you how Maddox likes me—"

Maddox cleared his throat. "Yes, well, enough of that." He drank his coffee. "So, are you just passing through? Like, in Mission City? Because we've got forests, but the interesting ones are in the interior of the province."

"I'll be doing a couple of lectures at the University of British Columbia as well as a few out here at the University of the Fraser Valley. I'm working with a land-management group as part of a municipal project. Mission City has a working forest, and I'll be part of that project. I want to replicate some of the husbandry practices back home."

I chanced a glance at Ravi.

His eyes had gone a little glassy.

Maddox, though, seemed more engaged. At least, if his body language was any indication. "I used to do back-country rescues," he offered. He pointed to his husband. "Pediatric nurse."

"Both important jobs." I eyed him. "Used to?" *Crap, was that too nosy? I'm always stepping in it...*

"Rescue gone wrong. Bum knee." He gave me a small smile. "These days I do diaper duty and cybersecurity freelance work."

I would've pegged him in his mid-forties. If these were his first kids, he'd gotten a bit of a later start. Ravi, though, was under thirty for sure.

"And dog watching." Ravi raised an eyebrow.

"Isn't that dog *sitting*?" I was curious. Perhaps they called it something different in Canada.

Ravi barked out a laugh. "Oh, if Princess Sofia didn't belong to us, then yes, it would be dog sitting. But we are responsible for the irascible mutt...so it's dog *watching*."

Maddox glowered.

My phone vibrated. I yanked it out of my back pocket to send the call to voicemail. Oh, wait, the number was Canadian. I glanced at Maddox across the table from me.

He nodded that I should take the call.

"Hello?"

"Mr. Hargrave?"

"Yes, this is he. Or that's me." I barely knew what time it was, let alone, apparently, my own name.

"Oh, I'm so glad I caught you. My name is Ethel Thistle."

Ethel...oh, my new landlady. "Nice to speak to you, Mrs. Thistle. I was just grabbing some dinner before—"

"Oh, then I'm so glad I caught you."

My stomach sank. "Yes?"

She sighed. "My daughter has been living with this asshole."

I glanced at the table, somewhat comforted to see no one could, apparently, hear her speaking. "Okay."

"Anyway, she finally left the horrible man. Just this morning. And I was so glad the basement suite was empty so I could give it to her—"

"Would this be the basement suite you promised me?"

"Well." She clucked her tongue. "You're a young man with prospects. I'm sure you'll find something. My daughter has two young children. Wouldn't be right for them to be on the streets, now would it?"

"Could they not live with you? We have a contract. I signed a lease and sent you a deposit."

"I've sent the money back." She cleared her throat. "I guess you could sue me for breach of contract..."

But I wouldn't.

And she knew it.

I blinked several times. *Need to remove these contact lenses.*

Right...like *that* was the problem.

"Do you..." I swallowed. "Do you know anywhere else that might—"

"In this rental market? Not a chance." She paused. "Oh dear, that sounded callous."

That *was* callous, but my mother taught me that if I couldn't say something nice, that I was to hold my tongue. "Well, thank you for letting me know."

"Best of luck, young man." Then she cut the line.

I pulled the phone away from my ear and stared at it. I'd rented this place eight months ago for my six-month stay and I'd emailed every month to ensure everything was fine. My last email had been just before I left Canberra. Which had been more than twenty-four hours ago—what with the flight to Sydney, the layover, the flight to Hong Kong, the layover, and finally the flight on to Vancouver. Still, in that short time, my plans had all gone to shit.

"Waffles for Ravi and Montreal smoked-meat sandwich for Maddox." Sarabeth laid out the plates. From the server who'd followed behind, she snagged two smaller ones. "Chicken fingers and fries for the munchkins."

Victor and Violet both clapped their hands in glee.

"And a burger for the Aussie." She put the plate down before me. "With a large helping of poutine. Hey, what's your name?"

"Uh...Dean." I swallowed. "Dean Hargrave."

"Well, welcome, Dean. Anyone need anything else?"

"Nope, this is perfect, Sarabeth, thank you." Ravi offered a wide grin as Maddox occupied himself with cutting the chicken fingers and accompanying fries into little bits. He put a portion of the meal aside—I assumed to take home afterward. Truthfully, I had no idea how much toddlers ate.

Sarabeth took off, and Ravi placed a hand over mine. "We'll find you a place to live."

I let out a shaky breath. "That easy, eh, mate? She made it sound impossible."

Ravi and Maddox exchanged a look.

Finally, Maddox winced. "Rental vacancies are pretty low in Cedar Valley. We've had an influx of new people. We're close to the university in Abbotsford and, well, Canada's accepted a pile of new immigrants."

"I'm second-generation Filipino Indian." Ravi cut a slice of waffle. "My family settled in the next province over— Alberta. In Calgary, in fact. Lovely place. Crappy provincial politics. But that suits my conservative parents. I'm happier here."

I'd read something about British Columbian politics. A bit more left-leaning to centrist these days. The federal situation was different, but none of that mattered. "I..." I picked up my fork and poked at the melted curd cheese and gravy-covered fries that was traditional poutine. "I suppose I should find a hotel. I've got a bit of extra money." Not much, though. I'd been doing okay back in Australia. And our currency was pretty close to par with Canada's. If I'd been ten klicks south of here, in the US, I'd be screwed.

"The Grand Hotel was recently renovated." Maddox offered that up.

Ravi added a bit of whipped cream to his waffle. "Right, Aaron something. Who's with Noel. He was American, right?"

"Aaron's a dual citizen now that he's married Noel. And I popped in to see the renovations—Aaron's done an amazing job." He glanced at me. "That place used to be a bit of a dive..."

"I suppose..." Even just the thought of spending money overwhelmed. "Maybe an Airbnb?"

Maddox put down his sandwich and snapped his fingers. "I know."

"Know what?" Ravi dabbed a fry in a touch of ketchup and handed it to Violet.

She smushed it in her fingers, then jammed the whole thing into her mouth.

Ravi caught my bemused notice. "A treat. We normally feed them, you know, healthy food."

"No judgement here. I don't know anything about kids."

"Ah, well." He pointed to himself. "Pediatrics."

I nodded. "Crazy." I loved kids. From afar. I didn't have siblings or any close cousins.

Maddox had yanked his phone from his back pocket and was scrolling.

Does he have a magic solution? I eyed my heavenly smelling food. Although I was starving, my stomach in knots meant little appetite.

Ravi cut another piece of waffle. "Share, Mad. Poor guy's dying of curiosity."

Maddox glanced at his husband. "Adam."

In response, Ravi's fork clattered to his plate with a clang. "You're kidding me."

"Well…why not? When I spoke to him, he said something about financial problems." He winced. "And I probably shouldn't have said that. Truthfully, I'm not even sure why he told me…"

Ravi's eyes widened. "Okay, first—you didn't tell me you spoke to him—"

"Was, like, two months ago. Not a big—"

"Don't interrupt me."

Maddox chuckled. "Go on, love of my life." He bit into his sandwich, likely deciding a response wouldn't be needed.

"Second…" Ravi scratched his nose. "You're suggesting that we ask Adam to take Dean on…as a boarder?"

Wordlessly, Maddox nodded.

"Yeah, but…" Ravi wrinkled his nose.

In distaste? In confusion? I just didn't know him well enough to guess. "You think he might be willing?"

"He's a recluse," Ravi countered. "He doesn't do people."

Maddox swallowed. "Well, he speaks to me." He winced again. "Okay, spoke to me. A couple of times. The last time I met him walking Chip he looked super stressed. Wouldn't tell me any details, but he muttered, 'Money. Isn't that always the problem? Don't worry, I'll work it out.' So he might be open to this. God knows, he has the space."

Ravi arched an eyebrow.

"Okay, first time I met him, Chip had gone missing, and he was looking for her. Apparently, she escaped from the house when he was having a grocery delivery."

"Chip?" I had to ask.

"Adam's dog." Ravi nudged his plate as if in contemplation. "And recluse is almost too generous a word. I've never met the guy, and he lives just down the street. I mean, people live on our street because they want to be isolated, but he takes that to a whole new level." He eyed Maddox. "Financial trouble?"

"I didn't ask. I helped him look for Chip, and we found her." He met my gaze. "Adam has a Golden Retriever. Great dog. Just seven months old at the time. She just spooked. He's...overprotective of her."

Ravi snorted. "Like you're not with Princess Sofia."

Maddox glared. But, after a moment, he appeared to relent. "Before I ask him though, tell me a little about yourself."

"Uh." I considered. "I'm twenty-eight. I've been at the University of Canberra for almost ten years. First as an undergraduate student. Then as a graduate student and now as part-time faculty. I'm in Canada on a work visa. I've got a job with the District of Mission as well as days where I'll be lecturing and teaching at the University of British Columbia in Vancouver as well as the university in Abbotsford. I can provide a reference from my old landlord in Canberra, as well as one from the Dean of the Forestry Management program." I winced. "Except they're both in bed. Asleep."

Maddox considered me. "Do you have anything on you that confirms your position with the forestry service or the university? You understand, I don't want to land Adam with a con man. And how long do you need the room?"

I pointed to my rental. "I have paperwork from Mission City about my position as well as papers from both universities. I had everything ready for customs. In the end, they only looked at the work visa." I scratched my beard. "I did have an apartment set up for six months. At this point, though, I'm willing to take anything. Longer term would be better. So I don't have to move again," I clarified. "But anything would be amazing."

Ravi eyed me. "What's your budget for the rental?"

"I was supposed to pay fifteen hundred."

Maddox arched an eyebrow. "For an apartment? That's a great price."

"Oh? It's a basement. A one bedroom." I winced. "I don't know how Mrs. Thistle's daughter and two kids will manage."

"Better than nothing."

Maddox continued to eye me. "What kind of tenant are you? Some of the Aussies I've known were great guys, but heavy partiers, fond of their beer, and loud. That wouldn't go over with Adam. He's a...quiet guy."

"I don't drink or party. I'm certainly not loud." I winced. "But I look like a guy who could do all those things."

Ravi snickered. "I knew some straightlaced students at nursing school who would totally let loose. Looks can be deceiving."

"I have a Friday beer night. Look, I'm all about the academics. I worked damn hard to get this job. I'm not going to blow it for the sake of a party."

Ravi cut a slice of waffle. "You seem like a nice guy..."

"I am." With no way to prove it, of course.

"Do you like dogs?" Maddox poked at his food, watching me closely.

"I love dogs. All dogs. Never met one I didn't adore. I couldn't have them when I was younger. When I get a spread of my own, I very much plan to get one."

Maddox nodded. "I'm going to step outside to make the call. I'll be back." Without asking me if I wanted to board with a recluse and an overprotected dog, he slid from the booth and headed out of the noisy restaurant.

"I'm not going to warn you about Adam. Just...well, you'll

see for yourself." Ravi met my gaze with dark-brown incisive eyes.

"What's he like?"

He shook his head. "I don't know—never met him. But Maddox told me the guy's tragic story. And I could tell you, but it's not my place."

Oh my God, you have to tell me what I'm walking into. Yet I didn't say the words. I had to be respectful of this Adam guy, as well as whatever relationship Ravi felt he had with him.

"On the plus side, you won't be far down the road from us." Ravi pushed a piece of chicken closer to Victor. "We'd offer you a room, but it's set up for the next foster kid, and we never know when that call might come. We're on the emergency list." He considered. "I suppose we could've called Stanley and Justin. They're on our street as well." He pursed his lips. "Except that place is pretty chaotic as well. They've got their son Angus and their foster daughter Opal. Stanley is Maddox's ex."

He grinned wickedly. "The stories on our street... Oh, and the old cabin just sold. We're waiting to see who moves in. That thing is going to require massive renovations. The former owner was a bit of a hoarder. The kids just wanted to sell the place." He glanced at me. "And you didn't need to know any of that."

No, I really didn't. Except I was a friendly guy, and if I saw people on the street, even strangers, I'd say *hello*. Growing up in a suburb in Perth, I'd been tight with my neighbors and mates. "Okay...what can you tell me about Adam that doesn't break confidentiality?" I wasn't certain what kind of privacy Ravi felt he was violating, but I wouldn't ask him to step out of whatever bounds he'd created.

"He's mid-thirties. Nasty accident about ten years ago. Made national news because, uh... Right. I suppose you can search for him on the internet. The local paper tried to do an article on the ten-year anniversary. Let's just say that didn't go over well. People got really mad at Ulysses, the managing editor. People around here are protective of their own. I learned that when Maddox and I got together. He'd been a solitary guy, and people were wary of me just barging in."

"But they got over it."

He winked. "I won them over with my charm. Oh, and there's a nursing shortage in the area, so I get extra love when I wear my pink scrubs."

"Papa." Victor pounded his cup on the table.

"No, I'm Daddy." Ravi grinned.

"Want Papa."

"Papa will be—"

Even as he said the words, Maddox slid into the booth. He grinned at Victor who offered a toothy grin in return. Then he turned his attention to me. "Adam agreed. He's got a whole section of his house that he says he can rent out. You'd get your own room and bathroom, share a kitchen. He's getting it ready for you now. I've settled up the lunch bill, your burger's on me. Sarabeth's going to bring some containers. Or we can stay..."

I eyed my burger. The news I had a place—at least for the night—should've brought relief. And it did. Just not enough to bring back my appetite. "Yeah, containers would be great." I sipped my milkshake. This, I could manage.

Twenty minutes later, after everyone else finished eating, my food was boxed up, the kids had been cleaned up, and then we headed to the parking lot.

Maddox and Ravi loaded the kids into the SUV. They stopped and gazed at each other for a moment before Ravi handed over the keys. He turned to me. "It's a bit of a tougher terrain." He eyed my rental. "You're swapping that out, right?

We won't be getting snow, but the back roads can be treacherous."

"I'm returning this tomorrow and getting a municipal truck for the summer. They said it's all-wheel drive."

"That's good." Maddox patted the SUV. "This is fine most of the time, but a good sturdy truck is even better."

They hopped into their vehicle while I slid into mine.

The drive wasn't too challenging. Just a lot of hills. We climbed one, then up another. All still within civilization. Then we drove past a vast pile of row houses. Finally, we headed into some wilderness.

The houses I glimpsed were farther back from the road—some even obscured by the trees. So many trees. Several different kinds, familiar from my intense prep for this trip. I focused on keeping up with Maddox. I would learn more about the trees once I started working tomorrow.

I turned onto another street, noting the name as I passed it. I'd likely need a map to find my way back to town. Hopefully, the municipal truck had GPS. I was pretty good with old-fashioned maps, though. Just had to remember that the sun was in a different position up here.

Maddox stuck his hand out the window and pointed to a letterbox as he kept driving.

What...? Ah, likely he was pointing out his house.

We took a gentle turn to the right as the road curved. I suspected the green sign meant this was a cul-de-sac although we hadn't reached that bit yet. The road made another gentle right curve, and we headed up a gravel road.

And climbed.

And climbed.

The engine in my little rental car revved as I pushed her harder.

Maybe I should've left her on the street. Except we

continued to climb. I was decent at judging distances, and by the time we pulled into a clearing, I'd say we'd gone several hundred meters, if not half a kilometer. Was this a road? I hadn't seen any pull-offs or other driveways. *So the guy owns all this land?*

Wow.

The house was...spectacular. Like it had stepped off the pages of a French Gothic novel. It resembled a chateau with gray stone walls, a dark-gray slate roof, and even a turret. *Here? In a British Columbian forest? Someone had way too much time and money on their hands.*

Maddox pulled into a mini parking lot next to an SUV.

I parked next to him and got out.

We met behind the vehicles.

He met my gaze. "So Ravi told me that he said a bit about Adam's past. Just...don't ask questions. I'd say don't search either, but you seem like a curious guy."

I wasn't certain how to take that. I could certainly be respectful, if that was what was required of me.

"Ravi and the kids aren't getting out. The fewer people Adam sees, the better, I think."

"Ah." At that moment, I was tempted to drive back to Mission City and take a room in the Grand Hotel. A strange sense of foreboding overtook me.

The massive oak front door opened, and a man stepped out, his head turned, looking sideways at us.

I tried to take him in all at once, while also not staring.

He was fair, with almost an English complexion, rosy cheeks and pale skin. His medium-brown hair was shaved close at the sides, but long on top—brushed back from his forehead in an artless manner. He'd left his sideburns long, which made me tingle at the masculine contrast on his fair skin. He hadn't shaved in a while, and I wondered how prickly that scruff would be. His nose was almost cute on his face, but those lips were full. Kissable. Pillowy puffy redness. All in all, he was handsome—but in an utterly masculine way. Then he faced us, and I realized what Maddox had been hinting at.

An angry, mottled scar, probably from a burn, twisted most of the left side of his face.

Chapter Two

ADAM

FUCKING HELL, WHY DOES HE HAVE TO BE SO CUTE?

And I wasn't talking about my adorable neighbor Maddox who I'd secretly crushed on from a distance for about six years. When he'd been single, I'd almost approached him. He was a wounded recluse. I was a wounded recluse. We were both gay.

That had felt...almost possible.

Before I found the courage, though, he'd met Ravi. I didn't know much about the sunshine-happy nurse, but he made Maddox joyful, and that had curbed most of my lust. I didn't touch men in relationships.

You don't touch men at all.

Whatever.

This new guy? Dean Whoever, that Maddox was landing in my lap?

Jesus.

His reddish-brown beard was a shade darker than Maddox's red-gold. And while Maddox chose a close trim, Dean favored the bushier look. His bald head shone in the bright sunlight, and for an Australian, I felt like he should've been...more tanned? Both men topped six feet, and both were solid muscle and build.

Like a bear.

Maddox was more of a teddy bear.

Dean, though, I couldn't judge.

Just...fuck my life, he was exactly my type. Maddox hadn't said the Aussie was gay for sure, but he had told me the guy was cute and had checked out both Mad and Ravi in an interested way. Not predatory...but not neutral either. Since both men were so damn attractive, that didn't surprise me. Mad had told me his gaydar pinged loudly, trying to reassure me that this Dean wouldn't turn out to be a 'phobe. That was *not* going to be the problem.

Again, fuck my life.

Maddox waved. "Hey, Adam."

Be sociable. You desperately need the cash. I would never have said yes if I hadn't been reeling from looking at my bank statement right before Maddox called. For that blinding moment, this crazy scheme had seemed logical, almost miraculous. Now, I was going to have to turn the guy down to his face. Or... not. I stepped forward, not bothering to wave. "Hello, Maddox."

"This is Dean. Uh...you said your last name was Hargrave, right?"

Dean nodded. He held out his hand to me. "Good to meet you."

I hesitated.

When he started to pull his hand back, I reached out to shake his.

At least it's not your left hand. Yeah, that one I kept in my pocket.

As he gripped me, something shot through me. Like a jolt of electricity. Of awareness. Yeah, the guy was gorgeous in a very masculine way...but this was more. Way more. Despite the urge to yank my hand back, I gripped tightly and waited for him to let go.

His amber eyes met mine and his pupils widened.

Oh shit.

Well, he'd be sticking to his part of the house, I'd be sticking to mine, and we never had to meet day-to-day. We'd be totally fine as complete strangers.

Yeah, pull the other one. "I'm Adam."

"Adam." He extended the word just a touch. Like he was feeling it out? Like he was waiting for me to add a last name? Well, that was never going to happen. He might search me anyway, but I wasn't going to make it easy for him.

Am I really doing this? Panic flared inside me, but the idea of rejecting Dean and sending him away sat sour in my stomach. And I did need the money. *Desperately.*

"Why don't you grab your stuff and come inside?" I turned to Maddox and offered as best a smile as I could manage. As always, the right side of my mouth curled more easily. I angled my head so the left side would be out of Dean's line of sight. "Did you, Ravi, and the kids, um, want to come in?" I didn't have a single thing to offer, and my house certainly wasn't childproof, but they'd come here, and it was probably damned time I did the polite thing and met my neighbors. I shoved down the bit of me that wanted to run and hide, and tried to look like I meant the invitation.

Maddox's eyes went comically wide. Then he winced. "The kids are past their naptimes and there'll be hell to pay if we don't get them down shortly." He tipped his chin at Dean. "But since Dean's sticking around, I'd love for the four of us to get together. Maybe the two of you can come to our place one night? Or Ravi and I can find a sitter."

Does he not want me around his kids? Afraid I'll scare them with my face?

"Probably not." I pivoted and went back into the house.

Leaving the door open, I moved to the living room where I could gaze out from behind the curtain and not be seen. Chip whimpered from behind the den door, but I didn't want her getting out. Later, I could introduce her to Dean. Hopefully they'd get along.

I watched as Maddox and Dean walked back to Dean's car. Together, they unloaded a couple of suitcases and a rucksack. As they walked back to the house—two burly gingers with red hair shining in the sunlight—I forced myself back to the entry-way. I eyed the suitcase Maddox carried and judged I could probably carry it. I held out a hand.

Maddox waved me off. "Nah, I got this—"

"I'm perfectly capable." My hackles rose.

"Maybe you can show us to my room?" Dean glanced between the two of us, clearly not wanting an argument.

Inwardly, I winced. "Of course." I straightened, but my head still barely reached their shoulders. I hated feeling small. I hated that I liked feeling small. I'd worked with guys bigger than these two, and size never used to impress me, but after years of isolation I felt loomed over. "This way." I turned and strode toward the main staircase. "There's a back entrance and back stairwell that I prefer you use—I'll show you that. For now, you might as well know the other points of egress. Should anything happen."

But it won't. That's why you installed a sprinkler system as well as three kinds of smoke and carbon monoxide detectors.

One couldn't be too cautious.

I waved to the left. "Kitchen. Laundry room behind it. Those are the only main floor rooms you'll share." Was that too harsh? But I desperately needed my own safe space. I couldn't handle this stranger appearing suddenly in random places around my home, face-to-face. *Fuck, no.*

After we ascended the grand central staircase, I led him to the right, down a narrow corridor. That opened into an

GABBI GREY

entryway to the back stairwell. I pointed down. "That's where you'll come in. Yours is two more floors up." Then I pivoted and headed up the back stairs. Fortunately, my housekeeper, Ingrid, had done a thorough clean just a couple of weeks ago. *Spring cleaning*, she'd called it. Like the seasons mattered.

Like anything matters.

"Uh, I have a housekeeper who comes twice a week. If you need anything, you can let her know." Once we were on the second floor, we followed another narrow passage to the last staircase. "You'll be on the third floor." I led them up and, once I arrived at the top of the stairs, I opened the massive oak door. I had to push firmly to get it open. *Should I get someone to look at that?* As Maddox and Dean followed me into the room, and I again saw nothing but a sea of muscles, I figured Dean would manage.

"Oh my God, this is the turret room." Dean put his suitcase down, let his rucksack slip from his shoulder and dropped that as well. Then he hustled over to the window and threw the heavy velvet drapes open.

For the first time, his accent struck me. I'd known he was Aussie, of course, but the exotic variation in inflection hit me, his drawl rough and warm. Oh well, we wouldn't be interacting, so it didn't matter what he sounded like. Even if his voice did little things to my insides.

Focus.

"This is your private space. There's a washroom." I pointed. "Fresh towels and sheets. Ingrid does laundry on Mondays, so ensure everything is down in the laundry room and make certain to pick it up when she's done. I want minimal disruption." Because if anyone fucked with my schedule, there'd be hell to pay. I paid Ingrid a good salary to keep things as stable as possible. "I assume you're working during the day."

Dean turned from the window—and the stunning view

across the valley—and faced me. The afternoon light, so bright in this room, shone off his bald head.

Does he shave or did he go bald early?

How old is he?

Why the fuck does that matter?

"Yeah, I go in at nine and am supposed to be off at five. I have to drive into Vancouver a few times to give lectures at the University of British Columbia, and some days I'll go over to the university in Abbotsford."

"That sounds busy."

He shrugged. "I like to keep busy."

"Well, I'm a late person. Late to rise and late to bed. So you may have the kitchen between eight and eight-thirty as well as five-thirty to six-thirty."

"Okay..." He drawled the word. "What if I'm late?"

I blew out a breath. "I'm in the kitchen from ten to ten-fifteen in the morning, two to two-thirty for lunch as well as eight-thirty to nine in the evening. Just...don't come around during those times. I'll write it down for you, so you don't forget."

Maddox gazed back and forth between the two of us.

Likely thinking I was too obsessive. Too rigid.

You have no idea how hard this is for me.

No one ever visited the house, let alone lived here in my space. I'd thought everything was worked out, and then the email came—*delay, review, two months, interest*—the near-fatal words swam in my mind. *I have to do this. I can make it work. It's not forever. Not for long.* Maddox said he had a good feeling about Dean, and after watching Mad help catch and comfort my lost dog, I trusted his good heart. "You're good with twelve hundred a month and you provide your own food?"

Maddox snapped his finger and held out his hand. "Car keys? You forgot your leftovers. That should see you through until tomorrow. Unless you want to shop tonight."

Dean dropped the keys on Maddox's palm. "I want to pass out and sleep for twenty-four hours. Unfortunately, I have to drop off the rental in the morning and report to work by nine."

"I'll run and get your leftovers."

I scratched my chin. *Need a shave.* "You can have some of my food for breakfast in the morning. Just this once." We'd need to label things in the refrigerator. *Fuck.* The realities of this house sharing began to hit home.

"Great. That's awesome, mate."

Mate? Oh, right. An Aussie thing. I didn't want to be his *mate.* I wanted to be his landlord. He'd said he could pay three hundred a week, and that would work for me, enough to stave off disaster. Until my cash-flow situation improved.

Maddox disappeared down the stairs.

"I suppose..." I glanced around. I was itchy to get away from Dean and into my own safe space, but I was—stupidly, unavoidably now—committed. "We should probably meet Maddox in the kitchen. You can put the container in the fridge and then, when you're ready for dinner, you can eat."

He glanced at his watch. "Is it really two o'clock?"

"Yes."

"Um..." He squinted. "If it's all right with you, I'm going to nap first, eat dinner, and then crash for about twelve hours. I'll be up early so I can..." He gestured around the room. "Unpack my fucking bags and, you know, all that shit. Oh crap."

I arched my right eyebrow. A talent I'd always possessed.

"Swearing," he said, his cheeks turning an adorable pink.

"Doesn't fucking bother me." I wasn't going to tell him that, in my old industry, that we'd all sworn like proverbial sailors. I still did—on a regular basis. Just, these days, the words were spoken in my head. "Oh, are you allergic to cats?"

"Nah, I love cats."

I moved toward the staircase. "Maurice hardly ever appears. Always ensure your door is closed, though, or he might come and hang out without permission."

"Well, I don't mind if he does."

"And dogs? Any allergies there? Chip's a golden retriever."

"I love dogs as well. I can't wait to meet her."

Sharply, I looked at him. "How did you know Chip is a girl?"

"Uh...Maddox mentioned she'd gone missing and, you know..." He scratched his chin. "And when he said *she*, it kind of struck me because I would've thought a Chip would be a *he*, but I'm very much live and let live, so I figured I'd just go along with it because I don't have any problem with dogs or cats—I love them, in fact." He took a breath.

Jesus, does he always talk in run-on sentences?

"Yes, well, fine. I doubt she'll come up here, but make sure you never accidentally close her or Maurice in." A while back, Ingrid accidentally closed Chip into a room. I'd been in a panic for almost an hour while I searched the entire house, mostly fearing she'd escaped again and dreading that I wouldn't find her. She'd been asleep in a patch of sunlight in the second guest bedroom, not even aware of the stress I'd been under.

"Should we go downstairs to meet Maddox?" Adam frowned and rubbed his face. "I could've fetched those leftovers myself..."

And yet Maddox likely saw what I saw. An exhausted man who couldn't keep his eyes open. Resisting the urge to touch his arm, which was so unlike me, I pointed to the bed. "Why don't you sleep? I'll stick your food in the fridge." *Yes, stay here, and let me adjust to having you in my space.* "Maybe take a nap, eat, and then go down for the night? Adapting to time zones..."

"Travel a lot, do you?" The moment the words left his mouth, a look of horror crossed it. "I'm so sorry. That was..."

"Insensitive?"

"Well." He rubbed his face vigorously, mussing his beard.

I cleared my throat. "At one time, I traveled the world. Now, I never leave my property." I pointed to my face. "I wasn't always so hideous. Once upon a time, people didn't turn in disgust. Children didn't point. I didn't hate myself." I swallowed the bile and pain. "Rest. I'll see you...whenever." With that, I spun and headed for the door.

"Adam?"

Shoving down the tingle in my chest when he said my name in just *that way*, I halted. But I didn't turn.

"I don't find you hideous. Believe me. Plus, you saved my ass from wandering around looking for a hotel I couldn't even afford. That makes you fucking awesome. Thank you for opening your home to me. Just...thanks, mate."

Without acknowledging him, I kept right on going. I wasn't his *mate*. I wasn't his friend. I wasn't anything to him except a roommate. No, not even that. I was a landlord.

Which reminded me—I needed to get a contract from him and some kind of payment. Had he opened a Canadian bank account, or would he wire me the money? When I'd jet-setted around the world, all of that had been taken care of for me. I'd had a credit card with a massive spending limit and no worries.

How far the mighty have fallen.

As I arrived at the bottom steps, Chip's whimpers reminded me I'd completely abandoned her. I hurried over to the den door and opened it at the exact moment the front door opened.

Of course, my baby girl bolted. "No!"

And, of course, she paid me no mind.

As I rounded the corner in a panic, the front door slammed.

Maddox stood there with some takeout containers in one hand and his other palm held up in the universal *stop* gesture.

To my shock, Chip sat, staring up at him.

"Nice try." Slowly, he held out his hand.

She sniffed, then headbutted him.

Another shock, because I'd never seen her do that before. Maybe she remembered him from when he'd rescued her?

Then, more in keeping with the dog I knew, she sniffed the takeout containers.

Maddox chuckled. "Uh, no to that as well."

I moved to him.

He handed them over. "Fifties hamburger. The man has good taste."

After a moment, I cocked my head.

"Best burgers in all of Mission City. Well, Cedar Valley, as far as I'm concerned."

"Ah." The containers were heavy. *Did Dean eat anything or was he too stressed about finding a place to stay?* "I'll put these in the fridge. He said he planned a nap, to eat, and then a long night."

Maddox nodded. "You're a good man, Adam, for doing this."

I winced. "I need the money."

He glanced down at his shoes. "Yeah, I remembered you saying that. I didn't tell Dean anything else about you…"

"I appreciate your discretion. Did you mention the money to, uh…" I pointed upward.

"Yeah. Ravi wanted to know why I thought of you. Why you might say yes."

"Well, I hope Ravi won't go blabbing to the rest of Mission City—"

"He won't." Maddox met my gaze, his blue eyes flashing. "He really won't."

I believed him. "It's just a brief hiccup. Everything should be smoothed out in a few weeks."

"That's great. I mean, Dean's here for six months, but if you don't want him around that long, just let him know. I'm sure he can find another—"

"Six months?" My eyes widened. "I offered six weeks."

"Uh..." Maddox scratched his beard—something he often did. Did his itch the way mine did? Not enough to convince me to shave, though... "He'll try hard, and we'll ask around for him. Ravi and me, I mean. But the market's tight, and I don't get the feeling he's got a ton of money. I mean, he's going to be working for the municipality—they're not known for handing out tons of cash for their employees."

He wasn't wrong. I'd have to be judicious in what I asked Dean for. Enough to cover my shortfall, but not so much that I impoverished him. Twelve hundred a month seemed fair, but I'd have to find a way of ferreting out if I was charging him too much. Especially if he stayed longer, after my finances recovered— *No, he's not staying longer.* "Well, thank you for thinking of me." I guess. I was still reeling from the impact, good and bad and *sexy, asleep up in my spare room.*

"First person I thought of."

Really? Why? I was only memorable for one thing now. I bit down the nasty remark on the tip of my tongue. Then I realized I held the containers in both hands and Maddox hadn't once stared at my left hand. He truly was a respectful guy.

He waved. "I better go. Violet's liable to blow a gasket if we don't get home soon."

"Right."

"But I was serious about having you and Dean over. The kids would love all the attention."

"I'll frighten your children." An echo of what I'd said upstairs to Dean.

Maddox tilted his head. "No, you won't. Of course you won't. They're toddlers. You could have two heads, and if we treat you the same as everyone else—which we would—then they're not going to know any differently. When they're older...well, we'll cross that bridge when we get to it. They need to learn to be respectful of everyone—"

"I don't want to be a pity lesson."

"An empathy lesson," he shot back. "You don't need pity. And you'll never get it from me. You lived. And maybe you've got it rough..." He let the sentence trail off.

Because Frederick died. That's what he'd been about to say. I should be grateful because I still drew breath and my twin brother was dead. Had died a horrific death. Before my very eyes. Yeah, I had it rough. But I'd lived.

Except, every day I rattled around this old house, alone and useless, another little part of me died. How often did I wish to join my brother in eternal rest? Enough that I had a stash of sleeping pills, should I ever decide I'd had enough of the struggle.

Maddox waved toward the door. "You have my number. If things don't pan out and Dean's desperate, we can always give him the couch for a few days. Or I'm sure Stan can give him a room. We both just..."

"Kids."

"Yeah."

"Stranger." That Maddox had saddled me with. I wasn't a vulnerable child, but I still gave him a narrow look.

He cocked his head. "I mean, I didn't ask for a background check, although I'm pretty sure the municipality did. I'm a pretty decent judge of character, Adam."

"You seem to be laboring under the misapprehension that I'm a good guy who needs protecting from him, not the other way around."

With that he gave a salute and avowed, "You *are* a good

man," as he let himself out. He closed the door with a bit more force than necessary.

Chip whimpered. Then gazed up at me.

"Yes, darling, time for your walk. I get the message."

My property was almost twenty acres, stretching from the street all the way down to the municipal tree lot behind us. And stretching out a bit from each side of the house. Not quite a square. A decent rectangle.

The demarcation of the property was a fence, but my darling girl could jump that fence. And, when delivery drivers arrived, I opened the gate for them. I'd done that for Maddox once I knew he was on his way today. Which reminded me... I'd have to give Dean the code.

I glanced out the window to see Maddox's taillights disappear.

Leaving me truly alone.

Well, except for Chip the dog, Maurice the cat, and the Australian stranger in my turret room.

I shifted the takeout containers to my right hand, then I stretched out my left, trying to ignore the puckered skin and the way my fingers ached at the pull.

Chip brushed against my hand then licked it.

"Okay, walk now. Later, we brush you."

I could've sworn she rolled her eyes.

Money crisis solved. Stranger will be gone in six weeks. We're going to be okay.

Chapter Three

DEAN

I AWOKE WITH A START, COMPLETELY DISORIENTED. A pitch-black room, a luxuriously comfortable bed, and impossibly soft sheets.

Canada.

Adam.

Castle.

Right. I checked my watch. Eight-fifteen.

Shit, shit, shit, I'd be late to work on the first day. *Oh wait, that looks like sunset. Phew, it's evening.* Sam was always encouraging me to switch to the twenty-four-hour-clock feature on both my watch and my phone. I resisted because I always had that moment of hesitation. Of having to do maths in my head. Maybe if I just did it all the time, recognizing the right hour might become as easy as a twelve-hour clock?

Nope.

Just not a priority today.

My stomach rumbled.

Hmm, Adam's list of times to avoid the kitchen included eight-thirty. If I pissed and ran down to the kitchen, surely I could zap the food and be back up in my room by that time. Canada had microwaves, right?

Right?

Well, I'd never find out if I didn't get my ass out of bed. Thankfully, I'd remembered to remove my contacts. I tossed on a pair of glasses and headed to the bathroom to piss, thinking about that terrific espresso milkshake. I'd have to go back to Fifties. Maybe with Ravi, Maddox, and the kids?

After washing my hands, I hustled down the back stairs.

Despite having no experience with kids, I'd taken a liking to Violet and Victor. Quite adorable characters.

Oh good, the massive chef's kitchen was empty. All gleaming surfaces, modern appliances, and just general pristineness. My mum had never kept an organized kitchen. Or house. I'd pretty much grown up in chaos. Although I'd sworn to do better, I never really had. My kitchen was disorganized, my important papers everywhere, and neglected mail piled on my bedside table. I'd managed to wrangle everything before coming overseas, putting every-thing in storage, but I was quite certain I'd left things undone.

Oh well. Your phone works. People will call.

I opened the massive fridge, concerned about leaving fingerprints. The containers from the restaurant sat promi-nently in the middle of a surprisingly full fridge. Man, this guy ate a lot. Or maybe he wasn't alone? Maddox gave me the impression that no one else lived here, but that might not be true.

Oh, that one was labelled dog food. Fresh dog food. As I examined more labels, I found the same thing. Only for cats. Okay, well, that cut down on the amount of human food—

"What are you doing?"

I nearly dropped the takeout containers I'd grabbed. I pulled them against my chest and closed the fridge door. Since

I hadn't turned on the lights, Adam was only illuminated by the fading light of the crested sun.

Twilight was upon us, and night would soon follow. This close to the equinox, sunshine was plentiful. Back home, they were locked in winter.

Quickly, I glanced at my watch. Eight-thirty. *Shit*. "I'm so sorry, I'll just go." I headed to the back stairs.

"You haven't heated up your food."

"No." I barely slowed. "But it's your time, and I can eat it cold, and—"

"Stop."

My foot rested on the first step. I was *this close* to escape. I didn't need to escape, of course. Just that I didn't want to piss him off and break his rules. There weren't many...but this one had been described in great detail. I winced inwardly. "Okay. If you can just point me to the plates."

He'd advanced toward me and now he held out his hands.

Without hesitation, I placed the containers in them. I needed him to see I was prepared to treat him like all my other acquaintances.

Even if he was unlike anyone I'd ever met.

"You don't appear to have eaten much for lunch." He put a plate with the food in the microwave. Then he removed a plastic lid with ventilation holes. "Always use this—prevents splatter and decreases the amount of work for Ingrid."

The housekeeper. Right. I liked that he thought of her when he did things.

"I'm setting it for fifty seconds. One minute is too long."

Okay, good to know. "Uh, thanks, mate."

Finally, he met my gaze. The gray of his irises was almost gone, his pupils wide because of the lack of light.

Although I couldn't see them, I already knew the color, storm-cloud gray, slate gray. Had essentially memorized it this afternoon while somehow not staring. The shadows minimized his scars, his pose looked less aloof, and for a moment, he seemed like any bloke I might hang out with.

And that kind of thinking is dangerous. Because if I saw him that way, then he'd be fair game to hit on. I had to remind myself he hadn't asked me here to be friends, definitely not anything more. A guy who hadn't met the neighbors in years must have deep wounds and barriers I shouldn't go blundering over. Truthfully, that thought hurt. Not only did I find him attractive, but I was attracted to him. I wasn't minimizing the scars and the pain they implied, but they didn't define how I saw him. The idea that someone like Adam had locked himself away so long—well, I couldn't know what drove him, but if it had been superficial cruelty on someone's part, I might have to knock a few heads together when I found out who.

The microwave beeped.

The clacking of nails drew my attention to an entrance from what I'd assumed was the dining room.

"Halt."

The shadowy figure of a canine stopped and immediately went into a sit position.

Adam muttered, "Always about the food." He removed my plate from the microwave and placed it on the counter. "Let it cool for a moment."

"Uh, okay. Do you, you know, want me to take it back to my room now? Because I'm totally fine—"

"You may stay to eat it." He wrinkled his nose. "How could you sleep after having the smell of food in your room?"

Easily. I'd lived in dorm rooms for years with the smell of food, funky socks, and BO from a certain roommate. Sleep came easily to me. Still, I didn't need to share all that information with him. My mouth had a tendency to get away from me, and that was *not* going to happen here. In this house. With this man. "May I say *hello* to Chip?"

The dog whimpered in response.

Adam sighed. "I suppose. Chip, friend. Dean. Go."

I'd wondered if she might hesitate, but she didn't, instead barreling over to me. I dropped to my haunches and held out my hand.

She skidded to a stop just before me and sniffed my fingers.

An overhead light turned on.

I blinked several times in what I considered overly bright light.

Chip took advantage of my momentary confusion and licked my hand. Then she pushed forward to lick my face.

I giggled.

"Chip." Adam's voice snapped.

But his dog paid him no heed as she continued to lavish me with love and affection.

In response, I scratched her chest and belly and rubbed her ears. I'd always wanted a dog while I was growing up, but we barely money had enough to feed ourselves, let alone another being. My neighbor had a shepherd she let me spend time around. I'd grieved when he'd passed at the age of thirteen.

"Chip," Adam tried again.

This time, reluctantly, she pulled back. She gazed into my eyes with the most intense brown ones. As if finally taking me in. As if finally seeing me. She cocked her head.

"Friend, I promise."

She nuzzled my hand one last time before heading back over to Adam.

I rose and, as Adam petted the dog on the top of the head, I reached toward my burger. I figured it'd be cool enough, and—

"Stop."

Naturally, I stopped. And met Adam's gray-eyed gaze. "What?"

"Your hands." He appeared truly horrified.

What... Oh. I moved to the sink, squirted some soap into my hands, and set about washing them. And yeah, I should've thought of that myself. Perhaps because I spent so little time around animals, it hadn't occurred to me.

As I turned the water off, a tea towel was thrust at me. Dutifully, I dried my hands. When I searched for a place to put the damp towel—my mother always hung it on the oven handle and I did the same—Adam grabbed it from my hands.

"Just eat."

I couldn't tell if he was angry or if he was always that abrupt. Quickly, I took my plate to the kitchen table, which sat six. To me, that was a lot of people, and I suspected the dining room sat even more.

Chip plopped herself at my feet and gazed up at me.

"Please don't feed her anything."

"I won't." I eyed the dog. "Papa has spoken."

"What did you say?" Adam, who'd had his face stuck in the fridge, shut the door and headed over.

With the bright light, I could make out his features—and he was clearly angry. I held up my hands. "I was just being cheeky. What do you call yourself around the dog?"

He blinked. "What?"

"Well...you know..."

His furrowed brow indicated clearly he did *not* know.

"Okay, so my neighbor had a shepherd. And I'd always call him my buddy."

"Chip has a name."

"Right, but then I'd tell him that I was his buddy."

"But you have a name."

I sighed. "I guess...if I had a pet...they'd be like, you know, my child. So, I'd want to be their dad. Or, in Chip's case, her *papa*." I stuffed a fry in my mouth and grimaced at the still-cool gravy. Well hungry men couldn't be choosers—

38

He snagged my plate and took it back over to the microwave. Without me asking, he zapped it for about half a minute. As soon as he plopped it down before me, I ate the burger and poutine in silence. He prepared himself a salad.

I continued to eat my burger and poutine—oh my God, true heaven—and eyed him as he stared blankly down at his salad. "That was great, thanks, mate."

"I didn't do anything."

"You zapped it for me. And I was starving. It hit the spot." I placed my hands on the table and began to rise.

"You don't..." He winced.

At this angle, I could only see the right side of his face as he continued to look forward.

I glanced at the spot where he looked, but I only spotted what I knew to be the backyard. "You have a pool?" *Right, because that is what's really important right now.*

He cleared his throat. "You may use it."

I waited for him to appoint times, but he didn't. Maybe he didn't use it often? Slowly, I sank back into my chair. I assumed he'd been about to say that I didn't have to leave. I would have, of course. My allotted time had long been over, and he'd asked for solitude at this point. Perhaps he needed it at the end of the day? *Or he just doesn't want to be around you.* I tried not to let that sting. Yeah, I could be a loud and boisterous guy, but I'd tried to tamp down my general enthusiasm since I'd stepped into this house. Gratitude and deference were, I believed, what I needed to express.

Finally, after what felt like forever—but was probably about a minute—he grabbed a fork and then headed over to join me. He sat at the other end of the table, as far away from me as he could get. He speared a piece of lettuce, contemplated it, then clearly contemplated me. "I don't normally eat with other people."

"Okay..." *Does he want me to go? He told me I could stay...*

"My face..." He frowned.

Oh. "Look, it sucks if it makes it hard for you to eat, but I don't fucking care what it looks like. People have come in and out of my life who haven't been—"

"Normal?" With a slow bite.

I winced. "I'd never use that word. Like, my mother was severely dyslexic. Only diagnosed near the end of her life. I often wonder what her life would've been like if she'd known from the beginning. If she'd had the supports in place to help her. Instead, she struggled with poverty for most of her life. By the time I was finally in a position to help her...she was gone." I swallowed hard, trying to push down the lump in my throat.

"She's dead?"

"Yeah."

"I..." He placed his fork on his plate. "I want to say I'm sorry, but the words always feel hollow. I am sorry you've had to endure pain—because I assume you have. If I take the untimely death of my own parents—"

"You lost them both?"

He cringed. "Yes. My parents are deceased. They died when the yacht they were aboard caught fire. Burned to death."

This time, I winced. "I'm sorry—" Automatic.

His gaze shot to mine. "Before that, my brother died by fire, and..." He swept his right hand up and down the left side of his body. "My family doesn't do well with fire. So there are to be no open flames in this house. No matches, lighters, wood fires, or even gas. Everything is electricity, and if that goes down, I have three solar-powered generators and plenty of battery lanterns. My car is electric as well, although there's a minute risk of an electrical fire in the engine." He pulled his lower lip through his teeth. "I have determined that is an acceptable level of risk. But I built a freestanding garage away from the house. If the car catches on fire, we should be safe."

He hesitated. "I suppose I should give you a remote to the garage so you may store your vehicle there. And you'll need the code for the gate."

I could tell from the way he dragged the last words out he wasn't crazy about the idea. "I suppose. Although I'll bet the work vehicles are kept on a lot in the open air and not in a garage. Apparently, it's about ten years old and so not likely to attract a thief. I hear there's a lot of car theft in Canada."

Adam cocked his head. "I might've read something about that on the news." He raised his fork. "I don't really pay attention to things that don't affect me." He took another bite of the salad.

"Uh..." I pondered that. I was a news junkie. I devoured stories from all around the world and had been regularly checking the British Columbia page of the Canadian national broadcaster to get a feel for my new home. Mission City almost never came up—I figured that was a good thing. "Sure. But you read the local paper, right?"

Again, Adam scowled. He really did look extra menacing when he did that. "There's a community newspaper box next to the mailboxes." He pursed his lips. "I suppose I'll have to give you the street address so you can get your mail sent here."

I squinted. "Mail? You mean like letters? In the post?"

He squinted back. "Well, yes."

"Oh, right." I waved him off. "I don't actually use the mail for anything. My mate Sam promised to send a care package, but he's sending that to work. Likely to have tongues wagging. Just the way he likes it."

"Your...mate?"

"Uh, yeah. I mean, Sam and I go way back. Since he moved next door to us just before high school. Which I guess maybe isn't that far back, but fifteen years feels like a long time."

"When you're young, I suppose it is."

I cocked my head. "I'm twenty-eight. You're not much older."

He pursed his lips. "A bit."

"Like how much?" I challenged. Whoops. That might seem rude. Some people were super touchy about their age. I was the opposite. I had no problem getting older and wiser. Might be a good thing, Sam would say.

After what felt like forever, he finally responded. "Thirty-seven."

So, like, nine years. What was the big deal? Except...his accident had been ten years ago. He'd been my age. I couldn't imagine such a life-altering thing happening right now in my life. Of course, my mom had been thirty-seven when diagnosed with cancer and forty when she died. I tried to never think of that. Because, as I climbed closer to that age, I worried I might have a ticking time bomb inside of me.

"What are you thinking?" Adam's tone bit.

"Of my mom." Even as I said the words, I knew I'd regret them.

"Why?"

"Just..." I raised the bun on the burger to determine how much meat I had left. Answer? Plenty. "She died young. I mean, she had me when she was young. and she died young, and there couldn't have been much fun in her life, you know?"

"How old?"

"Forty."

"That's older than many get." He cut a slice of tomato in half. Then, he put the large piece of the vegetable—which most people considered a fruit, but I didn't—in his mouth, effectively cutting off the conversation.

I ate the rest of the burger and devoured the poutine. I'd never had cheese like this before. Cheese curds, I'd read. The taste settled, along with the gravy, and I smiled.

"You wear glasses."

My gaze snapped to Adam's. "Uh, yeah, sometimes."

"Earlier, though, you were not wearing them."

"Nah. I really prefer contacts. These glasses—" I indicated my black plastic frames. "—are annoying. They make me look geeky." And, because I was nearly blind without assistance, the lenses were coke-bottle thick. I wasn't vain—well, maybe a little—but they even distorted my face when caught from the wrong angle.

"You're finished eating."

"Yeah."

"You must be tired. Go to bed."

Stunned, I just sat there for a moment. Was he *suggesting* I go to bed or was he *ordering* me to go? "I'll just clean—" I started to pick up my plate.

"I'll do it. Just go."

Chip whimpered, presumably at her master's sharp tone.

What the actual fuck? Did I do something?

Well, I could stay and ask—risking his ire—or I could head to bed.

I skedaddled.

Chapter Four

ADAM

I HADN'T MEANT TO BE SO ABRUPT. HE LIKELY thought I was certifiable. And although I didn't believe in joking about mental illness, I often wondered about that myself. Dr. Lana Cho, the burn specialist who'd cared for me after the accident, had strongly suggested counselling but I couldn't bear the thought of exposing myself to a stranger. The first time the counselor at the hospital stopped by to speak with me, I saw her expression freeze into an emotionless mask when she saw my wounds. I had her banned from my room. Dr. Cho could heal my flesh, and I'd take care of the rest without that kind of pity.

She'd transitioned my care to Dr. Marco Raymond, a friend of hers who was a family doctor here in Mission City. He'd picked up the mantra of recommending I attend counselling. Resisting proved more challenging as each year passed. He kept suggesting I chat with a psychologist named Kennedy Dixon. Apparently, the good doctor owned Healing Horses Ranch in the Mission City hills—near where I lived. After I questioned how horses performed *healing*, Marco explained that the ranch provided equine therapy as well as canine support animals. In desperation one night, I'd researched. Plenty of former patients said great things.

I'd written off those words as having somehow being coerced. Because who would admit to being in therapy? Let alone that they'd been helped?

Glasses.

Dean wore glasses. When he wasn't wearing contacts, apparently. And that shouldn't have been a big deal. It certainly shouldn't have triggered me. Dr. Marco wore glasses. Ingrid wore glasses. Neither were the thick, dark plastic frames and those heavy lenses that I'd noticed as he turned his head. The way they warped Dean's face, so different and yet so familiar, had almost stopped my breath. Neither of the others reminded me of Frederick and how he'd been nearly blind without his glasses.

I should've been the one to die.

One of us could've saved the world. The other liked to look pretty and have people fawn over him. Little surprise the depth of loss cut so deep. Even if I'd had the kind of mind Frederick did, I still couldn't have accomplished what he had during his brief life—or picked up the mantle to finish what he started.

Slowly, I rose. I scraped what food I hadn't eaten into the compost bin, and then I set about putting everything into the dishwasher. Even with the addition of Dean's plate, it wasn't near capacity. Despite having a deep well, I was cautious about the amount of water I used. Hell, caution ruled everything I did. Taking in a stranger was the height of recklessness. Unlikely he would kill me in my sleep. But he did have the ability to upend my quiet existence and destroy the peace I'd worked so hard to achieve.

Chip whined. Likely unimpressed with me just leaning my hip against the kitchen island and contemplating the state of my life. So I didn't know what was going on in the world? I'd shut myself up for a reason. Nothing else mattered. No one else mattered.

I petted her head, then tapped my thigh, indicating I wanted her to heel and follow me.

Instead, knowing what was coming next, she darted to the mudroom and sat next to the door.

I rolled my eyes, donned my coat, and attached her leash. I shoved my feet into my boots, even though we were mostly past the rainy season and little mud remained. Next, I put on the headlamp and flicked it on. Sometimes we went farther than the motion-sensor lights covered—often all the way down the driveway and back. We'd get good cardio climbing back up the hill.

Finally, I put in one earbud and cued the audiobook I was listening to. Only one ear because I needed to be able to hear what was going on around me. I wasn't likely to be attacked by a bear, but I'd prefer to know before it happened.

Or maybe not.

Bear maulings aren't a thing. The coyotes aren't going to attack. Hell, even the skunks will probably leave you alone. The only nocturnal creatures I tended to see were raccoons. Vicious little creatures who usually gave us a wide berth.

As my favorite narrator's voice filled my ear, I tried to focus on his words. I'd recently found a new author I enjoyed as well, and I was making my way through her back catalogue.

Chip's sniffing ability was legendary—at least in my mind —but tonight I insisted on a brisk walk. She could sniff on the way back. During the day, I could let her off leash, but I didn't feel secure at night. I needed to see her at all times, whereas in the day I could be a little less vigilant.

We headed down the hill, and she pulled to the side of the road. I stepped with her, and as soon as we stopped moving, she squatted. "Good girl."

I could've sworn she rolled her eyes. My dog with massive

amounts of both energy and attitude. She'd replaced Froufrou —my mother's lapdog—who I'd somehow wound up with.

Everyone died. Of course you got the dog.

Yeah, there was that.

That purebred Bichon Frisée'd had an attitude a mile wide. Only, when left with just me, she'd...grieved? Mother didn't go anywhere without the dog. The day she and my father had gone out on the yacht, to get away from life—and likely to escape the pain of my brother's death—they'd fortunately left Froufrou at home with a dog sitter. She would've died in that fire as well.

I pushed the image from my mind.

Chip pulled at her leash, dragging me deeper into the woods.

I angled my head, so the lantern lit the way.

In the end, she didn't go far. Just enough to have some privacy while she...did her business.

Scooping was my least favorite part of owning a dog, but we walked through these woods all the time, so it didn't make sense to not scoop. I did *not* want to step in dog shit. Hence, always having multiple bags in my pocket.

We continued to meander down the driveway. When we arrived at the gate, and I found it secure, I turned Chip toward home. "Let's go."

As much as I felt like running, my lungs weren't up for it. And I hadn't worn my running shoes. So we hoofed quickly back up the steep incline.

By the time we crested the hill and could spot the house, the lights on sensors triggered on and bright illumination covered the driveway and the house. I winced that the light might wake Dean—especially if he hadn't closed the blackout blinds.

I needn't have worried. Light poured from his room in the turret. I could've given him any number of rooms, but I'd decided the turret would be a treat—and was the room farthest from mine. Less possibility of running into him. Even before I'd known he was a gorgeous lumberjack kind of guy, I'd worried how interacting with another person would mess with my head.

And yet... I'd enjoyed dinner. At least until I'd rudely dismissed him. Because the glasses had brought memories of Frederick. Which was about the dumbest reason ever.

Breathing hard, I took a moment to regroup.

In that instant, a shadow approached the window.

And stopped, clearly gazing out.

For once, I wished I hadn't installed such bright lights.

I had nowhere to hide.

Do you want to? Or do you want him to see you?

God, what a stupid question. Of course I didn't want him to see me. Not the real me, certainly. The beast behind the mask of civility. The man who had once been seen as one of the most gorgeous men in the world. Women and men alike had flocked to be within my realm because I was the epitome of beauty. Of privilege. People admired me. People wanted to be me. To be near me.

Now I lived in a castle alone with no one but an overly enthusiastic dog and a diffident cat to keep me company.

Dean raised his arm in an almost-wave before lowering it.

I managed a quick nod he probably couldn't even see as I strode to the house, heading around to the back. In the mudroom, I stripped out of my sweat-soaked clothes.

Chip didn't need drying off, so I let her dart into the house.

Then I considered my state of undress as I tossed my smelly clothes onto the laundry pile. To make Ingrid's life easier, I should've installed a washing machine nearer my bedroom. Alas, something like that would be mega expensive. Certainly right now, I didn't have the funds.

As a chill set in, I decided to risk being seen and to just boot to my room. Thankfully, I didn't encounter any wayward Aussie wanderers. I hopped into the shower and let the hot spray work out some of the tension in my muscles.

Then, because I couldn't get rid of the images of Dean flashing in my mind, I took myself in hand. So rarely did I do this, that my cock kind of needed some coaxing. Although I hadn't lost my ability to have sex after the accident, my libido had nosedived. First from the unrelenting pain and the meds, but even now, when the pain was a sometimes thing, I could go weeks without the urge to get off. Tonight, that urge was roaring back. I didn't look at myself as I stroked my shaft. I braced my left forearm against the shower wall, ignoring the twinge in my tight shoulder. Instead, I focused on doing everything I could to make myself feel good. To bring myself to some kind of satisfactory conclusion. I slid my thumb over my sensitive slit, enjoying the little jolt of electricity that shot through me.

Eventually, my balls drew up and I came.

Hard.

Harsh breathing filled the space as I tried not to imagine coming in Dean's ass. How he would moan my name. How he'd want me. How he wouldn't care about the scars. How he'd beg for me to take him.

Then reality crashed in. I gazed down at the puckered and marred skin that covered my left arm and torso. An image of my face flashed through my mind.

He'll never want me. Not that way. Not any way.

Beauty and the Beast was a fantasy, and even then, despite all the money and books and roses, they only got to be happy when the ugliness curse fell away and she got her handsome prince. No kiss would ever end my curse.

Chapter Five

DEAN

RETURNING THE RENTAL CAR AND NABBING THE pickup truck proved to be the easiest part of my day. The municipal complex, with city hall, the storage buildings, and the various vehicles, sat on a main road, so that proved easy to locate. The actual worksite for today wound up being more challenging. I'd assumed I'd be paired with someone, but since I had my international driver's license, I was handed the keys and sent on my merry way. Up into the hills north of Mission City. I had to cross one of the hydroelectric dams to get to the service road I was looking for. Noting the visitor's center location, I promised myself I'd drop by one day to check it out.

The rutted service road climbed higher as I passed diverse stands of mature trees. The towering height of the local conifers blew my mind, even though I could recite the climactic and soil conditions that caused that optimal growth. I wanted to examine all of them all at once, but that was ridiculous. I had months to do this. When I spotted another municipal pickup truck, I hoped I'd arrived.

A petite woman stepped out from the shrubs and waved.

I shut down the engine and hopped out. "How ya going? I'm Dean."

She grinned. "Even without the accent, I would've guessed. I'm Ruksana, but please call me Roxie." Her dark-brown eyes lit with evident amusement.

Her grin was infectious, and some of my stress slipped away. "What're we doing today?"

"We've got a team of researchers coming up from the university. They've got a pile of experiments going on at various places in the forest. They don't really need an escort, but I like to ensure they have peace while they're working."

I eyed her. "Who might give them trouble?" I hadn't spotted another car, but—

"We've had a couple of bear sightings."

My eyebrows shot up. "For real? I might see an actual bear? Like...black or brown? Because there aren't grizzlies around here, right?"

"Actually, we've got black. There are brown bears in Cedar Valley, but closer to Harrison Lake and Hope. Anyway, it's the brown bears you really need to watch out for."

I gaped. "But not the black or grizzly?" We didn't have them back home and, although curious, I wouldn't have actually said I'd go out of my way to spot one.

"Well, pissing off a bear is never a good idea. Just give them a wide berth. You've got bear spray, right?"

I blinked.

She grinned. "Oh, I can tell you're going to be fun."

Huh. "Well, at least you don't have to worry about drop bears here."

Her eyebrow arched. "I understood you only had koala bears in Australia. And koalas aren't proper bears—I know that. They're marsupials. The whole pouch thing is adorable and..." She squinted. "Drop bears?"

GABBI GREY

"They're part of the koala family. Well, the more vicious, larger, and carnivorous cousins."

She held my gaze. "How come I've never heard of them?"

"Well, we have a reputation to uphold. 'Roos and koalas and—"

"Venomous snakes. Venomous spiders. Crocodiles. All kinds of creatures that'll be happy to kill you." She wagged her finger at me. "You try to come across all warm and fuzzy, but I know better."

"Right. We warn tourists about the drop bears—"

She snagged her cell phone from her back pocket. "Reception out here isn't great, but they installed a new tower that—"

"Go ahead. Google it. Plenty of sites." I tried to whistle, it came out vague. Aussies loved their drop bear tales. There were plenty of sites about them. She wouldn't catch me out.

She pocketed her phone. "You and me..." She grinned. "I think we're going to get along just fine."

A rumbling sound caught my attention, and I turned to see a big rig heading down the road.

"Timber truck."

I could barely hear Roxie over the noise.

"We have a few come this far, as we've got a small clearing project going on right now."

Patiently, I waited for the truck to pass, even as Roxie waved to the guy driving the rig. "That common?"

She shrugged. "We've got two clearing projects this summer. We're creating a new campground up closer to Stave Lake, and the municipality has approved a long-term lease of public land to a charity. They're building a wildlife-rehab center of sorts. They haven't finalized the details, but I think it's going to be pretty cool. Again, it'll be a private not-for-profit using crown land."

"*Crown land?*"

"Owned by the crown. Well, the federal government. You're part of the commonwealth as well, right?" She removed her hat, wiped sweat off her brow with the back of her hand, and plopped it back on. Her black hair stuck to her temples while her ponytail went halfway down her back.

"Yeah, commonwealth. But we don't say things belong to the queen or king—whoever that might be at the time."

"I still hesitate when I go to say king." She eyed the sun. "It's going to be another scorcher."

Hot. Great. I nodded. "We're heading into winter back home. Not cold like you folks, but definitely not hot."

"I'm sure you know Canada stretches from one ocean to another and from the arctic down to America south of us."

"Yeah."

"Well, winter in most of the country is a hell of a lot colder than here. Southwestern British Columbia is pretty much the warmest place in the country during the winter, and although we can get damn hot, we don't tend to have the unrelenting heat of the prairies. The ocean can bring temperate winds." She pointed to a felled tree. "And also brutal windstorms."

"Straightline winds? No tornadoes here, right?"

"Yep. Occasionally tornadoes over water, but that's super rare."

"Good to know." I cleared my throat. "What do you need me to do?"

Roxie clapped me on the back. "I can see you're going to be a hard worker. We're going to get along just great."

Eight hours later, as I tried to unknot my muscles under the hot spray of the small shower next to my tower room, I had no doubt of her words. She was quite a dynamic and spunky person. Quick wit, quick praise, gentle corrections, and someone who knew how to get the most out of her people. Since she was to be my supervisor for the next few months, I considered myself lucky.

As I dried off, I ran through the material I wanted to cover in my guest lecture next week at the local university. Today I'd been especially fascinated with discerning the differences between the Douglas fir and the Grand fir. Roxie showed me some of the older trees, and I couldn't fathom they were seventy to eighty meters in height. As tall as a twenty-story building. Those kinds of lengths boggled the mind.

I'd gone to Tasmania to see the Centurion—the tallest eucalyptus tree in the world. That'd been taller, so I probably shouldn't have been in awe of the Canadian trees, but it was one unique specimen. Here, you saw towering firs around every corner, butted up against strip malls and in people's back yards. Most of the tallest trees back home were located in either Tasmania or the state of Victoria. Not so much in Perth, which was the capital of Western Australia. WA's tallest trees were located south of the capital where there were jarrah and karri forest. And, of course, the giant tingle trees. I loved tramping around the South-West forests. They were so easy to get lost in and just roam wherever you wanted.

Very unlike the city of Perth where I'd grown up which was the second most isolated capital city on the planet. And Aussie's fourth largest city. Easy to get misplaced in a place like the back streets of Perth too. A different kind of lost to the forests. One that wasn't nice.

I'd been lost, so to speak, until Sam popped into my life in my early teens. He'd recognized me as a kindred soul. His family had recently been forced to sell their farm and move into the city. He was kind of lost in the sea of technology, concrete, and humanity.

I was lost because my mother worked all the time, and I was alone for much of that.

Sam brought me home, and his parents welcomed me in as if I were one of their own. Suddenly I had two adults who cared, a brother of sorts who adored me, and other siblings to round out the package.

My mom had been understanding—and even supportive —of my making friends. She'd likely seen my misery, but had been too busy surviving to help me deal with it.

Early on, I recognized I was gay. And that Sam was as well. But for all his surfer-boy, blond-hair, Aussie god look, he didn't attract me. He had tons of admirers—male and female —but we never saw each other in *that* way. Which meant our friendship always had been, and always would be, on solid ground.

Plus, Sam had been and was still a player. So the opposite of me. He was living the high life in Sydney. Running his tour company and enjoying the company of men whenever he had time off. Business first, with him, but he always had time for a roll in the hay.

I was also business first. But sex with a bunch of strangers didn't work as a stress relief for me.

After slipping into my sleep pants and a T-shirt, I headed toward the door. At the last minute, I threw on socks.

Although the temperature was hot outdoors, the castle was cooler. Delightfully chilly air flowed through the vents even up in my room, suggesting central air conditioning. Which begged the question of just how old this castle was. Had it been built much earlier and the air con added later?

I couldn't see the ductwork, so that was likely embedded into the walls. Which, to my mind, meant it'd been part of the original design. Which meant this place wasn't as old as I might've thought.

Plodding down the stairs, I mentally reviewed the groceries I'd bought after work. I was nearing the end of my allotted time in the kitchen for the evening, but Adam wasn't due for a bit, so I figured a few extra minutes should be okay.

I nearly tripped over Chip, who bounded up to me and

tried to wind her way through my legs. "Hey, girl. How's it going?" I headed to the fridge to retrieve my rotisserie rosemary-and-spices chicken. A tad expensive to buy it cooked, but no way was I going to be able to do anything so elaborate myself. I was a decent cook, but not for something like that without a damned good reason to spend two hours in the kitchen. Maybe not even then. I nabbed a plate, then started slicing off pieces of the chicken.

Chip watched me in clearly rapt fascination.

I pointed the knife at her. "No way, Missy. I happen to know you get lots of good food." I'd never seen her fed, but her coat was healthy and shiny. She was just the right weight, and Adam obviously took great care of her. So no, she wasn't suffering from being starved. I had yet to meet Maurice, but I didn't figure he was hard done by either.

After putting some frozen corn in a bowl, I zapped that. I added a slice of fresh-baked buttered bread to the plate, zapped the chicken, then grabbed a can of soda and sat at the table.

Still, Chip didn't take her eye off me.

I pierced a piece of chicken with my fork. "I'm not giving in. I don't even know if you're allowed..." Crap, almost said the 't' word. "And even if you are, I'm not sure your papa would want me to give them to you without his supervision."

"She's allowed some treats."

Whirling, I found Adam in the doorway between the dining room and the kitchen. I grinned, trying to quell the panic at being in here past my designated time. Again. "Hey."

He pushed off the wood and shuffled over to a container I hadn't noticed before. Truly incongruous with the sleek modern kitchen. Everything in here was brilliant white or slate gray. The ceramic jar he snagged was deep purple with lilac-colored bones on it in a haphazard design.

Chip raced over and sat at her master's feet.

Said master removed a bone-shaped treat and snapped it in half. He offered half to the dog, who took it gently.

"You realize that only giving half a treat doesn't actually mean an entire treat." I'd seen a meme about that somewhere, and it felt true, even if it wasn't.

He arched his right eyebrow as he made his way over to me.

I'd oriented myself when I'd come home. The kitchen, in the back half of the house, faced the forest. Due north. Although the outside wall was all glass, it didn't offer as much light as, say, my room. Still, Adam's features were clear in the light. My gaze didn't linger on the scars, but they were impossible to miss.

He held out the rest of the treat to me.

After a moment, I took it.

Our fingers brushed. He could've dropped it into my hand, so I couldn't figure out if the touch was deliberate or accidental.

I maintained eye contact, trying to discern his feelings. Whether that little connection meant as much to him as it did to me. I didn't touch people. That wasn't my thing. I hugged Sam—but no one else now my mum was gone. Certainly not students or other faculty. And as sweet as Roxie was, and likely a ball-buster to boot, I couldn't imagine her hugging a colleague. I got the feeling Ravi would offer one up in a heartbeat. Hell, maybe even Maddox. I had no interest in getting touchy-feely with them. But what did touch mean to Adam? Was that brush of fingers a careless moment or a meaningful gesture?

"Make certain she does something for the treat."

Chip whimpered.

I grinned. "Something?"

"Sit. Down. Shake a paw." Adam scrunched his nose.

"Just...not speak. I spend enough time trying to get her to not bark her head off."

"Sit."

Chip plopped her butt.

"Shake a paw."

She cocked her head. Almost like she was saying *mate, I already obeyed one command...you want two?*

I held my ground.

She finally yielded and held her paw out for me to shake.

I shook her paw. Then, as I gave her the treat, I grinned. "She's got enormous paws."

Adam sighed. "She's going to be a big dog."

"And you're working on training her? Is she still a puppy?" She looked pretty big to me.

"Nine months. So still a toddler. I've tried a number of obedience books, but nothing's working. Froufrou was already trained, so I didn't—"

"Froufrou?" I didn't even try to hold in the laughter.

"My mother's dog."

His tone had me instantly regretting my outburst. He layered grief into those words. No missing it. "You, uh, inherited the dog?"

"After my parents' passing, yes."

I wanted to ask more questions. How did he survive the grief? How did he put one foot in front of the other? Perhaps, most critically, did he feel the same acute pain that lanced through me when I acknowledged I was alone in the world? At least when it came to biological relatives I knew about.

"Do you have siblings?"

If I tried to put the next twenty seconds into words, I'd have said pain like nothing I'd ever seen crossed his face, then he spun, and he bolted from the room.

Chip stared after him, whimpered, then turned to me.

"Go after him. He needs you."

She hesitated.

"No treats." I held up my empty hands.

Those were, apparently, the right words. She made a beeline for the dining room. Moments later, the clacking of her nails on the grand staircase reached me.

And then a resounding silence.

Jesus, foot in my mouth again.

As I zapped my food again, I replayed the conversation. Clearly, the mention of siblings triggered him. He'd endured the pain of remembering his parents, but couldn't cope with whatever had come next.

I poked my chicken—my appetite having fled. But I'd put in a hard day's labor, trekking through the forest with the environmental-studies students from the university. I knew a lot about biodiversity, of course, but to see it in action in an unfamiliar environment was amazing.

Roxie promised tomorrow was going to be both hotter and tougher. So I shoveled the food down, cleaned up after myself, and headed upstairs. I might be able to sneak in a video call with Sam if he hadn't started his tour for the day. Maybe he'd have some grand insight for me.

Chapter Six

ADAM

STUPID. STUPID. STUPID.

Yeah, so what else is new?

As much as I wanted to bolt outside and run for the forest, I didn't have Chip's leash. I could've left her behind—I had no doubt Dean would take care of her—but I couldn't do it. As it was, she was barely through the bedroom door before I slammed it shut.

She delivered a sharp *what the fuck* bark.

"Sorry, girl."

Clearly unappeased, she continued to stare at me.

"I...panicked."

She cocked her head.

"Stupid, right?" *I shouldn't be calling myself stupid...even if the word fit.*

Frederick's smarts always outshone my less-than-stellar grades. I'd convinced my parents little things like academic success didn't matter to a kid like me. By the time I was thirteen, I was raking in the modeling contracts. Mostly catalogue and stock photos, at first, but I was soon gracing the catwalks in Vancouver. And then farther afield. I barely graduated from high school. But by then, I had an enormous pile of money my mother insisted be beyond my reach. She gave me an allowance and put the rest away in long-term investments locked inside a trust her death hadn't ended. Investments I now needed and couldn't access. The next increment wasn't to be released until my next birthday. Six weeks from now. I usually had a cushion, but disastrous unexpected repairs that had eaten into this year's allowance and done in the last of my savings. The basic bills were paid automatically—electricity, cable, and internet. Anything else that might crop up was not. My advisor had, respectfully, suggested I find some kind of employment.

A job?

Me?

Looking like I did?

Not to mention the other health crap that followed me around and loomed large as a specter in my life.

She'd talked about some kind of online gig. Where I didn't have to show my face.

Great.

What on earth did a thirty-seven-year-old former international fashion model who could barely open a browser know about...computer shit? I could post to Instagram. I knew how to host Facebook parties.

If those were even still a thing.

I hadn't touched social media in ten years. Lots of stuff that'd been big at the time was no longer. And stuff I'd thought would be a flash in the pan had totally taken off. What remained constant, though, was that no one wanted to hear from me. Unless to hear me go over the details of the crash. The pain of losing my only sibling. The devastation of my parents dying mere months later—

I'd cut my throat before I let their deaths become my cash cow.

Which brought me right back to the present.

Temporarily broke.

A nosy roommate.

A dog who needed to be fed.

She eyed me.

I knew *that* look. Sighing, I wandered over to the bedside table to check my phone. No messages. Not that I'd expected any. The phone never rang these days. Well, except by the clinic to remind me of my upcoming appointments. I swiped to my calendar. I had one coming up next Tuesday, so they'd call Monday. And I'd try to cancel. And Hortense would give me a hard time and point out Dr. Marco was staying on late just to see me.

She was a meddling woman with way too much time on her hands, and Marco was a man who seemed much older than he was. At forty-seven, he had plenty of good years to go. But he'd gone gray early—during his mid-twenties, Hortense had once confided—and he didn't try to hide the lines in his face.

I fingered the crow's feet at the corners of my good eye. I used to moisturize religiously, and had sworn I'd have whatever surgical intervention was necessary to maintain my youthful appearance. Now, all my skin care was aimed at care and feeding of the damned scars and I rarely looked in the mirror. Not just because I couldn't bear to look at the scars, but because I didn't need the reminder of who I'd once been. My latest scruff threatened to become a full-on beard soon, which wasn't a good idea because it didn't grow evenly over the scar. I'd grown a beard a dozen times, long, short, wild man, trimmed close, and I'd shaved off every attempt. It always made me look even worse than I already did.

As if that were possible.

After checking the time on my phone, I calculated Dean would likely be long gone from the kitchen by now. If not out the door, down the driveway, and back to Mission City. At least my dog still loved me. "Are you hungry?"

Chip woofed.

I petted her head as I headed out the bedroom door. I could've trod carefully down the stairs, but I stomped. If he was in the kitchen, he'd have enough of a warning to clear out. If he was back up in his room, he wouldn't hear anyway.

Chip being the priority, of course, I poured her food into a bowl and set it by the table. As I straightened, a piece of paper and a single red rose caught my attention.

I'm sorry.

He was sorry? He hadn't done anything. Unless he was sorry for having picked one of the roses off the vines that climbed the west side of the castle. I recognized that bloom. I'd always found them fanciful and, truthfully, hadn't done much with them. My gardener promised they weren't doing any damage to the stone and that she'd trim them as necessary—so I'd left them alone.

Mindful of the thorns, I traced my finger along the stem from the cut up to the petals. I fingered one.

A red rose?

Weren't they for romance? I'd gotten quite a few bouquets in my day—usually as congratulations for having done a good job. Come to think of it, I dated a guy who'd once bought flowers for me. Why had I dumped him? Probably because someone better had come along. More influential. Better able to help me climb to the top. And I couldn't remember that guy's name either. My teens and twenties had been a blur of men, parties, shows, shoots, beds, and airplanes. No wonder Mom had locked down my money.

I suppressed the urge to rip the petals off and shove the entire mess down the garbage disposal.

Why? Why did Dean have to be such a nice guy?

More specifically, why had I come into the kitchen before

my allotted time? I'd known he was in here, and instead of keeping my distance, like I should have, I'd traipsed in and interrupted his dinner. Then there'd been the moment our fingers touched...

I tromped into the dining room, opened the cupboards at the bottom of the curio cabinet, and located a small vase. Telling myself I was all kinds of an idiot—and yet doing it anyway—I put the rose into the vase, adding water. Then I set it on the center of the kitchen table.

And stared at it.

For a really, really, really long time.

I blinked. Several times. Then I sniffed. *Am I allergic to the damn thing?* Yeah, that would just make my day.

Chip, who'd finished eating, sat beside me.

At times, her nervous energy threatened to unhinge me. Then she'd have these moments of preternatural calm, and that would flip me out in a different way. It was almost like she knew I needed her strength. Yet a puppy of less than a year old could not possibly be that intuitive.

Better do more reading.

I thought of the business card sitting on my desk.

Torah Dixon, dog trainer.

Dr. Marco had recommended her when I'd complained about...something Chip had done. I'd been mid-ramble when he'd opened his desk drawer, drawn out the card, and handed it over.

I'd stared at the card.

He'd said something about having lots of patients who had pets in need of training and that Torah was the best.

In that moment, I'd questioned why a doctor felt the need to keep a dog trainer's business cards in his desk. Later, when I'd snuck a peek as I was leaving, I'd spotted a dozen different cards. I couldn't read them without risking getting caught. Up to that point, I'd just thought doctors did, like, medicine shit.

Only as I'd driven home had I acknowledged Dr. Marco did a shit ton more than that for me. Part counsellor, part cheerleader, part facilitator... He'd set me up with a nutritionist. Whose advice I disregarded. As much as I believed I ate well, some of my numbers were out of whack.

He'd tried to explain.

I'd patently ignored.

What was the point of good health? That just meant I'd live longer.

I eyed the fridge, thinking of the lettuce I needed to eat before it rotted.

Then I thought of what I really wanted for dinner.

And decided I'd share.

Ten minutes later, I stood at the closed door of Dean's room. *What the fuck are you thinking? You were horrible to him earlier. You think dessert will make up for that?*

Well, not really. But I had to try. I balanced the two small bowls with spoons in my good hand and knocked on the door. A hollow thump resounded under my scarred knuckles.

No answer.

Great. So I'd leave and—

As I spun, the door flew open. "Hey, sorry mate. I was on a call with my mate Sam and..." His amber eyes widened. "Is that ice cream?"

I held back the *duh*. But it was a near thing. I cleared my throat. "Yes. My secret stash. I...thought you might want some."

"That's brilliant." He glanced behind him. "Do you want to come in? It's, uh..." He cleared his throat, much as I just had. "A bit of a mess."

Suggesting we go back downstairs appealed, but I didn't want him to go through the trouble. "I don't mind mess...if I'm not intruding."

He held the door open wider.

I held out the bowls for him to take one, my bad hand subtly tucked behind me, then followed him inside. Where I'd expected...chaos, I saw only an open suitcase, a few pieces of clothing scattered around, an unmade bed, and a pile of computer stuff on the desk. "It's not so bad."

No missing his wince. "I really try to be more organized. It's just...not my forte. I loved my mom, but she was a bit of a disaster. And I swore I'd do better when she...you know...." He swallowed. "But I still struggle."

"You have different priorities." I indicated the suitcase. "You know you're free to unpack. Unless you're not planning to stay—"

"No." He expelled the word loudly. "I'm staying as long as you'll have me. I trust you'll tell me when you need me to leave." He sniffed the ice cream.

"I..." In my mind, I replayed our various discussions about how long he'd stay. I'd thought a short period of time, but if he stayed longer, I'd be in a better position financially. "How long are you here?"

"At least until the end of October. It's a six-month contract."

"Through to the end of fire season."

"Yeah." He sniffed again. "Okay, I'm clueless. What flavor is this?"

"You might not like it."

He laughed. "It's ice cream."

"Oh, you might be lactose intolerant. I didn't think of—"

"I'm not, mate, but thanks for asking." He poked his spoon into one of the scoops. "Are you going to tell me...?"

"Try it." I managed a smile. "I want to see if you can guess."

"Right-o. Here goes nothing." He siphoned off a bit on his spoon. He put the spoon in his mouth, then dragged it out, puckering his lips as he did. After a moment, he met my gaze.

I watched his Adam's apple bob as he swallowed.

He shook his head. "Absolutely clueless. I mean, this is a great flavor. Canadian...something? I'd think, I dunno, maple or bacon or—"

"You don't have bacon in Australia?"

"Well, I read about maple bacon potato chips. Or ketchup flavor. I definitely want to try ketchup chips."

"That could be arranged."

"Your eggnog ice cream's melting, mate." I snickered.

He laughed. "No, I've never had eggnog ice cream before. My mum hated eggnog with a passion, so this wouldn't have gone over well with her. Me? I love the stuff. Wish I could drink it year-round."

"Yeah, me too. There are recipes and stuff, but..."

"Too much hassle?" He took another spoonful and let out a moan.

That went straight to my groin. What were we talking about? Oh, yeah. Homemade eggnog. "Pretty much."

He saluted me with his spoon. Just before he put it in his mouth, he said, "I'll make you some one day soon."

"That would be nice." I set my bowl on the dresser, apportioned a bit of the delicious ice cream for my spoon. "And, uh, thanks for the rose."

Our gazes held. Finally, he said, "My pleasure."

I ignored the little butterflies in my belly and proceeded to eat my dessert. And if I kept the right side of my face turned to Dean and the stiff side of my lips out of his sight, well, I was there, eating, with a relative stranger. I would take that win.

Chapter Seven

DEAN

THE NEXT FOUR DAYS, I WORKED LIKE A DOG ON THE job and then came home to eat dinner with Adam. Every day, he'd been lurking near the door when I came in and muttered "I have too much food. Join me in half an hour," and I didn't say anything about deviating from our allotted mealtimes. In fact, on Friday night, when he handed me a plate of steaming pasta with a side of green beans with melted butter as well as garlic bread, I nearly wept.

As we sat, Chip at our feet, Adam as always turned sideways so I only saw him in profile, I tried to find a topic of conversation. The past three nights had been subdued, but I felt like maybe tonight we could...bust out? Break free? Back home, Friday nights were the one time I had a beer and put my feet up. The rest of the weekend I did chores and prepared for the next week. I always wanted to be one step ahead—whether on the jobsite or in the classroom.

"Do you, uh, consume alcohol?" I speared a green bean and then, finding some courage in the vegetable, met his gaze as he sat across from me at the table.

"Drink?" He didn't turn to me but his gray eyes darkened.

"Once upon a time, I was the life of the party. Mimosas for breakfast, cosmos for lunch, champagne for dinner."

I'd never tried any of those. Sounded...saccharine. "But now?"

He let out a long sigh. "I was drunk before the accident. I wasn't driving," he quickly added. "But I was wasted. We had a family party that night. I drank to excess and made an ass of myself." He winced. "Frederick, my brother, was always the peacemaker. He should have shoved me into a taxi and sent me on my way, but he bundled me up in my extravagantly expensive coat, shoved me into his car, and drove me home. Only we didn't make it."

Inwardly, I winced.

"The ultimate irony was the guy who T-boned us was also wasted. He hit Frederick's door, trapping him. Then the guy's engine exploded. The flames leapt through the shattered driver's window, and..." He swallowed. "My brother screamed and screamed, and I tried to pull him out, but he couldn't get his seatbelt undone. Then someone opened my door and dragged me out. And I shouted and begged, and then our car exploded as well."

I did my best to try not to betray the horror I felt down to the marrow of my bones.

He pushed his plate toward the center of the table, clearly done with eating, even though he'd barely consumed anything. "I was in a coma for ten days. Then..." He turned toward me, indicated his face and swept his right hand down the length of his chest.

I'd glimpsed his left hand, as well as visible scars on his neck, but he always kept his arms and torso covered. Long-sleeve shirts, despite the heat. Possibly why the castle was always kept so cold. "I want to say I'm sorry. Because I am. That's...horrific."

"Those screams haunt me."

My chest constricted. "I can't imagine." Well, possibly I could, if I went to the darkest place of my psyche, but I wouldn't allow that. I had to press forward and see the positive parts of life. Otherwise, I'd descend rapidly again. I'd gone to the dark place when mum passed. I didn't want to go back.

He shook his head, as if trying to shake off the memory. The haunted expression in his eyes told me he hadn't managed. Still, he asked, "You drink?"

"Just a beer or two to end the week. Friday nights," I clarified. "And a couple when Sam and I go out."

"Sam's your...mate?"

I grinned. "Like an Aussie mate, not an American mate. And I assume Canadian is the same?"

He considered. "Yes, if I hear mate, I think of mating."

"Right. Well, for us not so much."

"You and Sam never..." He made some weird gesture but I figured I knew what he meant.

"No."

"Ah."

"But he's gay. Like me." I shoveled some lasagna into my mouth so I'd have time to consider the answer to any question he might ask. I was pretty sure he'd figured it out. Just like I was pretty sure Ravi and Maddox had as well.

"Ah." He toyed with the crumbs of garlic toast on the side plate. At least he'd eaten that before I'd turned him off the rest of his meal. "There seems to be a lot of that going around." He sipped his water.

He hadn't shared either way, and I hadn't wanted to presume. "Going around?" *I'm surprised he didn't run, but at the least, he's going to be in a dark place.*

"Maddox and Ravi. Then Stanley, Maddox's ex, and Justin moved in just down the road. Married now, of course."

"Right."

"And me." He met my gaze. "But you already suspected."

I held up my hands. "I would never presume. Even if I suspect, I'd never go there without an invitation." Wait, did I word that correctly? When fatigue was weighing me down, sometimes words didn't come as easily.

"An invitation?" His right eyebrow arched. "Do you often get invitations?"

My mind flashed to Sam and his many, many, many conquests. And boomeranged back to me and my paltry few. "That's Sam's jam. I mean, I'm not going to say *no* when asked out, but that doesn't happen all that often."

He gaped. "Why not? You're attractive, clearly intelligent..." He waved his hand in the air as if searching for a third compliment.

"Charming?" I grinned.

A sigh fell from his lips. "You know what I mean."

"I do." I scooped the top layer of cheese off my lasagna and contemplated it. "The thing is, with guys like me, people assume I'm..." I popped the cheese in my mouth.

"A top?"

I nearly spit the cheese out. Then I tried to inhale, which sent me into paroxysms of coughing.

"Need water?"

"Uh...no...?" My eyes watered even as I grabbed the glass of water and slurped some down. I drank so much I was lucky I didn't cough that up as well.

"You okay?"

"Sure...?"

Adam pulled his plate back toward him, used his fork to cut a bit of lasagna, and stared at it. "I've learned not to make assumptions. I might be tall, but I've always been a twink. People see twink and think bottom."

Jesus, please save me. "That's not what I was trying..." I strove to take another breath. "I don't know if I'm a top. What I meant was that they assume I know how... Guys my age can't imagine I never, that I'm..." God, how was I supposed to say this without sounding like an idiot?

"A virgin?" His tone rose in disbelief.

My fork clattered to my plate.

So did his. "I'm sorry. I didn't—"

I tried to wave him off, even as I needed more water. *Fucking hell.* After another long pull, I blinked several times.

"You all right?"

I nodded.

"Not going to choke?"

I shook my head.

"Okay, well, that's good." He eyed his forkful of pasta, meat, and cheese.

Three of my favorite foods.

Finally, he met my gaze. "How do you get to thirty and still be a virgin?"

"Twenty-eight."

He rolled his eyes.

I laughed. "Yeah, mate, fair question." I considered. "Sam...takes up a lot of space. In a good way. People gravitate to him. Like I did. And..." I offered up the best smile I could. "You've got the Australian blond god and, at the time, a kid with acne and gangly limbs. I was taller than him, but I hadn't grown into myself, if you know what I mean. I was awkward, and he was...awesome." I smiled a little wistfully. "Then I went to uni, and he headed to Sydney. He had access to unlimited gorgeous people— tourists and locals. I had to work my ass off so I could keep my grades up."

"Really? You went to university and didn't hook up with anyone?" He appeared truly shocked.

"It *does* happen. I met a lovely young woman who...wasn't interested in dating and sex and *all that crap* as she put it. We hung out, roomed together. It felt disrespectful to bring anyone home. She's now a marine biologist living on a boat with her husband and I'm...a tree hugger."

"So she became interested in *all that crap?*"

"Turned out she was demi. At the time, she thought she was sex-neutral ace. She definitely thought I was."

Adam tilted his head. "Are you?"

"No, mate. I am definitely sexually attracted to certain people, and I'm definitely happy to wank off thinking about them." *Jesus fucking Christ, did I just say that?*

"And yet you haven't..." He made that weird hand gesture again.

"Uh, no." I shrugged. "I'm awkward and I get fixated on my work, and I'm not naturally brilliant so I have to study like a bitch to pass. By the time I graduated with my Master's degree, everyone had paired up. Then I started working for the forestry service and teaching, and..."

"That ship had sailed?" His eye held a little twinkle of genuine amusement.

"Well, yeah. My mum had to drop out of uni when she got pregnant with me. She never went back. Her greatest wish was that I graduate and *make something* of myself. And yeah, if I'd had sex with a guy, I couldn't have gotten him pregnant—"

Adam snorted.

"—but I could've derailed myself and my dreams. I wasn't willing to take that risk." I scratched my chin. "By the time I was ready, the world had passed me by."

"Seriously?" He pursed his lips. "There aren't any gay bars in Mission City, but Vancouver's just a short drive. You must know that, since you came from the airport."

"Yeah, but—"

"So why not head down to the West Side? Davie Street is where you should point your GPS."

"Adam."

"What?" He blinked.

73

"Okay." I put my fork down. "Even if I wasn't exhausted beyond all rationality, do you really think I should head out, less than a week after arriving in Canada, and go down to a gay bar more than an hour's away and, what...hook up with some random dude? Just so I can lose my virginity?"

He frowned. "When you put it like that..."

I almost—almost—said I'd go if he came with me. He wandered around this mausoleum every day and, as far as I could discern, never went out. I might've been wrong, of course. Because I wasn't here during the day. Perhaps he did go out. To brunch at Fifties, or to grab a latté at Starbucks, or to buy fruit at the local market. Even though Ravi had never met him...

No, I knew to the depths of my soul that he never left the property.

In the end, I just offered a tired smile. "I'm pooped. I've worked in forests for years, and although the fresh air is invigorating, the humidity in this place is brutal. I thought you lot were temperate and summer wasn't due to arrive for another month."

He held my gaze for a long moment. "The weather's been unseasonably warm. If you think it's humid now, just wait until we hit mid-July." He indicated my plate. "You going to eat more?"

I eyed the food, now grown cold. *Waste not, want not.* "I'm not sure." I pointed to his plate. "You need to as well."

"My figure..." He winced. "Ten years on and that's still my standard answer to everything." He straightened. "Thank you for your concern. I'm truly not hungry anymore."

"Maybe some ice cream?" I batted my eyelashes. We'd had a scoop of eggnog ice cream after dinner every night this week.

He wagged his finger. "We've got less than half a container left. I won't be able to replenish until November."

I stilled. "Oh, you should've said something. I didn't need—"

He rose. "No, but you enjoyed. I'll survive without it. There's always tiger tail."

I blinked. "Say what?"

"Never heard of tiger tail ice cream?"

Rising, I wracked my brain. I grabbed my plate and followed him into the kitchen. "Can't say I have. That a Canadian thing?"

"Yes. I think you can sometimes find it in the States, but it's a truly Canadian thing."

"Ah." I scraped my leftovers into the rubbish bin. I would've done compost, but the pasta had meat, which meant rubbish. "So what is it exactly?"

"Orange ice cream with ribbons of black licorice."

I winced. "Who the fuck thought that was a good combination?" I swallowed down bile at the thought of black licorice.

Adam, after having scraped his plate, put it in the dishwasher. "If you don't mind, I'll run and get my phone and search who invented—"

"Stuff it." My phone sat in my back pocket, but I wasn't going to get us off track. "So you keep that vile stuff in the house?"

"Sure." He blinked as if surprised. "I have All Sorts as well. A little stash."

"More black licorice?" He didn't have an ounce of fat on him anywhere, but skinny people ate candy just as much as fat people did. I was definitely in between. All muscles and bulk.

Unlike Adam who was all sinew and lean.

I put my plate in the dishwasher. "Well, you have your tiger ice cream. I'll just pass tonight."

He stood right before me. "You said you wanted ice cream."

"Yes."

"And now you're saying you don't because you don't want to use up my stash of eggnog."

"Well—"

"That's very considerate of you." The frown on his brow made his annoyance clear.

"I try—"

"I'm an adult, Dean. If I say I want to share my ice cream, even knowing it will run out sooner than expected, then I'm allowed. I'm perfectly able to cope without eggnog until November."

"Right." I believed him. And gratefully took the bowl with two scoops that he offered a few minutes later. With great suspicion, I eyed the orange-and-black-goo concoction in his bowl.

"Do you want to try some?" He tried to pass the bowl to me. *What if I take it? What if I try something I know I'll hate? Does that show how I feel?* For that matter, how did I feel? Like we'd broken through a barrier tonight. Like somehow things that had once felt impossible now felt possible.

He started to pull the bowl back.

"Sure." I hovered my spoon over his ice cream, trying to find a spot with only orange cream. The damn black crap seemed everywhere. Still, I scooped a small amount that appeared mostly orange. After another moment's hesitation, I put the spoon into my mouth. As much as I wanted to just swallow quickly—like I had when the wasp had flown into my mouth that one time—I tried to savor. To taste, at the very least.

Sort of like an orange creamsicle.

I almost dipped my spoon in again.

Our gazes met.

He held out the bowl, indicated he didn't mind the double dipping.

Bravely—and mostly because he was putting his trust in me—I took a bit with black. Again, I tried to savor.

Then I swallowed quickly so I wouldn't gag. I took a huge spoonful of eggnog, stuck it in my mouth, and let the ice cream melt. And then winced.

"Ice cream headache?" Adam's eyes sparkled as he spooned some tiger tail, even after I'd had some.

I wasn't a fan of germs, by any means, but I wasn't as diligent as some people I knew. I'd pegged this man, with his need for order and routine, as being a neat freak. Obsessive. Or nearly so. What did it mean that he was welcoming my germs? "Yeah, a bit. Hey, do you want to watch a movie?" Along with my beer, I often watched a movie Friday night. Sometimes with friends. Usually by myself. I was good at keeping my own company. Sometimes, I could be the life of the party. Other times, I tried to keep things on an even keel. Tonight should've been one of those nights—especially after the week I'd had. Yet I was willing to venture into dangerous territory.

By spending time with the prickliest man I knew.

The *gay* man who, although he hadn't shown any interest in me, intrigued me to no end. *And he double dipped with me. That means something, right?*

Chapter Eight

ADAM

A MOVIE? WITH DEAN? THAT SOUNDED SO deceptively easy and yet also so challenging. I cleared my throat, staring down at my ice cream where I'd invited his spoon. Twice. *What the hell am I doing?* I was in a freefall, bits of who I once was leaking around the burned remains, and it was terrifying and exhilarating. "There's a media room in the basement."

His eyebrows shot up.

I chuckled. "The castle was built about fifteen years ago. By an entrepreneur with more money than sense."

"How did..." He twirled his spoon in his ice cream, pressing small bits from the scoop against the side of the bowl. To what end, I wasn't certain.

"How did?" I offered the prompt.

He glanced around. "How did you wind up here?"

"The million-dollar question." My gut clenched. "Why don't I give you the full tour?" Well, not my bedroom, but the rest of it, anyway.

"Sure." He dug into his ice cream with renewed vigor, increasing my guilt. I'd pretty much ruined dinner. And, while

I was remembering him choking on cheese, how the hell was this...beautiful man... a twenty-eight-year-old virgin? I ate my ice cream, careful not to get a headache. I rarely indulged in sugar. And I definitely shouldn't have had it every night for the past five. But he'd been so gleeful. He's offered such an infectious grin. I couldn't figure out if he was an introvert or an extrovert. For me, the question was straightforward. Used to be an extrovert and now I was a complete introvert. I didn't do people. I used to love Davie Street. Now, the thought of returning to my favorite haunts held zero appeal. But Dean was an intriguing mystery.

We finished our dessert about the same time, and Dean grabbed both our bowls, put them in the dishwasher, added soap, then started the machine. Finally, he clapped his hands. "Let's get this show on the road."

"Such enthusiasm."

He winked. "I get to see your lair—that's pretty cool to me."

I rolled my eyes. Something I'd been doing a lot since I met this man. "Well, this is the kitchen. After the accident, my lawyer wanted to find me a place to settle. Somewhere permanent. He'd thought a condo in the city." I laughed. Harshly. "Yeah, me. In the city." I led Dean into the dining room which sat an insane sixteen people. "Like I said, the owner of this place was some kind of tech entrepreneur. Anyway, he put all his money into a product that failed. Spectacularly. He'd mortgaged this place, and if the bank foreclosed, he'd wind up with nothing. My lawyer saw the opportunity and pounced." I pointed to the china cabinet. "The plates and stuff came with the place. Just about everything came with the place. I spent so much of my earned money on frivolous things, that I had little in the way of possessions."

"No savings?"

"Uh...not really. Enough for this place, but it cleaned me

out. My business manager had me put aside ten percent, but that got eaten up pretty quickly between the hospital and rehab."

"Don't you have universal healthcare?" He gazed between the gold-accented crockery and myself.

"Sure. But it doesn't cover everything. And I didn't have private insurance, so I had to come up with cash to pay for stuff that wasn't covered. Then my parents died. They'd left their estate, which wasn't much, to my brother. Who'd died. The money's tied up in a trust that I don't have access to until I turn forty."

Dean winced. "That was harsh. Because you're gay?"

"Because I wasn't responsible. They weren't wrong. Before the crash, had I gotten ahold of money, I would've spent it. They didn't change their wills, then they died and..." I sighed. "By the time my lawyer fought for my fair share, little remained. My lawyer bought this place for me with what I had, and I moved here." I opened the china cabinet and handed Dean a plate.

He whistled.

"Yep. Cheesy, wouldn't you say? Over-the-top. And there was a time when that suited me just fine. Now? All I can think is they need to be hand washed and what a pain in the ass that is." I took it back from him, placed it back on the pile, and closed the door. "Plus, if there's an earthquake, even as secure as this thing is—" I pushed against it and it didn't move. "—I still see it all being destroyed."

"You're thinking the big one?" He rested his hand against the back of one of the chairs. "I heard that was a west-coast thing."

"Well, sure. Like, we're overdue or some shit."

He held my gaze. "And you moved here."

What...? Oh. "I didn't expect to live long. Earthquakes were irrelevant."

Slowly, he nodded. "Yeah, I figured that's where you were leading. And yet, you didn't die."

I thought of all the skin grafts. The pain. The desire to just fade away.

Dean telegraphed his next move.

I could've pulled away. So easily, I could've stepped back. Mesmerized, though, I didn't.

He reached out, inch by inch. I watched his hand approach mine. When I didn't pull back, he said, "Okay?"

I nodded, a tiny, stiff, centimeter, but a nod. I reached out, an equally tiny amount.

Dean's big rough fingers snagged my good right hand in a gentle clasp.

I didn't flinch. I didn't panic. I also couldn't deny the clenching feeling in my gut. Aside from Dr. Marco and my specialists in Vancouver, aside from an occasional handshake I'd usually dodged, this was the first time someone had touched me in ten years. Ingrid knew to stay well away. I never saw other people. That just wasn't a thing.

"Show me the rest of your house, Adam. And then we can watch a movie." He stifled a yawn, not letting go of me.

"If you can stay awake."

"If I can stay awake," he confirmed.

Still holding hands, we moved into the living room. "I was really glad the first owner was all about tech. I worried this place might be all chintz and floral, but he'd gone for the modern look." Plenty of leather, chrome, dark wood, and recessed lighting.

As if reading my mind, Dean added, "These rooms are really dark."

I pointed to several lamps. "If you turn everything on, you can get some brightness."

"But you prefer the dark."

"Uh..." I met his gaze. "Yeah. I mean, I go outside and

stuff, so that's not it. I'm not a vampire." I tried for a laugh. It came out as forced. Because that's what it was. "Chip needs lots of fresh air and sunlight." And with the castle being set well back from the road and surrounded by forest, we could go all around the property and never be spotted.

Said dog was fast asleep on her bed in the kitchen, having consumed her dinner with all due haste.

I turned toward the stairs. "I'll show you upstairs."

Dean pointed to closed double doors.

"No."

His amber eyes widened at my sharp tone. "Okay."

I gripped his hand tighter, lest he consider pulling away.

He didn't. "Upstairs?"

"Well, I can show you my den first." I led him across the entryway to the other side, I opened the door and flipped on the overhead lights. Lights I never used. They flickered and one bulb died. "Well, shit."

"I can change that for you. No problem."

The look he gave me was so earnest. I didn't ask for help. If I couldn't do something, then I either hired a professional or it didn't get done. I could find a stool and change a bulb. I reminded myself he meant to be kind. "Sure. You can find lightbulbs in the pantry. Uh, don't worry about it, though. This room faces due south and gets tons of natural light."

"And at night?"

I eyed the laptop, sitting forlorn and unused. "I don't think I've ever come in here at night."

"Ah, you do everything on your phone, eh? Me too."

Truthfully, I didn't do anything on my phone, but I wasn't going to argue. "You just said *eh*."

"Yeah?" He cocked his head.

"That's a thing Canadians say."

He grinned. "Right. Canadians are known for incredible politeness, *eh*, and a-boot."

I wrinkled my nose. "Only easterners say a-boot. Really, just mostly Newfoundlanders. People on the other side of the country."

"Gotcha. We have plenty of weird quirks. And yes, occasionally Aussies say *eh*."

"Ah. We're also known for French."

"Mon cher, je t'adore."

I blinked. "You know French?"

He grinned. "I took a class in my first year of high school. Compulsory. The langue d'amour."

Amour. Paramour. Beloved. Love. And adore was pretty straightforward as well. What had he said? *Mon cher, je t'adore.* Like, Cher? As a Canadian, I was probably supposed to know this...but French classes from high school felt like a million years ago. I shook my head.

A laugh burst out of him. "I said I love you and I chose the love language."

"For a virgin, that seems like an odd choice."

Another laugh. "Maybe I studied French so I'd stand a chance of losing my virginity."

I smiled. "How's that working for you?"

"I'll let you know. It's showing promise."

Chapter Nine

DEAN

WHEN I'D STUDIED FRENCH FOR A YEAR, I NEVER envisioned putting it to practice on a prickly Canadian gay man who shied away from intimacy at every turn.

Somehow, I'd managed to hold his hand through our entire tour of the second floor. Well, the four guest bedrooms and three bathrooms. Seriously, a guy could use a different toilet each day of the week in this castle and still have spares. I'd only ever shared bathrooms. My john in the turret was a dream come true.

He'd pointed to the main bedroom without inviting me in, and then guided me up to the attic space. I loved the dormer windows, and could envision sitting in one on a sunny day, soaking up the rays, and reading my favorite book. Part of me was disappointed the cavernous and empty room wasn't full of boxes and antiques. Given the castle was only fifteen years old, it made sense not enough time had passed for treasures to have accumulated. Back home, we'd lived in a flat, so no hiding spaces there either. "This is a great space." I wandered over to one of the dormers and gazed out the window that looked out over the dark backyard and toward the forest. A few distant lights glittered across the valley and the sky above the trees shone with stars. "Great view."

"Sure."

I shifted my gaze back to him.

He shrugged. "I've never actually been up here before."

"Oh." I'd reluctantly relinquished his hand when we'd taken the narrow staircase up here, but now I reached for it again.

His noticeable hesitation before reaching back was a fraction less than the first time I'd done this. *Just give him time.* "I just think this is a lovely space."

"We could..." He looked around. "There's a bathroom just below. I suppose we could move your furniture up—"

I hovered my index finger in front of his lips. "Shh. Uh, no. I'm staying in an actual turret in an actual castle—"

"Not an actual castle—"

That index finger, which I'd lowered, went right back. "In an actual castle with stone walls and everything."

"Sure. Okay."

"I'll stick to the turret room." I glanced around. "I'm just thinking that there are so many things you could do with this space."

"What would you do?" He considered me. "If you had an unlimited budget and all the time in the world?"

Two things I'd never have. Still, I had a good imagination. I pointed to the southern dormer. "I'd set that up as a reading nook. With pillows and a wool blanket for the cold winter days. The view of the valley in the daylight must be stunning."

He tilted his head. "It is. And I can see what you're envisioning."

I pointed to the northern dormer. "I'd set up a desk there. I mean, if I could do anything in the world, I wouldn't need a desk. But I do, so I'd put it there. Splendid view of the forest. Less direct sunlight." I spun to the eastern wall. "I'd put a television with a massive u-shaped couch. For when my mates come over and we want to watch the game."

"Okay. I don't think I've ever watched a...game...but I can see why that might work."

Finally, I pivoted to face the western wall. Part of that space was curved inward so the turret room could exist. "I'd put a bed. Like a king. Or bigger."

"I'm not certain they make bigger. Although I've heard of the California king. You planning an orgy?"

I offered him a wicked grin. "Nah. But I'd want to cuddle up and be comfortable and I'm a big guy." I looked up at the sloped ceiling. "Unless they soundproofed the roof, I'll bet you can hear the rain. I'd lie in bed during a rain shower, and just..." I blinked. "Sometimes I think rain is the closest we get to...the divine universe."

"God," he prompted.

Considering him, I chose my words carefully. "I'm not into formal religion. I identify with the spiritual practices of the Aboriginal Australians. The land was there long before an ignorant European ever stepped foot there."

He eyed me. All my red hair, amber eyes, and light skin.

"Yeah, I did that DNA test thing. Ninety-nine-point-some-thing northern European." I wasn't going to tell him I did the test because I wanted to know if I had a family out there. Some fourth cousins were on the website, but nothing closer. I was stunned because I'd assumed everyone was registered these days. That I'd hoped to find my father after my mother's passing shouldn't have been a consideration—but it had been.

"I've never done the DNA thing." Adam wrinkled his nose. "I know where I come from."

"But you might discover you're not alone."

His gaze sharpened, those gray eyes turning stormy. "What would I do with family? They might see the castle and think I have money—which I don't. They might feel sorry for me. I don't need that shit."

Perhaps I should've been cowed by his raised voice, but all I saw was a man alone in the world and unwilling to reach out. I couldn't blame him. How often had he tried in the past? Or had he erected these walls just after the accident and only hardened them in the intervening ten years? Made them impenetrable?

Which made my attempts all the more futile. And the more ridiculous.

And yet you're still holding his hand.

"What would you do in this space?"

Adam laughed. "Nothing. It's fine the way it is. I keep it sealed off so I don't have to pay to either heat or cool it. In fact, I'm surprised it's this cool after the hot day we had."

"It's clean." I'd noticed. No dust. No signs of disuse.

"Ingrid." He shrugged. "I told her not to bother with this space, but she never listens to me."

I had yet to meet this woman. I was incredibly curious as, to my knowledge, she was one of the few people he actually interacted with. "I'll have my sheets downstairs on Monday morning."

Something flickered in his eyes, but I didn't know him well enough to read the emotion.

"That's great. I've, uh, told her a bit about you. She's going to clean your bathroom this week."

"Right-o. Except I'd like to take out the trash myself. How does that work?"

He cocked his head. "Do I want to know?"

"What? Oh, no, nothing like that." Clumps of tissues covered in my spunk because I kept wanking off to the image of him? No, he didn't need to know about that. "I just..." I blew out a breath. "I'm used to doing things for myself. I don't like imposing on people. If she gives me the cleaning supplies, I'm happy to do the room and—"

He snorted.

I desisted. And waited.

"I hired Ingrid because she's a perfectionist. And I compensate her well. Truthfully, unless your standards are medical-grade hygiene, she'd likely lose her mind. She cleans and I don't ask questions. I recommend you do the same."

"Got it." I squeezed his hand, the skin warm under my touch. "You said something about a movie?"

"Are you certain you're not too tired? We can call it a night, and—"

"You haven't shown me your media room." I grinned wickedly. "Something tells me this is going to be very high tech."

"Okay." He wrinkled his nose. "Very high tech—fifteen years ago. Everything still works, so I haven't upgraded the equipment."

"So, no..." I trailed off. I probably didn't even know the latest technology in electronics. 4k or something like that? I could search for it, of course, but what would be the point? "Fifteen years is fine. I grew up with a tube television. Everything is great."

"They still have those?" He blinked.

"Poor people do, yeah."

"Ouch."

"Not complaining. I got to watch a lot of great old movies on that thing. I kept wanting to buy mum a new one, but..." I blinked. "I donated the old one to a new immigrant family after mum passed. She'd have gotten a kick out of knowing it found a good home."

"You must miss her."

"Yeah, yeah, I do. Almost ten years." I eyed him. "About the same amount of time for you, right?"

He nodded. "But..." He winced yet again. "I didn't have that kind of a relationship with my parents. They tolerated me and my *antics*, but were clearly waiting for the day I grew up and found a proper job."

I squinted. "Proper? Okay, so you bought this place. Out of the ten percent your business manager made you save."

"Yes." Wariness tinged his voice. "I had a mortgage."

"But you paid a down payment?"

"Yes." Still eyeing me. "A million dollars."

"So you'd made..." I did the math. "...about ten million dollars by the time you were, what, twenty-seven?"

"A bit more. What's your point?" His brow furrowed.

"Just... I think about how long it'll take me just to make a million. Like a fricking long time. Like fifteen or more years. And that's gross, not net. Saving twenty bucks feels impossible most days, yet you made enough to save a million."

"Canadian," he said dryly.

"Which is almost on par with Australian, so I know what I'm talking about. I'm saying..." *What am I saying?* "Even if your parents thought what you were doing was frivolous, you still earned more than most people will in their lifetimes. Certainly more than I ever will—and I've got a good job."

"My work wasn't frivolous." His voice shook. "I made people smile. I showed them beauty. Not just my own, but theirs as well. I showed them what was possible. And, thanks to me, a number of fashion designers in Vancouver got their start. Working with me gave them a cachet. Got them exposure. And I did a lot of charity work." Yet another wince. "Okay, like, *some* charity work."

"Adam—"

"No, I have to say this. I was shallow, Dean. I wanted to believe everyone was beautiful, but I judged. Often harshly. And maybe now—" He pointed to his face. "—this is God's punishment for that arrogance."

"Adam—"

"But I'd give it all back. In a heartbeat, I'd give it all back. I'd do anything to change places with my brother. But I can't. And that's what's slowly killing me from the inside. That I lived, and he died, and it should have been the other way around."

Chapter Ten

ADAM

DEAN GAPED AT ME.

Or, at least, that was how I perceived it. For a very long time, he didn't respond to my outburst. To me saying the words aloud that I'd never said to anyone except Dr. Marco. During one of my darkest, dark periods when I'd found the burden of survival almost too much to bear. He'd wanted to send me to an inpatient facility. I'd refused. I'd promised him I was just talking—that I wasn't going to kill myself. And I hadn't.

But I'd come damn close that time.

And several times before.

And a couple since.

But here I was, with a handsome Aussie staring at me, and this was nothing like those low moments. Unless I'd unloaded too much on him.

"Still want a movie? I might not be great company."

He cocked his head. "Do you think something you've said has changed my mind? That I'd decide you'd be better left alone?"

I tried to pull my hand away, but only a token effort. I didn't really want to lose that touch.

He held fast. I couldn't read his expression.

Is he curious? Is that sympathy? "Pity is a patronizing emotion. I don't want it and I certainly don't need it."

"Who said anything about pity?" He arched an eyebrow.

"I just thought..." What did I think? I wasn't even sure anymore.

Dean stepped closer. "If you need to talk, I'll listen. If you're hurting, I'll try to make it better. If you need help, I'll help you find it. I'm not a professional for emotional stuff, but—"

"You're here." The words felt foreign to me. No one was ever *here*.

One corner of his lips raised. "Yeah. And it started because I needed a place to stay. But...I like you, Adam. The past few nights, I've enjoyed myself, spending time with you."

I wanted to mock his words. Because who could possibly enjoy my surly and rude company? And yet, as I gazed into those gorgeous amber irises, I believed him. His sincerity shone through. He really did like being with me.

More fool you.

"There is a movie I'd like to watch." I eyed him closely. "Barbie."

He grinned. "I have to say that surprises and delights me. Surprises because, well, I didn't see you enjoying something like that. Delights, because I haven't seen it either, and I had it on my list." He kept my right hand in his as he dragged me down the stairs.

Holding on through the narrow attic staircase proved a little harrowing, but he appeared dedicated to gripping as tightly as possible. *Does he think I'm going to bail? I'm the one who suggested the movie.*

And he, being clever, had figured out which was the

doorway to the stairs leading down to the basement. As we hit the very bottom, he stopped short.

I nearly knocked him over.

"Wow, Adam, this is..." Slowly, he moved farther into the space, still holding tightly to me.

Looking around the room, I tried to see it from his eyes. A massive screen sat at the far end, with twenty reclining chairs on tiered risers—like a real movie theatre. To one side of the room was a gaming center with a huge u-shaped couch, a big screen, and two hand-held controllers. At the other end of the humongous room sat a fully functioning bar. I didn't have any alcohol, for obvious reasons. I didn't drink and no one ever came over. Regretting I couldn't offer him a beer, I tried to think of what was in the fridge.

Dean guided me to the pool table in the center of the room. "You play?"

"Uh...no. Like I said, everything came like this." The green-cloth surface was hidden beneath a gray vinyl cover. The cue and balls were neatly stored in a rack on the wall.

"You fancy a game sometime?"

I blinked. "I don't play."

He waved off my concern. "That's okay. We can, I'm sure, find something to occupy our time. I'm a really good teacher in some areas." He squeezed my hand. "Just like I think there are things you could teach me."

Before I could respond, he headed toward the bar, me still in tow. "I'm assuming you've got soda or something?"

"Well, yes, I think so."

"Great. Too bad you don't have popcorn or something. I'm peckish."

"Probably because you didn't finish your dinner."

He glanced back at me. "You're probably right."

"And I do have popcorn."

We'd arrived at the bar, so he halted, finally releasing my hand.

I shouldn't have missed that tight grip, but I did. His look of excitement when he met my gaze did something wonderful to my insides. I could do this. I could offer him something that would make him happy. "We have an air popper stored under the counter." I guided him around the bar with four stools to the little food preparation area.

He whistled again. "Sink, microwave, fridge. You've got everything you need. Without any windows, you're completely cut off. You could survive the apocalypse down here."

"Yeah." I spent a fair amount of time down here. By myself. Hiding from the world. Enough time so Ingrid dedicated a decent amount of time to keeping it clean and stocked. "What would you like to drink?" I pointed to the mini-fridge as I grabbed the air popper, two bowls, and the popcorn kernels.

As I set everything up, Dean put two Canada Dry ginger ales on the counter, along with a container of butter. "How often do you eat popcorn?"

"At least once a week. Ingrid ensures the butter's always fresh." Lest he think the small stick had been around for a while.

"I'd like to meet this Ingrid. She sounds amazing."

"Uh, yes." Of course, they wouldn't meet—Dean would always be at work while Ingrid was here. Ingrid was older than me by a few years, and a damn attractive woman. And single, as far as I could tell. Although I could admit to not really paying that much attention. Dean had admitted he was gay, but might he also be bi? I shook my head. He'd likely meet dozens of people as the summer wore on while I'd remain holed up in my—

"Hey." He snapped his fingers.

I was startled.

"Where'd you go, mate? I was asking if ginger ale was okay. I mean, I figured it probably would be, since you have a lot of it in your fridge."

And because no one ever comes down here, so it must be mine.

He didn't have to say the words. They were as plain as anything. But he chattered on like he hadn't heard the unspoken weight. "I've never seen an air popper like this one. Show me how it works?"

"Yeah, sure." So I did. And within a few minutes, we settled into recliners next to each other. With me to his left, of course. Because if he was going to look over at me, at least he wouldn't see the scars.

The movie turned out to be enjoyable. Not what I'd expected at all, but that wasn't surprising. I didn't read reviews and rarely watched television. The movie had barely entered my radar screen except I'd met Ryan Gosling once, in another lifetime. Back when I moved in the *it* circles.

A light snore drew my attention. I had purposely focused on the movie so I wouldn't obsess about the man next to me. The man who became more attractive every time he opened his mouth. He was damned attractive, but that wasn't what drew me in. With his every word, every gesture, he exuded a kindness I'd never really known in my life. My parents were, according to the blogs I'd read, good parents. They provided. They disciplined. They accepted my homosexuality—even though they weren't thrilled. And they cut me off when my behavior became outrageous, verging on self-destructive. Oh, and they never forgave me for killing their cherished better son.

In the hospital, for one crazy moment, I'd considered telling everyone I was Frederick. That we'd swapped wallets and clothes and that their favorite son was still alive. No one would've believed me. Ask me any science question and the truth would have been revealed. But clearly they wished—if one of their sons had to die—that it would've been me.

Of course, I'd wished that too. So that truth shouldn't have hurt so much.

Carefully, I extricated the popcorn bowl from Dean's grasp. Both his and mine were empty, so I stacked them and put them on the seat next to mine. Then, slowly—after having wiped the butter off my hands—I stroked his cheek with my right hand.

His nose twitched.

In the recessed ambient lighting around the room, his beard shone almost the amber color of his eyes. Eyes that now fluttered open.

"Oh crap."

Despite myself, I smiled. "We can watch it again another time when you're not so tired."

"But I was enjoying it." He pouted. Honest to God, stuck his lower lip out and gave a good old pout.

God, he had such kissable lips.

He licked them.

Our gazes locked.

My chest tightened. Ten years. I hadn't felt a single bit of attraction for ten years and now, this forestry-management specialist—whom I totally saw in my lumberjack bear fantasies —was licking his lips again. "We should…"

"I want to kiss you."

His words were like a slap to the face. "You can't."

He cocked his head. "I reckon that's a hard limit for you, so I'll respect that." He gazed down at my denim-clad crotch. "But there might be something else I could do…to show you how much I like you."

"I, uh, like you too." Something compelled me to continue as he eyed me. "Dean, honestly. I can't say I would've let just anyone stay. Maddox's recommendation and, I don't know, your obvious trustworthiness made it easier to say yes. But..." I swallowed. "I'm hoping you'll stay until the end of your contract. Why look for somewhere else? You're pretty settled here." I traced my finger along the shell of his ear.

He angled his head into the touch like Maurice did when he was in one of his less-fickle moods.

Experimentally, I stroked down to his earlobe and fingered it.

He moaned.

Bolder still, I scratched down his cheek, feeling the crinkly softness of his beard.

"Yeah, mate, keep that up and you'll have me ravishing you in less than a minute."

"But you don't do that." But was that true? Virginity meant different things to different people. I'd given and received a fuck ton of blow jobs before I'd moved on to anal. Maybe he was all kinds of—

He snagged my hand and slowly pressed a kiss to the palm. "I want to ravish you. To try, anyhow. Whether or not I do is entirely up to you." He met my gaze.

"No kissing," I whispered.

"Right-o."

"No touching my face. Or my chest on that side."

"I can respect that." He eyed my crotch with the rock-hard erection straining at my jeans.

"Yeah, that's allowed. Welcomed, in fact."

He licked his lips. "How does this... Do we, you know...?"

I didn't know. Was he talking about logistics of how to actually give a blow job? "Maybe I should go first? Give you one?"

"Nah, mate. Now I've decided, I don't want to chicken out."

"If it's a matter of—"

"Shh." He lowered the foot rest of his recliner.

I followed suit.

He positioned himself between my thighs that I spread for him. Then he sank to his knees.

At once, I wanted to protest. A thin laminate floor covered concrete. There wasn't a square of carpet in this entire house. Something about the last dude being averse to vacuuming. Ingrid did it anyway, but to get the dirt. I had a couple of area rugs and—

Telegraphing his move, he placed his hands on the button of my jeans.

I nodded.

He unbuttoned them, then lowered the zipper.

My cock strained against my boxer briefs. A spot of cum stained the dark gray.

"Ah. I wondered if you were a boxer or jocks man." He gazed up at me. "I should've known you were both. Or neither, depending on your perspective."

Perspective? From where I sat, I just wanted his mouth around my cock as soon as possible. Still, I managed a smile.

With the lightest of touches, he trailed his index finger along my length.

I shifted my hips.

He met my gaze as his fingers slipped into my briefs.

Wanting to help him, I grasped my jeans and underwear as I wiggled them over my hips, making sure my shirt stayed pulled low to cover the mess on my side. Once free, I gently guided my cock. In the light, a drop of precum shone.

Dean cocked his head.

I nodded.

He licked.

My entire world tilted on its axis, and I feared—or hoped —nothing would ever be the same again.

Chapter Eleven

DEAN

As I held Adam's cock in my hand, a feeling swept over me. Something I struggled to define. Because I'd waited for this moment since I'd seen Sam's cock in ninth grade. I hadn't been interested in *his* cock, but the idea of having another guy's in my hands kind of blew my mind. The idea of having one in my mouth was almost more than a fourteen-year-old kid could contemplate.

And yet, I'd known.

Gray, stormy eyes met my gaze as I squeezed experimentally.

He thrust up into my fist.

I grazed my thumb over his slit. Then I put that thumb into my mouth and sucked.

"Jesus, Dean, you'll be the death of me."

Grinning, I ran my hand up and down his length. I cocked my head, yet again asking permission without saying the words.

He nodded.

I angled myself so I could swirl my tongue around his crown.

A moan escaped. Although it came from him, it could've been mine as well. Continuing my journey, I speared his slit with my tongue, enjoying another drop of precum.

He bucked his hips again.

Slowly, I drew him into my mouth. Since I didn't want to gag my first time out, I took it slow and steady. I bobbed and went a bit deeper each time. I swirled my tongue around his cock as I tried to reconcile my mind to the fact I was actually giving a blow job. Experimentally, I grasped his balls in my left hand, feeling the soft and wrinkly skin. I'd handled my own sac thousands of times, but the differences were stark. If his moans and soft encouragements were any indication, I was getting this right. Who knew watching all those gay porn videos would prove helpful?

He ran his hands over my bald pate, making me glad I'd shaved my head this morning. The premature balding thing had pushed me to start shaving it years ago, and aside from worrying about sunburn, I was glad for the sensation Adam now elicited. Again, no one had ever touched me like this before.

With gentle pressure, he encouraged me to pick up the pace. So I did, following the guidance he provided. Of what he clearly liked. What was likely to get him off. What, hopefully, would bring him pleasure.

God knew, I couldn't get any harder, with my shaft pressing against my jeans.

"I'm coming, Dean." He harshly whispered the words. "If you don't want me to—"

I doubled down and sucked harder. Just as he touched the back of my throat, he came. I thought I was prepared, but as the salty liquid hit my tongue, I struggled to swallow.

He grabbed the back of my neck.

I whimpered, even as I continued to swallow.

He raked his fingers through my beard. "You want to come."

As I pulled off his flaccid cock, I gazed up into his eyes. "So bad that I'm going to explode."

Rucking up the right side of his shirt to expose a wedge of slim abs, he whispered, "Come on me."

I didn't need any other encouragement. Clumsily, I rose to my feet. I unbuttoned my jeans, unzipped, yanked my cock out, pumped three times, and came on his chest and abdomen. Dizziness threatened to bring me to my knees, but I fought to focus as I watched the white ropes of cum hit him.

Under hooded lashes, he ran his right finger through a little pool that had accumulated on his belly. He put that finger into his mouth and sucked.

Another spasm rocketed through me, and my deflating cock jerked in interest. Then, remembering I'd just come, it went limp again.

Our gazes held.

After a long moment, his eyes drifted shut.

Mindful of the fact I was still hanging out, I sank back to my knees. In turn, I laid my cheek against his thigh.

He stroked my head.

This. This is what I've always wanted. Why now? Why this man?

Yet, even as I asked the question, I knew the answer. He spoke to me. Called to me in an authentic way that no one else ever had. Had I met him years ago, I would've known he was the one. And not because of his scars or his loneliness. But because of the genuine and deep man beneath the surface. He held others away even as he craved contact and it was an honor he let me see that craving.

"Woof."

I startled, finding Chip in front of me. I hadn't even heard her nails on the laminate floor. "Do you need to go out?"

"Woof."

Adam blinked his eyes open and chuckled. "At least she's good at expressing her needs."

I thought of my sticky, soft dick and laughed. "Well, clearly cocks don't disturb her."

"I'm not certain she knows what they are." He grinned ruefully. "I have to take her out."

"Why don't you let me? I know where her leash is. And there are baggies, right?"

"Uh, yeah."

"Or I can stay here and clean up." I eyed his chest, abs, and cock. "I don't think you want Ingrid finding jizz on your leather recliner."

He furrowed his brow. "Well...huh. I was going to say she's probably seen worse. But if she has, it hasn't been with me. I don't..."

"Yeah. I get it. It's why I don't want her taking out my trash."

After a moment, he cocked his right eyebrow.

From my angle, I had a good look of his entire face. The scars were there, but I barely noticed them. All I saw was a debauched man who looked like he could fall asleep on the spot.

"Tell you what—I'll take Chip out and then clean up down here. Why don't you clean yourself up and go to bed?"

He snorted. "You're the one who did physical labor all day, and you're offering to take care of my dog *and* clean up?"

"Of course." I winked. "I consider it my reward."

"For?"

"For giving my first blow job." I licked my lips, still able to taste him.

"You..." He blinked. "I knew that was your first, but...you were pretty damn good."

My chest puffed out. "Thank you."

"I think you're welcome." He smiled. "If you're willing to take Chip out, I'm happy to take care of the recliner. Ingrid has spare cleaning supplies in the storage closet. I found them when I spilled soda one day."

Slowly—unsteadily—I rose. After tucking myself in, I nodded to Chip. "Out?" That was the word I'd heard Adam use.

"Woof."

"Well, okay then."

I resisted the urge to bend over and kiss Adam as I headed away. *No touching his face.* Clearly kissing fell into that category. I'd kissed a few guys before. Never seriously. Never with someone I was coming to care for.

When we arrived in the mud room, Chip sat patiently while I clipped on her leash. I stuffed a couple of baggies into my jeans' pocket and then glanced through the window to outside.

Dark.

I searched in the cubbyholes, which reminded me of primary school, until I located a headlamp. With a bit of adjustment—Adam's head was a bit smaller than mine—I made it work and we headed out. The night air was cooler than the day. Even a slight nip in the air. Not enough that I regretted not putting on a jacket. I needed the chill. To wake me up. Although I should've been starting to shut down. God knew, I needed sleep. And my only plan for the weekend was to do some grocery shopping, and that wasn't pressing, so I had no plans tomorrow. None.

Chip squatted near a bush.

Turning slightly, I gave her some privacy.

Then realized how truly ridiculous that idea was.

She finished, and we continued to meander down the driveway. I'd surreptitiously watched Adam walk her several nights this week. Sometimes he strode purposefully down the driveway, other times he let her meander. I hadn't discerned a pattern, but if she was inclined to sniff everything, that suited me just fine.

What's Adam doing right now? I probably should've been more insistent about cleaning up. The idea had been mine and, even now, my cheeks heated. Giving a blow job shouldn't have been a big deal. Sam had been fifteen when he'd done it. And had, as far as I could calculate, probably given over a thousand in the intervening years. Sam always loved to share his conquests. Yet, never once, not in all the years I'd known him, had he judged me. He'd casually asked me a few times if I wanted him to hook me up. He'd visited Canberra once, with the thought of heading straight to the gay bar. With the intention of finding someone for me.

I'd begged him not to. I knew myself. A one-night stand wasn't my jam.

He'd tactfully opened a discussion about demi and ace. I'd assured him that I didn't believe myself to be either. Simply put, I wasn't in the right place for a relationship in that moment—neck-deep in research papers and preparing for my future career in academia. His offer, although tempting, wasn't appealing enough for me to put myself out there.

But pretty much since the moment I'd met Adam, that desire simmered within me. Not pity. Of that, I was certain. Something about him...the loneliness? The determination to keep the world out? And yet the deliberate intrusion into my allotted dining times to make my life easier. Making me dinner, no less. Although I was pretty certain Ingrid had cooked much of what we'd eaten. Still, the thought was what counted.

And tonight? The rawness of his emotions still ate at me. Not pity, though. No, something deeper. Physical attraction, to be sure. His slender body appealed. His crooked smile endeared.

His cock impressed.

I'd had that in my mouth. A crooked smile tugged at my lips. *I gave a man a blow job. No not just a man, Adam. I made him come.*

Chip pulled toward the trees. As I followed, she stopped short and squatted again. Ah, obviously I'd need a baggie. I dug into my jeans pocket, retrieved one, and struggled to get it open. In the end, I had to lick my fingers. By the time Chip finished, I was ready. Quickly I had everything done. She looked up at me.

I shrugged—trying to convey whatever came next was up to her.

She cocked her head.

"Home?"

She headed that way.

I could always give her a longer walk tomorrow.

If Adam let me. To this point, I hadn't asked about spending more time with Chip. She was often within reach of her master, and I'd located numerous dog beds around the castle.

Also, I'd yet to spot Maurice the cat. I'd seen his fancy litter box in the mudroom, but had never actually caught him using it. And given the size of the place, I suspected he and I could go the entire six months without spotting each other.

Six months.

Adam asked me to consider staying the whole time.

Well, duh. No-brainer there.

But would he ask me to join him in bed tonight? Did I even want to? Was this all happening too fast, or just exactly fast enough?

I didn't have an answer to that question. Since Chip didn't appear to either, we headed home.

Chapter Twelve

ADAM

THREE DAYS.

As I sat in Dr. Marco's waiting room, I obsessed over... everything.

When Dean and Chip returned from their walk, I thanked him without meeting his gaze, then practically dragged the dog upstairs and closed my bedroom door.

God only knew what Dean had thought of that childish reaction.

Saturday and Sunday, I'd stuck to my allotted kitchen times and had spent the rest of the time holed up in my den. Reading. Or so I told myself. More like pacing incessantly and obsessing even more. Both days, I'd taken Chip on long walks around the property. Checking the fences, I told myself.

I was feeding myself a lot of crap.

Avoiding the house, was the truth of it all.

Monday night, I courageously prepared grilled salmon, roasted baby potatoes, sautéed mushrooms, green beans, and fresh-baked rolls. I hadn't baked them, but that wasn't the point.

At seven-thirty, long after I'd realized he wasn't going to make the meal, he'd texted to say there had been a spot fire, and he'd been assisting the fire department to ensure it didn't get out of control.

I'd wrapped everything up, left a note, and had gone to bed.

Hortense, Dr. Marco's receptionist, watched me. She intimidated the hell out of me with her black hair in an efficient ponytail and her dark-brown eyes always scrutinizing me.

I used to work with a woman with the same dark skin—the color of mahogany. Imani's career success as a model eventually parlayed into acting, and she had a recurring role on a television series filmed in Vancouver. She texted me periodically.

I never texted back.

"What?" I tried to scowl, then remembered that wasn't a good look.

She shrugged. "You seem...different." She eyed Chip. "And I'm always glad to see my precious girl." She, in fact, had been the one to suggest I bring Chip.

I'd shown her a picture when I'd brought the puppy home. Totally out of character for me.

Hortense said they allowed service animals, therapy dogs, and personal-support animals.

I pointed out Chip was none of those three.

She pointed out that she made the rules in the office, and if she decided Chip was a personal-support animal, then that's the way it was.

Like I was going to turn down the opportunity to bring my adorable puppy with me. Plus, socialization was important, and Chip didn't get enough of that. Now, she saw Hortense, Dr. Marco, and often one or two people wandering down the street when we were in the parking lot. If they expressed interest, I'd let her interact. I always wore my cap down low and kept my head ducked.

Still, most people spotted the scars. Some stared. Some turned away.

A precious few acted like it was no big deal.

Chip's tail swished on the ground.

"She's starting training soon."

"Torah Dixon?"

"Yeah."

"Best trainer in—"

A young woman darted from the back and scooted out the door without acknowledging either Hortense or me. Not that I expected anyone to, but her demeanor spoke of someone wanting to be left alone.

I could relate.

Hortense rose. "I'll show you back."

Of course, I could find my own way. Had done this twice monthly for almost ten years. Still, she ran this clinic with an iron fist.

I sat on the chair next to the exam table.

"We'll see you in two weeks." She petted Chip. "You be good for Torah."

Chip woofed.

Hortense laughed. Then she headed out, closing the door behind her.

Leaving me alone with my thoughts.

Fortunately, I didn't have to wait long before Dr. Marco arrived. He sat on the stool, wheeled over to the computer, tapped a few keys, then scrutinized whatever he saw.

Well, likely my blood and urine test results.

"Adam."

"Yep."

He met my gaze. His dark eyes always drilled little holes

into me. This was the one person I should really be listening to.

But I didn't always.

He indicated I needed to sit on the exam table, which I did. Reluctantly. Then he took my blood pressure. And sighed.

I squirmed.

"You know I care about you, right?"

"Yeah." He often said this. And I believed him. He cared about all his patients. That's what made him such a great doctor. With great empathy, though, came great responsibility. He treaded a fine line between cosseting me and tearing me a new one.

"Have you been following the diet Ankita had prepared for you?"

Ankita was the dietician who worked with several of the medical clinics in town. Nice woman. I didn't like anything about the meal plans she suggested.

"I'm eating healthy."

Dr. Marco arched an eyebrow. "I'm not going to have you write out a food journal."

Because the last six times you tried, I didn't do it...

"But if you're not following her directions, then you're not getting the nutrients you need." He removed his glasses and pinched the bridge of his nose. "The infection after the scars did a lot of damage, Adam."

I winced. Dr. Cho included the information in my file that had been passed to Dr. Marco when he agreed to take me as a patient.

Unsurprisingly, I didn't want to talk about my past.

Just as unsurprisingly, Dr. Marco did.

"Are you taking the supplements?"

"Sometimes." I could lie. Hell, I was incredibly tempted to. But I owed Dr. Marco the honest truth.

"We can have the pharmacy make blister packs for you. Then you don't even need to count them out."

"I can count them out," I snapped.

"And you can set an alarm to remind you—"

"I can remember," I snapped again.

He sighed. "Then why don't you?" He put his glasses back on. "Look, Adam, for ten years you've resisted counselling. I nagged and threatened and found therapists who would work remotely or by text, and you never followed through. I've been inches from having you involuntarily held a couple of times. I told myself that if I insisted, you might just stop coming in altogether. Stop seeing anyone at all. And that would be worse."

"Right. So can I go?" I started to slide off the exam table.

"No."

I shuffled back. "What if I promise to set an alarm and take the pills?"

He arched an eyebrow.

Yeah, I'd be skeptical too. I hadn't in the past...so why this time? I cleared my throat. "I, uh, have a roommate."

He sat up a little straighter, his dark gaze narrowing on me. Not for the first time, I noted the gray streaks in his short, dark-brown hair.

"You're living with someone?" Absently, he petted Chip's head.

"Well, sort of. He's renting a room."

"That's good." He scrutinized me. "What does this have to do with taking the supplements? Will he remind you?"

"No, nothing like that." So why was I telling the doctor? Nothing was really changing in my life. Except...I had company.

"Adam."

"Yep."

"I want you to see a counsellor."

110

"Nope."

He held up his hand. "This isn't really a request. You tell me you're not purging."

"I'm not." *Most of the time.*

"You tell me you're not suicidal."

"I'm not." *Not recently.*

"Well, see a counsellor for half a dozen sessions and put my mind at ease."

"Six appointments. You think I'll have enough to say to fill six appointments?" I didn't bother to hide my disbelief. My annoyance. "Dr. Marco, I don't have anything to say to anyone. There's nothing going on. I live my life. I have Chip and this new roommate—"

"And you're not taking your pills or taking care of yourself, Adam." He sighed. "The numbers don't lie, and yours are going in the wrong direction."

For the first time in this conversation, I had an ominous feeling. "What do you mean?"

"That pills now will help prevent or delay more-drastic treatments down the road. Or complications you don't want." He scratched Chip under her chin—right in her favorite spot. "You've got a dog who needs you."

As much as I wanted to argue, I couldn't. I'd supported Froufrou for a long time-through a variety of health ailments. Hers and mine. I probably should've let her go sooner. That would've been the humane thing to do. But I'd stubbornly clung to more time and had spent a pile of money trying to keep her going. In the end, she'd let me know the time had come. Her vet, Dr. Zephyra Dixon—trainer Torah's sister— had helped me grieve and then had encouraged me to get Chip.

Whom I hadn't named. I should've renamed her. But that would have been too much—

"Adam."

"Yep."

"You don't want complications. You don't want to wind up back in the hospital."

"No."

"Then do as I ask."

I pursed my lips. "I'll follow the meds regimen."

Dr. Marco nodded. Then he wheeled over to a drawer. He extracted a business card and held it out to me.

Reluctantly, I took it.

Healing Horses Ranch. Dr. Kennedy Dixon, PhD.

I actually snickered. "You've given me this before. *Another* Dixon."

Marco cocked his head.

"Torah...Zephyra..."

He nodded. "There are eight sisters in total, so it's hardly surprising you've encountered more than one."

Actually, given I barely left the house, meeting one felt monumental. Two felt like I was beating the odds. Three felt like *winning the lottery* territory. Then my mind screeched to a halt. "Eight sisters?"

Marco inclined his head. "Yep, eight."

"How many brothers?"

"None."

"What are the odds of that?"

He grinned. "You know, I've never calculated them. And I'm not going to right now. Kennedy's expecting your call. If you don't want to speak to her, she's got a handful of counsellors on staff, including Justin Bridges. You...have stuff in common."

I deadpanned. "He's gay."

A chuckle escaped Dr. Marco. "Well, since he's often spotted around town with his husband, Stanley, and their two children—"

"Stanley. As in Maddox Baker's ex?"

"Yes." He eyed me.

"Stanley and this Justin and their kids live on my street. Maddox and his husband and their kids live on my street."

"And yet I suspect you don't socialize with them." He tapped the table next to me. "I don't see a conflict of interest with you speaking to Justin, but do whatever works for you." He rose. "This is non-negotiable, Adam. Kennedy has some forms for you to sign, giving her team permission to speak to me about you."

"I think this is an overreach."

"Do you want me to go through the possible progression of your illnesses if you don't comply?" He started to sit back down.

"I'll go." Partly because I just wanted to get the fuck out of here. And partly because I'd already seen enough of hospitals to last a lifetime, and if I didn't take care of myself, I might just wind up having to visit one multiple times a week. I'd looked up progressive kidney disease, and it was no kind of party.

"See that you do." He gave Chip a final pet.

She preened.

He washed and scrubbed his hands thoroughly, dried them on a paper towel, gave me a salute, then left.

Chip gazed up at me.

"Yeah, I know."

Seven o'clock had come and gone. As much as I needed to get home, I didn't feel like cooking. Even if cooking meant heating up something Ingrid had prepared.

I opted for the A&W drive-thru, hoping for a cashier who knew me. Because of the car's configuration, my scars were always the first thing visible. Sometimes I'd go into the store, but that didn't tend to work out any better. I ordered my Mozza burger with onion rings and a root beer. I was about to pull away, when a thought occurred. "And throw in a chicken sandwich combo."

"Sure. Drink?"

"Cola." I hadn't noticed Dean drinking diet soda, so hopefully this was the right choice.

The cashier was one I'd seen before. She offered a genuine smile as she gave me the machine to tap. Within moments, I had my heavenly smelling food and was headed toward home.

Chapter Thirteen

DEAN

WE'D BELIEVED YESTERDAY'S FIRE HAD BEEN extinguished. Until we received a call late Tuesday morning that it'd flared again. Reignition happened. Well, more like we'd missed a hot spot. Roxie assured me the Mission City Fire Department were the best, and the flare was just *one of those things*.

By the time I hit the house that night, totally exhausted, I was ready to drop. Except I hadn't eaten since I'd scarfed down a protein bar at ten. Some ten hours ago. So food wasn't just a luxury—it was a necessity.

I removed all my clothes in the mud room and threw them all in the washing machine, setting an alarm on my phone so I wouldn't forget to put them in the dryer.

Only then, did I realize my mistake. I was down to my jocks with no way to cover myself.

That didn't seem right. Surely there must be a towel to dry off Chip. I didn't care if I wound up smelling like dog. I just didn't want to scamper mostly naked through the house, and—

"Are you okay?"

I whirled to find Adam standing in the door to the mudroom. He had a takeout drink cup in his hand and he took a long pull through the straw.

His Adam's apple bobbed as he swallowed.

I watched, mesmerized.

Then my state of undress came home to roost in the form of violent shivers. "Uh, I'm pretty rank. If you've got a towel—"

"I don't care if you run around the house naked." He appeared to consider. "Well, you'd have to take your underwear off for that." He indicated toward the kitchen. "I brought you a chicken sandwich, a cola, and some fries. Or you can share my onion rings…"

"Not a fan."

"Okay." He nodded again. "You have a shower and I'll warm up your food. I mean, I'm assuming you haven't eaten."

"No." I rubbed my face. "I'm starving. I'll love you forever if you feed me. Or I'll love Ingrid."

He chuckled. "No Ingrid. The fast food was all my doing." He cocked his head. "I don't know why, but I kind of assumed you'd need to be fed." He pointed to my goose bumps. "Go shower." With that, he pivoted and left the room.

I didn't need to be told twice. I hotfooted up two sets of stairs and was in the steaming shower within moments. Scrubbing off the soot and smoke smell was wonderful, and I would've luxuriated, but my stomach rumbled and vague nausea came over me in waves. Pretty soon, I'd be too nauseous to eat. Which was a complete contradiction. I dried off, then tossed on sleep pants and an old Dockers T-shirt. *Heave-ho. Freo heave-ho.* Which reminded me. Wasn't there a Derby Day coming up? Perth had two football teams, and when they played each other, they called it Derby Day. Being from South of the River, I was naturally a Docker fan. Those

North of the River, Eagles fans, were just loser weagles as far as I was concerned.

The scent of fried food carried me all the way down to the kitchen.

Adam sat with a plate before him while a second sat across from him with a silver dome above it.

Hurriedly, I sat. After he nodded, I raised the dome. The smell of seasoned meat, French fries, and ketchup assailed me. My saliva glands went into overdrive.

"This is brilliant, mate." I eyed the breaded chicken. "Thanks so very much. What did you—" *Oh crap, he just took a bite.* I waved for him to continue chewing. "So, the fire came back, which is weird, but this time we're sure it's out. And I'm sorry for coming home stinking. It's lucky you've got that separate room. And, for all the medieval stones and shit, this house has amazing ventilation."

He wiped his mouth, then swallowed. "Uh, yes, medieval shit."

I started to object, but he smiled. "State of the art. If the owner had held onto it for a few more years, when the real estate market turned, he could've gotten double or triple."

My eyes widened. "This place is worth that much?"

"Yes. The acreage it sits on increases the value. That and the privacy aspect. If someone put up an impenetrable fence, this place could literally become a fortress. I didn't buy it for that reason, but having this level of invisibility helps."

"No one ever comes onto the property?"

"Not that I know of. I have motion-triggered lights at night. I suppose I should set the alarm when I'm alone, but..." He glanced down at Chip.

She sat. Placidly staring at our food.

He met my gaze and shook his head. "She does *not* need a French fry. Her vet would have a conniption fit."

I wasn't going to argue, of course. I turned to Chip. "I'm sorry."

She cocked her head.

Then gave me what I termed *puppy dog eyes* as she flopped onto her belly and laid her chin on her front paws, still keeping both of us within sight.

"In case we drop something," Adam assured me. "Hasn't happened yet, but she lives in hope."

"Nothing wrong with living in hope."

Our gazes caught.

Something passed between the two of us. I tried to discern it, but he shoved a large onion ring into his mouth, effectively silencing me on that topic.

What's he afraid of? Why has he remained so cut off since Friday? Did I scare him? I dipped a fry in ketchup. "I got the food you left for me last night. I'm sorry you went through all that trouble and I wasn't here."

He waved me off. "Ingrid did it. You ate it, so she doesn't even know."

Ingrid might've made it, but I'd read between the lines that he'd thought we'd be eating together. And I hadn't made it home. Well, until very late. "The food was appreciated." I pointed to the food before me. "As is this. I should pay—"

"It's fine." He snapped the words. "I can afford a sandwich." He straightened his shoulders. "I used a coupon."

"Oh, that's brilliant, mate. Coupons are the best." Mum and I used to collect them when I was young. I'd never gotten out of the habit and, when I was clearing out my place so I could move here, I'd found an enormous stack. All of which had expired, so I felt vaguely annoyed at myself for not having used them when they were still good.

He laughed. "I'd never clipped a coupon in my life before the accident. We were...well-off. Better than most. By a bit." He looked around. "And I suppose I still am. House poor doesn't really count as hard done by. I have enough to survive on."

I wanted to ask about a dozen questions to do with his finances, but so not my place. "Mum and I had a little flat. I loved her, but she wasn't the tidiest of people. Don't get me wrong—everything was clean. Just...cluttered."

Adam shuddered.

"Right. So I've sworn to never be like that. But..." I shrugged. "I think it's genetic. The disorderly gene."

"Can't say I've ever heard of that." He took a sip of his drink. "I...didn't take care of my possessions. When something broke, I threw it away. If something got torn, I'd toss it as well. At least I usually remembered to give old clothes to our house-keeper who would donate them." He poked at his burger. "At least, I assume that's what she did. I just...didn't care." After a moment, he picked up the burger. "I regret not having taken better care. Of thinking only of myself." He bit into his burger.

I wanted to argue, of course. To say he hadn't been that bad. That he couldn't have been as selfish as he portrayed himself. Except I couldn't, because I hadn't known him back then. Reconciling that person to the man who'd taken in a virtual stranger proved challenging. And sure, he said he'd done it because he needed the money, but buying me a meal wasn't helping his finances. And eating with me each night—keeping me company—didn't improve his bottom line. He was a good man. I just had to find a way to prove it to him.

Before I could speak, though, he yanked out his wallet.

Uncertain of his intentions, I held myself still.

He pulled a business card out and dropped it on the table. Then he nudged it toward me.

Healing Horses Ranch. Dr. Kennedy Dixon, PhD.

I scrutinized the card. "Shouldn't that be DVM?"

He cocked his head.

"Doctor of Veterinary Medicine."

He snickered. "She's a psychologist."

"Oh, Yeah, didn't see that coming." I searched for some kind of indication, but couldn't find anything. "How do you know?"

"My doctor wants me to go to therapy."

This time, I cocked my head. "Your medical doctor?"

He nodded.

"Right. Well, like, if that's what he... He?"

He nodded again.

Phew. Didn't want to be accused of sexism. The last doctor I'd seen was a woman. "Right. So if he feels you need to go, why not? Is it the cost? I can pay a bit more in rent—"

"No, nothing like that."

Another phew. I was paying less here than I would've at Mrs. Thistle's house, but my paycheck would only stretch so far.

He shifted. "Now I have private health insurance. It covers quite a few therapy sessions. I got it after I got out of the hospital, and some of the physical care isn't covered, considered preexisting, but therapy is."

"And you're not certain about this...Kennedy?"

His gray eyes flickered.

Interesting.

"I guess...he asked me to go, and I have to do what he asks."

That caught my attention. I understood following a doctor's directions, but not *having to do* whatever they recommended. Still, none of my business. "Do you need my help to make the call?"

"Uh...no."

"You don't sound certain." I dipped another fry in ketchup.

Chip whimpered.

I shot her a glance.

She put one of her massive paws over her snout as if in protest for not getting a treat.

I snickered. Then refocused on the troubled man across from me. "How can I help?" I slid the card back toward him. "If you say you need to go, then you make the call."

"Except..." He fingered another onion ring which was surely pretty cold by now. Cold fries were doable...cold onion rings were just plain gross.

I tapped the table next to his fidgeting left hand and turned mine palm up, inviting his touch. After a hesitation, his scarred fingers landed feather-light on mine. I didn't close my grip, let him call the shots.

He stilled, his gaze shooting to mine.

"Do you need me to make the call? Because I'm happy to do it. Although a git with an Aussie accent might confuse them."

"I might have the choice of counsellor."

"Oh." I scratched my cheek. "I thought you were seeing this Kennedy guy. Oh, shit, gal? That's one of those names—"

"She's a woman."

"Right."

"One of eight sisters, two of whom I already know. And you don't need to know any of that."

Eight sisters sounded completely overwhelming. Still, as an only child, I would've been thrilled to have even one. "So you might not see Kennedy?"

"There's another counsellor there. Justin Bridges?"

I held his gaze, unsure of where he was going with this.

"Justin's gay."

"Okay?" I tilted my head. "Does your doctor know you're gay?"

"Yes."

"So did he suggest you speak to Justin or Kennedy? Or both?"

"Casually, almost in passing, he mentioned Justin, who's married to Stanley, and—"

I snapped my finger. "Right. Stanley is Maddox's ex."

Adam's eyes widened. "You know that?"

"Ravi mentioned something, I think. About how they all live on the same street. He seemed very Zen about his husband's ex-boyfriend living so close." I considered. "Do you know Justin? I mean, you're neighbors..."

"I only know Maddox. Even that was..." He glanced down at Chip. "A fluke."

She huffed.

"Okay." I tried to wrap my head around the problem. "So you're worried you might run into him on the street or something? Or that he might tell Maddox?"

"Jesus, I hadn't even considered that."

Oops. "I'm certain there's a patient/counsellor privacy thing. He won't tell anyone, I'm sure. So...talking to a gay counsellor...does that freak you out or something?"

He leaned back.

Still, I clung to his hand.

"I don't know." He furrowed his brow. "The idea of talking to *any* counsellor freaks me out."

I wanted to point out he had free autonomy. He didn't *have to do* anything. But part of me figured his doctor knew best. A good therapy session could be really helpful. I'd seen a student counsellor after my mum passed. Just a couple of sessions—to help me work through my grief. But well worth the effort. "Why don't you make a list?"

"Huh?"

"Like a list of pros and cons for each counsellor."

"I don't know each counsellor."

"Sure. But you know Justin's a gay guy and Kennedy's a

woman…" I floundered. "Uh, with seven sisters." I frowned. "No brothers?"

He shook his head.

"Huh, what are the odds?"

"Less than half of one percent."

A laugh escaped. "You calculated it?"

He scrunched his face. "I might've looked up the odds of flipping a coin eight times and landing on heads eight times in a row. Less than half of one percent."

"Okay." We were getting sidetracked—and that was my fault. I eyed the enormous clock on the wall. That traditional clock with roman numerals felt so incongruous in this high-tech house. Didn't fit in a medieval castle either, for the record. "It's past seven. If you call now, you'll get the answering machine. So leave a message saying you're calling for either Kennedy or Justin. Whoever calls you back wins."

His eyes widened again. "Chance? You want me to leave things up to chance?"

"I'm a fatalist, my friend. Everything's already pre-determined. You think you can change your fate, but you can't."

He blinked. "You don't actually believe that. Or why would you have taken a job on the other side of the globe?"

"I'm saying this was what was meant to happen. Mrs. Thistle's daughter was supposed to leave the asshole and move home so I wouldn't have a place to stay—" Him waving his hand in the air didn't distract me.

"And I was meant to meet Ravi and Maddox in the diner. Just like Chip was meant to go missing so Maddox would be able to help you find her."

"That's absurd. That removes free will from the equation. Every person makes a million decisions a day that impact their lives—"

"They only *think* they do. Really, all that's been already decided." I waited.

And waited.

And—

"That's bullshit. And you don't believe any of it."

I grinned. "Yeah, but I had you going there for a bit. Still, make the fucking call, Adam, before you lose your nerve. Leave a message. Deal with the rest tomorrow." I squeezed his hand. "I'm here to support you. Whatever you need."

Chapter Fourteen

ADAM

I'm here to support you. Whatever you need.

For reasons I couldn't even fathom, I believed him. He was here to support me. He did have my back. No matter what the outcome of the phone call, or even of the therapy session, he'd be here.

I flexed my fingers.

He let go of my hand.

I reached into my back pocket and yanked out my phone. Carefully, I dialed. Then counted the rings until the answering machine—

"Healing Horses Ranch. This is Rainbow Dixon. How can I help you?"

"Uh..." I'd put the phone on speaker, again for reasons I couldn't fathom. Now I glanced at Dean, panic rising in my chest. "Rainbow?" I stammered. "I was looking for Kennedy."

"Are you a client?"

"No."

"Oh, okay. Well, Kennedy's in a session right now."

"But it's night."

There was a pause. "Kennedy sees clients several nights a

week. As do some of our other counsellors. Not everyone can get out here during the day."

"Oh. Right." *God, how stupid can you be?*

"I can get Kennedy to call you back. It might be tomorrow, though."

"How about Justin Bridges?" Because that wasn't leaving things up to fate or anything...

"Justin doesn't work Tuesday nights, but he's here first thing tomorrow morning." She waited. "Is this urgent?"

"No." *Why is this so hard?*

"Rainbow?" Dean's soothing voice carried across the small space.

"Yes?"

"My name's Dean. And I'm just a friend of this guy. He wants to make an appointment. He's been told both Kennedy and Justin are wonderful counsellors."

"Well, they are."

"So who has the first opening?"

My gaze shot to him.

He shrugged.

Fucking hell. He was going with this pre-determined shit.

"Justin's had a cancellation for tomorrow night. Six o'clock."

"Great." He turned expectant eyes on me.

Somehow, Adam's steady gaze made me do what a hundred suggestions from Dr. Marcus hadn't. "I'll take it," I squeaked, then my throat closed tight.

I waved frantically at Dean, who smiled and told Rainbow, "His name's Adam. Granger."

"Fantastic. Adam...?" She paused, clearly waiting for me to respond.

I cleared my throat. "Yep."

"Would you be comfortable giving me your email address? I can send you the intake forms. You can fill them out and read a bit about the ranch. You can meet with Justin tomorrow night and you guys can see if you're a good fit. That okay?"

I rattled it off, struggling to piece together what had just happened. Then a thought occurred. "Did you say your name was Rainbow Dixon?"

"Yes."

Even I could hear the smile.

"Like Dixon as in Kennedy, Zephyra, and Torah?"

"Yep. There are more of us, but you probably won't see them tomorrow. You can find Sunshine at The Owl's Nest bookstore, Spring's an intern reporter with the Mission City Gazette, and the twins are still in high school."

"Twins?" I kept my gaze on Dean's.

He grinned.

"Yep. That's eight."

"Okay...well, thank you."

"My pleasure, Adam. I look forward to meeting you tomorrow night." She cut the call.

I sat, staring at Dean. "Did that just happen?"

"Yep." He grinned. "Everyone seems to be saying that a lot today."

I poked my cold burger.

He snagged both our plates. "I'm going to warm these up, we're going to eat them, and then we'll take Chip out for her evening constitutional. Then bed. For me, at least."

He offered that breath-stealing smile that had become achingly familiar to me. Before I could stop myself, I blurted out, "I'm sorry."

He cocked his head. "For what?"

The microwave beeped.

"For..." I floundered. "You..."

He brought my plate over to me, placed it on the table, then headed back to the microwave. "I...what?"

"Gave me a blow job, and I ran off."

127

"Oh, that." He scratched his beard. "I just, I dunno, figured you needed time to process it. Or you had regrets."

The microwave beeped.

He retrieved his food and joined me at the table.

"I don't have regrets."

Our gazes clashed.

"Well, only that, of all the men in the world that I wound up being your first. You could've done so much better—"

"Bollocks." He picked up a fry and examined it as if it contained all the wisdom in the world. "Well, bullshit, anyway. I have agency, Adam. I can do whatever I want. You were willing. I mean, you definitely consented."

"I did."

"So if you're having regrets, that's on you. I have none." He grinned. "I'd be game to do that again." He sucked the ketchup suggestively off his fry before popping it into his mouth, then poked at his sandwich. He lifted the top, snagged the wilted lettuce, then ate that.

All the time, I watched him with fascination. Here I'd been obsessing about this and, clearly, he had not. Or he was putting on a façade. I couldn't tell. Which pretty much drove me nuts.

"Eat your burger, Adam, or I might worry about you."

"I'm fine."

"Right."

"You think because I've agreed to go to counselling that there's something wrong with me."

He put his sandwich down. "When my mum died, I spoke to someone. Those sessions had a big impact on me. Helped me put things in perspective. If I needed to see someone today, I wouldn't hesitate. It's not weakness to admit you need help." He stared at me defiantly with a little jut in his chin.

"If I go—"

His amber eyes flashed triumphantly.

"If," I repeated.

He nodded.

"Then I think I should get some kind of reward."

"Well, I think that can be arranged." He cocked his head. "Why don't I go with you tomorrow night? I can sit in the car. I've got some reading to get caught up on. Then we can go out to dinner. My treat."

Everything up to the *out to dinner* appealed. If he went with me to the ranch, I was less likely to chicken out. If he stayed close, I'd feel his presence. "I don't eat out, Dean. For obvious reasons."

"I don't see anything obvious about it." He scowled. "Fifties has the best burger in town. Everyone swears that. Roxie? My boss? Can't stop raving about them."

A&W made a damn fine burger. I should know, since I'd just enjoyed one. "Let's...see? I believe you can do takeout with them. So we could order and then bring the food home with us."

He offered a cheeky grin. "Yeah, this is a nice place to hang out. A good home."

Something lit within me when he mentioned *home.* Specifically when he referred to my home, and not Australia. I motioned to his purple T-shirt. "That's quite the color."

"Oh, yeah. They're playing soon. I need to check, but I think they're playing their biggest rivals this weekend."

"You'll want to watch." Duh.

"I'm not sure there'll be a station that covers it."

"If you give me the particulars, I can call the cable company and figure out if there's a channel I need to add."

"You don't need—"

"I want."

"Oh. Okay. I'll text you the details." He smiled. "That would be great. Do you want to watch with me?"

"Will it be the middle of the night?"

He winced. "Yeah, probably."

"Well, with enough notice, I'm certain I can manage to make it." With my world-class insomnia, I *knew* it wouldn't be a problem.

We finished our food in silence and then, as if by mutual accord, he put the dishes in the dishwasher and I hooked Chip up to her leash. As we stepped outside, the mugginess of the night hit me. "You were out in this all day."

"Yep. We need rain. Badly." He matched my stride as we headed down the driveway. "And I'll even pick up the poop tonight."

I laughed.

He nudged me.

And that joviality—along with the meandering conversation about property lines, neighbors, and a few other things—carried me through that night and into the next day. I'd been tempted to invite him to my bed, but that felt wrong. Instead, I'd wished him a good night. After a decent night's sleep—the first in a while—I settled after breakfast to look at everything Rainbow had emailed me.

The intake form was pretty straightforward, although I hesitated on the reason for my visit. How much was too much? If I told them everything, would they decide I was too much trouble?

Not likely...they work with people even worse off than you.

If I didn't share everything before we started, would that allow me to keep some of my secrets?

Secrets are slowly destroying you. Now's your chance to get out from under them.

I hated when my snarky self had such good responses. In the end, I went for the obvious stuff—the accident, the scars, and the solitude. I passed over the bulimia, the unwillingness to take care of myself, and my new roommate. While I was at my computer, though, I dug through and found the file

Ankita had sent me. She'd coordinated with Dr. Marco and put together a vitamin regimen to complement the medication I was supposed to be taking. I opened my desk drawer and pulled out all the pills I was theoretically consuming.

After making certain none had expired, I pulled out the sorter and diligently filled each box with the pills for the next week. I contemplated setting an alarm, but all of the meds were either supposed to be—or could be—taken with food. So...just remember to swallow a pile of vitamins, supplements, and meds with each of my three meals. That shouldn't be difficult.

I snickered. If the notion was so easy, why had I been so resistant?

Perhaps something to discuss with Justin.

Then I read about the ranch. The testimonials were impressive. The theory about therapy dogs and horses felt a bit far-fetched. But I'd promised Dr. Marco I'd do this. While I was on the computer, I shot off an email to Hortense, updating her to pass along to the doctor.

Before I could shut it down, she sent back a quick *so proud of you* note.

That meant way more than it should have.

At five o'clock, Dean barreled into the house. "Sorry. At least I don't smell like smoke this time. How far is the ranch?"

"Fifteen minutes."

"Brilliant." He shot past me, as I sat in the kitchen, and headed for the stairs. "Quickest shower in the world. Then you can tell me about your day."

Despite having removed his boots, he still managed to make quite a bit of noise as he made his way up the stairs.

I gave my outfit another critical look. I'd started out in a suit with a crisp white shirt and a jacket. After sweating through that, despite the air-conditioning, I'd opted for a golf shirt with khakis. I'd decided that was too pretentious—and too much of my arm showed—so I'd ended up in jeans and a tan-colored henley. Probably too hot for this weather, but less revealing than any T-shirt I owned.

Before I could decide to change again, Dean appeared. His forest-green T-shirt showed his flawless chest and strong biceps. Those jeans hugged his hips perfectly, and his thick thighs were on clear display. I was sort of glad Justin was married. At least I didn't have to worry about him falling for the lumberjack who I could easily tumble over the abyss for.

I grabbed my keys.

Chip popped up.

"Sorry, sweetie, not this time." I snagged the dental treat I gave her when I had to go out.

She made a beeline for her crate.

I gave it to her, shut the door, and was in the process of hustling Dean out the door when he stopped me. "I can keep her with me."

"She'll be fine." Even as I said the words, though, I reconsidered. I'd spend the entire time worrying about her. If she and Dean could hang out—

He pivoted, went back, retrieved her, then, when they got to me, I clipped on her leash.

In the back of my SUV, I hooked her up to her harness, and she grinned.

"Oh, yeah. You got a treat *and* you're coming with me."

"Woof."

Dean grinned as he secured his seatbelt. "You're a softie, Adam."

"Hey, you were the one who convinced me." I pointed to the glove box. "Grab about five baggies. Just in case." I eyed my girl in the rearview mirror as I drove down to the road.

Well, this is going to be interesting.

Chapter Fifteen

DEAN

I'D SEARCHED HEALING HORSES RANCH ON THE internet during my lunch hour. So I'd had a decent idea where it was, how long it would take us to get there, and the basics of the ranch. Still, I hoped Adam might fill me in as his SUV ate up the miles. His castle and the ranch were both north of Mission City—in the hills—but at opposite ends of the vast land. In fact, the ranch was located very close to where we'd been working last week.

Although I would've been happy to fill the silence, I left that up to Adam.

Who appeared to be far into his head with contemplation.

So I held my tongue until he made a left turn and we passed the sign welcoming us to the ranch. We climbed up a long and winding driveway surrounded by some of the tallest trees I'd ever seen in my life. Very different from the bush back home.

Eventually the land levelled out, and we arrived in a lot. Adam picked a spot and pulled in. He set the SUV into park, pulled the parking brake, shut down the engine, and then... didn't move.

I waited.

Chip tried to stick her head between the seats.

I reached back and freed her from her harness. If Adam changed his mind and we headed out, I was certain he'd give me enough time to put his beloved pet back in her harness. I liked that he took such good care of her.

Glancing into the side mirror, I caught sight of a woman approaching slowly. She had a golden lab by her side. "Uh, Adam..." I pointed to his side mirror.

He took a deep breath. "You'll get Chip?"

"Of course."

We exited the SUV at the same time. While he stood, motionless, I opened the back door and snagged Chip's leash. As soon as she spotted the other dog, she strained. "Sorry." I shrugged. "Should have asked."

The woman grinned. "Ah, you're the *friend*. I'd recognize that accent anywhere." She held out her hand to Adam. "Welcome, Adam. My name's Rainbow." Her long, blue/black hair shone in the light. She stood just under six feet and had the palest blue eyes I'd ever seen. Paler even than Sam's. She wore a chambray shirt, well-worn jeans, and cowboy boots.

I nudged Adam.

Finally, he reached out to grasp Rainbow's hand, "Yes, Adam. Thank you."

"Okay, before we go any further...." I grinned. "Eight?"

"Yep. Kennedy's the oldest—and looks nothing like the other seven. There's Torah, Zephyra, Sunshine, me, Spring, and then the twins, Autumn and Summer."

"Jesus." Adam swore under his breath.

I chuckled. "Must've made life very interesting for your parents."

"My dad was a long-haul pilot. He was gone a lot of the time, which, I think suited him."

"Ah." Her poor mum.

Chip again strained at the leash, trying to get to the dog who sat placidly at Rainbow's side.

"This is Chip."

Rainbow advanced slowly, holding her palm out. When she got closer, she crouched. "Hello, Chip. You're most welcome here. We love when people bring their furry friends. Mostly dogs, but we've had a couple cats, a lizard, and a llama."

I coughed out a laugh. "A llama?"

She nodded. "An unofficial emotional support llama."

Chip licked her fingers and nuzzled against her palm.

"Golden retriever?"

"Yes." Adam petted Chip's head. "She's about nine months old. We're starting training with Torah soon. Probably should've done it sooner. I've been watching videos and reading books…"

"Nothing beats hands-on experience." Rainbow rose. "Torah's the best. That's not bias speaking. She's won awards and stuff. But you don't need to hear that from me." She gazed back and forth between the two of us, and I guessed she wasn't certain who to address with regard to Chip.

"Chip is Adam's dog." I grinned the smile that often had women—and men—swooning. I'd learned it from Sam, of course. "I'm just the friend."

"Not *just*," Adam muttered. "Jesus."

Rainbow grinned and eyed Adam. "Would it be okay if Tiffany says *hello* to Chip?"

"Of course." Adam sort of frowned. "I, uh, thanks for asking."

"That's okay. We stand on protocol until we set out what works for everyone. Tiffany's the ranch's therapy dog. And she has litters of puppies periodically. We re-home some and Torah takes others to train as service dogs."

"Wow, okay." I eyed Tiffany. "You're busy."

Tiffany woofed.

"It's fine." Adam shifted, gazing down at Chip. "She hasn't really been socialized."

As if that was no big deal, Rainbow grinned. "Well, if you're comfortable, we can introduce her to plenty of people and pets. Avery, another counselor, has Rex, an English Cream Labrador Retriever mix. He's a little skittish sometimes, so he's not an official therapy dog. But he hangs around and isn't shy with other dogs. Tiffany, of course, as you can see. And, if Chip's brave, she can meet the horses. Sugar, Sienna, Briar, and Fallon are all retired show horses and as placid as can be. They love both people and dogs. As long as the dogs stay out from underfoot." She eyed Chip. "You'll stay on a leash unless we know you're in an enclosed area."

Chip cocked her head.

Rainbow laughed. "Tiffany, friend."

Tiffany gazed up at Rainbow.

Her master gave her a subtle nod.

Then the dog advanced slowly toward Chip.

Who lunged.

Fortunately, I had a good grasp.

The more-mature dog approached carefully, but once she was within sniffing range, the two stuck their snouts together and inhaled deeply.

Chip stepped back and tried to lunge in what I knew to be her playful mood.

Tiffany lowered her head nearly to her front paws and pretend lunged.

Our dog barked and lunged as well.

They pretend to tussle.

I struggled to keep the leash out of the way. Up here, in the pristine wilderness, I probably could've let Chip off her leash. But I wasn't certain she'd come when I called.

Wait...*our dog*? Did I really get to think of her in those

terms? I'd only walked her a couple of times, and we'd cuddled a few more. But, somehow, she'd wormed her way into my heart. *I wish she was part mine.*

Eventually, the dogs subsided. Tiffany positioned herself next to Chip, and they both flopped onto the ground.

"Okay, time to get you—" Rainbow pointed to Adam. "—into the ranch and ready to meet Justin. I'm glad you guys came a few minutes early so we could do introductions. I'm assuming Chip's going to go with you into your session?"

Adam met my gaze, and I read indecision. Even a touch of panic. "Well—" I turned to Rainbow. "—our plan had been for me to hang around with her outside. We didn't want to leave her home alone." I pivoted to Adam. "But if Justin doesn't mind her joining Adam, I think that would be a good thing."

"Oh, Justin will be thrilled." Rainbow's grin couldn't have been broader. "Or I was going to offer up Tiffany. But if you think Chip can handle it—"

"Handle? What's there to handle?" Adam's voice was a little sharp.

Rainbow held his gaze. "Today's just an introductory session. A chance for you to get to know Justin. I'll be honest, though, and say sometimes these sessions can get intense. Highly sensitive dogs don't always cope well." She eyed Chip. "And some turn out to be troopers and of great comfort for their companion. I can't make a snap judgement, but I suspect Chip will be okay. Unless she's got issues—"

"Chip's fine." Adam was quick to assure.

I supported his decision, believing she would be. Now, I didn't actually *know* this, but I'd seen nothing in my time with her to indicate any kind of instability. Even when Adam got upset, she didn't bat an eye. She just went along as if this was the way things were. And, to her, she didn't know any better.

"Great." Rainbow pointed to my hand. "Why don't you give Adam the leash? And—"

"Hey, Rainbow." A deep, masculine voice came from the ranch.

I glanced over Rainbow's shoulder to see a man striding toward us. For a moment, I was taken aback. The man looked quite a lot like Maddox—beard, red hair, tall. Maddox might've been a bit more toward auburnish-gold while this guy was a touch closer to genuine ginger orange. Both men had full heads of hair and trimmed beards versus my bushy goodness and bald pate.

Why are you comparing yourself to these men? Adam's not likely to be any more interested in them than he is in you.

Yet still, a small part of me wondered. Adam and I had yet to truly acknowledge what happened Friday night. He'd given no indication he wanted a repeat, while I would've been thrilled to give—or receive—another blow job. And other stuff...but I was getting way ahead of myself.

"Justin, good timing." Rainbow grinned. "This is Adam, his dog Chip, and his friend Dean, who has the cutest Australian accent."

Heat crept into my cheeks. For one horrible fleeting moment, I wondered if she was attracted to me. Then that thought passed as she gave me another look. Did she get I was gay? It didn't matter, of course, but life was easier when everyone was on the same page.

Adam took the leash from me. "Rainbow said I can bring Chip into the, uh, session."

Justin's wide grin matched Rainbow's. "That's fantastic. We love all forms of creatures, big and small, beauties and beasts."

For just an instant, Adam stiffened. If I hadn't been beside him, I might not have noticed. He'd said something about being a beast once. Which I'd thought was total horseshit.

Either the counsellor didn't notice, or chose not to. He gestured toward the large ranch house.

After a long moment, Adam followed—Chip close at his heels.

Tiffany moved to my side and rubbed her furry shoulder against me.

I chuckled. "I'm not the one in need of therapy." I met Rainbow's cocked head with her intense gaze. "Truly...I'm good."

"Phew. Because I'm not a licensed therapist." She gestured with one hand. "Take a tour with me? Then, when we're done, you can join me in the kitchen while I heat my dinner. Or you can sit in the great room—which doubles as a lobby slash waiting area."

I cleared my throat. "I was just going to wander a bit. Maybe sit in the car?" I hadn't brought my tablet, but I could read on my phone.

"Whatever suits you. But I don't mind giving the ten-cent tour. So you'll be able to talk to Adam about the ranch...if he needs to."

Damn woman. She was right, of course. If I knew the facilities, then it'd be easier to converse with Adam about what he thought.

I let her lead me toward the stables.

Chapter Sixteen

ADAM

As I followed Justin into the ranch house, a sense of awe overtook me at the size of the place. I'd seen photos of the ranch—and of the counselors. Justin looked exactly like his photo. And greatly resembled Maddox. Which made me wonder about Stanley—Maddox's ex and Justin's husband. Obviously, the man had a type. I also wondered if Dean had a type. *Am I someone he looks at with physical attraction? Should I have offered a blow job last night?* He'd clearly been tired, and I'd been wired after making the phone call to secure this spot.

"This is the great room." Justin arced his arm as we stepped through the sliding glass door. The two-story space featured soaring wood beams and a high ceiling. "And we also use this space as a lobby or waiting area. Especially on rainy days." He indicated the seating area with two large, oversized couches, several chairs that looked amazingly comfortable, as well as a large-screen television. "Sometimes we have parents, guardians, or even siblings waiting for clients."

I noted a small play area off to the side with children's toys. "This is quite an operation."

"Well, we have four full-time counsellors. Our child psychologist is Dr. Denise Lang. Avery Stinson, our social worker, focuses on addictions and trauma counselling. Dr. Kennedy Dixon owns and operates the ranch, with Rainbow helping. Rainbow does some basic admin—enough to keep us moving smoothly—and she focuses on the horses and Tiffany." He paused and cocked his head. "Well, Kennedy uses Tiffany frequently in her sessions. As does Denise. As do I, on occasion."

I petted Chip's head. "Sounds like a busy dog."

"She is. Avery's pooch, Rex, does a bit of the heavy lifting as well, but mostly with Avery. He's not certified. Lovely little guy, but not always comfortable with emotional strangers."

"Ah...that would be a problem." As much as I was enjoying a discussion of all the therapists, I really wanted to get started.

As if sensing my frustration, Justin beckoned me to follow him through a kitchen. On the other side lay three doors. "Kennedy's office, our accountant's office, and my office." He directed me into the space.

The brightness of the yellow walls hit me first. Sunshine poured in through the open slats of the blinds, and I could see enormous trees just beyond the ranch. He also had a decent view of the parking lot. Ah, so he'd likely spotted us arriving. I quickly scanned, but I couldn't spot either Rainbow or Dean. What were they were doing?

"Why don't you have a seat?" Justin pointed to another oversized couch as well as two high-back chairs that didn't look as comfortable.

Do you deserve comfort?

"I...uh..."

Justin nodded. "I usually sit in one of the chairs. You can sit on the other or on the couch, totally up to you."

After a long moment, I settled onto the couch.

The counsellor smiled, then sat in a chair. His space spoke of happiness. The yellow walls, the soft furniture...even his desk, which faced the window, felt tranquil. Plus the ergonomic desk chair. Practical as well.

"I've introduced myself a bit, but let me fill you in on my credentials. I have a Master's Degree in Psychology and I'm pursuing my PhD part-time through Simon Fraser University. I've worked at the ranch since graduating with my Master's degree more than five years ago."

"How old are you?" I winced. "Sorry, none of my business."

He chuckled. "I'm terrible at gauging ages, so I'm always intensely curious about that myself. I'm twenty-nine, inching up to thirty." He met my gaze. "Your intake form says you're thirty-seven years old and single." He inclined his head toward the outside. "Dean seems like a nice guy."

"To accompany me here and ensure I didn't chicken out?" I petted Chip who'd taken up residence at my feet.

"Chickening out? Did you think you might?"

I huffed. "Dr. Marco said I had to come." I eyed him. "I filled out those authorization forms and the privacy stuff. So... did you speak to him?"

After a long moment, Justin nodded. "I got off the phone with him just before you arrived. He's...concerned about you."

His bright-blue eyes radiated empathy and, for just a moment, I sank into the comfort. Then reality struck. Hard.

"I'm fine. I don't know what he's going on about."

"And yet you're here."

I squirmed. "He practically ordered me here. But I thought he wanted me to see Kennedy."

Justin smiled. "And if you want, I can arrange for you to see her. She's a bit more... in demand than I am. I recently discharged two clients, and so my schedule's a bit more flexible."

"Discharged? Does that really happen? Do people actually get better?"

"Yes, they do. Sometimes a client only needs a few sessions —if the issue is short-term and can be dealt with quickly. Like getting over the loss of a loved one, an ended relationship, or something unforeseen knocking them off their stride." He held my gaze. "Sometimes the issue is more of a chronic and long-term nature. Mental illness, a situation that won't end, or just something that's been going on for so long that untangling and dealing with it can't be done in just a few weeks."

I grasped my left hand in my right. "Ten years."

"So you said. Dr. Raymond says you've been his patient for almost that length of time. Is this the first time he suggested counselling?"

"You know it's not."

"Perhaps. But I'd like to hear your side of the story. Why now, Adam?"

The sixty-four-thousand-dollar question. Which always seemed like a super weird number to me. But it'd been one of my mother's favorite expressions. *Stop stalling.* "Because Dr. Marco implied my numbers, as he puts it, are going in the wrong direction."

"Did he say why that was happening?"

"Something about not taking my supplements and medications. About not eating the right foods. And eating the wrong foods." I scowled. "I don't drink. No alcohol at all. I don't smoke anymore. No cigarettes. I don't even smoke pot anymore, much as I would love to."

Slowly, Justin nodded. "It's good that you're not ingesting toxic, addictive, and carcinogenic substances." He cocked his head. "But that doesn't mean you're not still eating and drinking things that might damage your kidneys."

I thought of the soda I drank way too much of. Or the fresh fruits and vegetables I rarely ate. The hydration I didn't maintain, and the pills I didn't take. I sat a little straighter. "I organized my pills. I'm going to take them." Even though I hated some of the side effects.

"Are you making a commitment to yourself? And to Dr. Raymond?"

"He said I can call him Dr. Marco." Somehow, that felt like something I needed to clarify.

"I can certainly call him that as well. I don't know him personally, but I've heard nothing but good things about him. Ten years is a long time. Finding, and keeping, a good family doctor can be tough."

"I don't know what I'm going to do when he retires."

"Well, that's a way off. But I'm glad you're thinking in the long-term."

"Like not planning to off myself tomorrow?"

"That's always a bonus." His incisive blue gaze settled on me. "You've never attempted suicide?"

"Why? Should I have?"

"Of course not."

"Just because of the scars—"

He held up his hands. "It's something I ask many of my patients. And I'll sometimes ask you to tell me where you are on a continuum. With one being incredibly low and in, let's say, psychic agony."

I winced.

"And ten being content, seeing the world optimistically, and everything feeling really good."

I eyed him.

He nodded, as if prodding me to answer.

"Like, I don't know, a five." I pursed my lips. "Okay, maybe a seven. I don't have any physical pain. Or, like, psychic pain. I just..." I waved my hand around.

Chip stirred, took stock, and resettled.

"I don't know what I'm supposed to do with my life. I

mean, I exist. And until I met Dean, I didn't really *do* anything."

"But that's changed?"

Tread carefully. "Having someone staying in my house has disrupted my routine. I thought I was headed in one direction..." *Breathe.* "But between his poking and Dr. Marco's insistence I be here..." I winced. "Life feels uncertain right now."

"Okay. Well, we have two choices. We still have some time on the clock. We can focus on today. Right now. How can we find a way to help you cope with the upheaval in your routine? What will make life easier for today?"

"Or?"

"Or we can get started on discussing the accident you talked about."

"The obvious reason I'm here." I couldn't keep the sarcasm out of my voice.

"I'm not here to judge." Justin adjusted himself, leaning forward slightly. "Your problems began ten years ago—"

"It goes back a lot further than that." *Damn—probably shouldn't have said that.*

"Okay...so do you want to start from the beginning? We might not get too far, but I'm happy to have you come back as soon as you're ready. I'd like to make this a regular thing until you're feeling more settled."

"Until I take my meds properly and my numbers stop trending in the wrong direction."

"If those are the benchmarks you want to set, that's fine with me. Sometimes we use tangible goals. Sometimes we aim for a feeling of well-being. Sometimes we just keep going until..." He hesitated.

I waved for him to continue.

"Until we realize there's nothing else that can be done. Nothing else to do."

"Or you acknowledge the client won't take care of himself and is wasting your time."

Justin settled back. "I can honestly say that's never happened to me. Maybe for Kennedy, but she's been doing this a decade longer than I have."

For a brief, fleeting moment, I wondered if I should switch to seeing Kennedy. Something told me Justin wasn't going to take any shit from me. Just as quickly, I dismissed the idea. Just because Kennedy was a woman didn't mean she wouldn't be just as tough. And, honestly, I liked this counsellor's no-nonsense approach to things. He called a spade a spade. And he might understand the added layer of being a gay man in small town British Columbia. In the bible belt of Cedar Valley, no less.

I took a deep breath. "We can start from the beginning. And..." I thought of Dean. "I'll keep coming back until I find this elusive *sense of well-being*."

Justin smiled. "I think we'll get you there sooner than you think."

Easy for him to say.

Chapter Seventeen

DEAN

THE RANCH IMPRESSED ME.

Rainbow charmed me.

Tiffany amused me.

The horses chuffed me to bits.

Yet, all the time, my mind was on the man inside. Talking to the gorgeous gay therapist. *Is he spilling his secrets? Is he sharing his pain? Are they talking about me? Is Justin saying a relationship with me is ill-advised?* Come to that, did we even have a relationship? We lived together, sure. But as landlord and tenant. Maybe roommates, if I stretched things.

I sat on a stool in the ranch kitchen, watching Rainbow make a stir-fry. How in the world had I gotten to this exact spot? Canada was my dream placement. I'd already spotted five different species of trees I hadn't yet encountered during our brief excursion around the property. Well, there were trails leading to more places, and we didn't see them all. Apparently, the entire property encompassed almost forty acres. Some was pasture, while much of it was forest. Amazing, Rainbow kept the entire place running—plus answered the phone when the accountant/business manager wasn't around.

"I'm versatile," she'd said.

I'd silently snickered because I was as well—and not in the same way. Or at least that's always how I'd seen myself. My imagination certainly gave me the impression I'd enjoy...lots of options.

Rainbow portioned out five plates of rice and then put stir-fry on all of them. The scent of chicken, garlic, peppers, and lemon scented the air. Before I could compliment her, she shoved a plate in front of me.

"Uh..."

"Did you eat dinner?"

"Well, no."

"Has Adam?"

I tried to recall. "I don't think so. I tried to suggest we could go out afterward. Like a reward or something." The memory hit me. "He, uh, doesn't go out often."

Rainbow speared a piece of chicken with her fork. She stood in the kitchen, opposite me, with her hip leaning against the counter.

If I were her, I'd have sat and taken a load off.

"The world can be a tough place. I know people who never venture out—and they don't have Adam's reason."

I appreciated that she understood. People could be down-right cruel. He was safe here. He might not be when he went elsewhere. "I don't know how to help him."

She forked some rice. "That's always a tough one. I mean, I say to be there for the person. When they want to talk. When they don't want to talk. When they need comfort, and when they need you to back the hell away."

"How do I figure out what's best? I'm a bit of an introvert, but I'll go out with people. Enjoy it, even. I want him to leave his self-imposed exile. To experience the world. I..." I pursed my lips. "I think—no, I know—he used to be a guy who traveled all around the world. Like, a lot. I don't even know how to relate to that. Aside from the flights from Canberra to Perth, all of three times, I've not really traveled. I mean, I popped over to New Zealand and Tasmania, but that's it. Then, boom, I'm halfway around the globe."

"I've never flown anywhere."

Her words took me a couple of seconds to compute. "Wait...your father's a long-haul pilot?"

She nodded.

"And you've never flown? Anywhere?"

"Nope." She grinned. "I'm a homebody, Dean. So's Kennedy, for that matter. She gets invitations from all around the world to talk about the success of Healing Horses. She almost never goes. Hasn't left the province in about three years. She says she's too busy." She shoved some rice into her mouth, then rolled her eyes.

I dug into the food, enjoying the lemony tang of the chicken.

She swallowed. "Sorry, stupid of me. Talk or eat, don't do both. Sometimes we're so busy we do that...but just within the family."

"Something tells me if you didn't, you'd never get a word in edgewise."

She threw her head back and laughed, and it tickled my insides.

"Oh my God, that's so true. With ten of us at the table— twelve, if one set of grandparents was over—we never had silence. Someone was always talking."

"How much of an age difference between the eldest and the youngest?"

"Nineteen years. Kennedy could easily be the twins' mother." She poked a red pepper. "Well, a young mother. My mother was twenty and my father twenty-three when they had Kennedy. That was more the norm back then. Well, maybe even before that" She glanced around. "Moonshine and Brian were very excited to get married. At least to hear my grand-mothers tell the story."

"Moonshine? Brian?"

"My mother and father." She eyed the pepper. "I swear, Kennedy really got the only normal name in the family. I suppose maybe Torah and my three sisters named after seasons were okay...but Sunshine, Zephyra, and I got stuck with the weird ones." She grinned. "And the Dixon sisters have quite the reputation in town." She ate her pepper.

"Adam said Zephyra is his vet and Torah will be doing the training for Chip."

She swallowed. "She'll be training you and Adam. Anything Chip learns is a bonus."

I cocked my head.

"Well, sure, she'll be training Chip as well. But most of her work focuses on you. Teaching you how to train the dog. She can't be there all the time—you can."

I didn't point out that I wouldn't be staying past early November. Adam had invited me to stay until then. And I'd taken him up on that offer. Whatever happened between then and the time for me to leave would be up to him.

"Oh boy, I smell something delicious." Justin appeared in the kitchen with Adam and Chip half a step behind. Tiffany immediately went over to greet Chip as if they hadn't met an hour ago.

An hour? Time had flown by.

Rainbow pointed to the plates. "Enough for everyone."

Justin winced. "Stan ordered pizza. Angus got the top score in the science fair." He met my gaze. "My son. He's all of twelve and already hates competition. He was upset he won because that meant other kids didn't."

"An egalitarian, eh? That's quite an admirable trait in a twelve-year-old."

He grinned. "You say *eh* too? Awesome."

I chuckled. "And you say *awesome*." The guy was about my age and had the brightest blue eyes that sparkled with amusement.

He hefted his messenger bag over his shoulder. "Gotta run." He turned to Adam. "Saturday."

Adam nodded, then met my gaze.

Justin departed.

Rainbow indicated a stool next to mine. "I didn't ask if you have allergies."

Adam looked over the food. "I don't...and this looks very healthy. Dr. Marco would approve."

I glanced at Rainbow to see if she'd comment, but she was already digging into her rice. I tilted my head toward the stool, encouraging Adam to join me.

After a moment, he did. He met my gaze. "Justin talked about unconventional therapy."

"Yep." Rainbow grinned. "I think that's part of our success. We like to think outside of the box. If that means feeding a couple of hungry guys, I'm happy to do it. Do you want a tour of the stables afterward, or do you want to save that for Saturday?"

"Uh, Saturday will be fine." Adam poked at his food. "Justin said eventually he wants to get me on one of the horses."

"Have you ever ridden before? I haven't." I snagged a snow pea and ate it, enjoying the crunch.

"Like for a photo shoot once. I think? It's a little hazy."

That, I couldn't fathom. How could one have been on a horse and not remember?

"Photo shoot?" Rainbow blinked. "You're a photographer?"

Adam cleared his throat. "I used to be a high-fashion model." He met her gaze. "Not anymore, though, obviously."

I hated that it was so obvious. He still had stunning gray

eyes, hair that looked touchably soft, and a lean body that both women and men would be attracted to. But the scars. Some people would be repulsed. Some would fetishize them. Some wouldn't be affected at all. The problem was, figuring out how to target the latter group—and only that group—was brutal. I glanced at Rainbow.

Who appeared about to speak when another woman breezed into the room. "Okay, another long day done and, oh —" She stopped short when she spotted Adam and me. Her lips widened into a brilliant smile. Her long, chestnut-brown hair hung loose down her back and her dark-brown eyes were incisive. She was around the same height as Rainbow and wore cowboy boots, jeans, and a buttoned-down collared shirt. She stuck her hand out to Adam. "Kennedy Dixon."

Rainbow grinned. "And the only Dixon sister who doesn't have black hair and blue eyes."

Kennedy rolled her eyes as he shook her hand. "We always joke about the mailman."

I chuckled as she offered her hand to me. "I'm Dean. That's Adam."

She gave me an assessing look before pivoting back to Adam. "We're glad you're here. If there's ever an issue, my door's always open. Well, except when I'm with a client, but you know what I mean."

Slowly, he nodded. "Yes, I do. Justin's a good guy."

Rainbow handed Kennedy a plate and fork. The recipient of the delicious food leaned against the counter and dug in. "Yes. We're lucky to have him."

I cocked my head.

"He's studying to get his PhD." Rainbow indicated her sister should eat and that, apparently, she had this. "He's doing it part-time, though, so he can keep up with his clients on the ranch. Busy guy."

"If he doesn't have time for me—" Adam began.

Rainbow shook her head. "He's got time. A couple of his clients have left recently. More success stories." She caught my gaze before shifting back to Adam. "It's critical our clients have support in the community—whether from their family, their co-workers, their friends, or their found family."

My ears perked up at that. My counselor had said something similar to me after Mum died. That even though I didn't have any biological family who might claim me, I'd surrounded myself with people who'd step in and be my *found* family. Like Sam was a brother to me. Almost beyond a best friend.

"I don't have any family left." Adam pushed the last of his rice around his plate. I was thrilled to see he'd eaten as much as he had.

"You've got me." I nudged him. "I'll be here for you."

"But for how long?" He met my gaze. "You'll be back in Australia before you know it."

"That's six months away." I willed him to understand. "And just because I'm on the other side of the ocean, doesn't mean I'll stop caring."

"You'll have your own life."

"And a Canadian friend who, as I've seen proof, knows how to use the phone and email and everything."

Rainbow sighed. "That's so sweet. I have to say, I'll never be lonely." She pointed to her back pocket. "Family group chat. Ten people. Someone's always got something to say."

"You mean Spring." Kennedy deadpanned the line.

"Well, yes." Rainbow rolled her eyes. "Or Sunshine's love life. Oh, have you guys headed over to The Owl's Nest? Dickens runs a great bookstore, and you could meet another Dixon."

"I, uh—" Adam winced as he pushed away his plate. "—don't go out."

I slung an arm around him. "You made it here today."

He gazed at me. "Because of you."

"And we're doing it again on, what, Saturday?"

"I can come on my own."

"Sure you can," Rainbow agreed. "But if you bring Dean, I intend to have him mucking stalls."

"Uh..."

Adam laughed.

Actually laughed.

Which is how I found myself mucking out stalls on Saturday morning.

Chapter Eighteen

ADAM

When Justin and I emerged to go riding, Dean was nowhere to be found.

Rainbow offered her trademark smile. "He mucked...and now he's looking at some trees near the back of the property. I've been meaning to get an arborist out for a while now. I feel guilty—"

"He'll love you for the work," I said, cutting her off. "He's most at home among the trees."

"I have to say, he didn't do too badly with the mucking. Are you ready to ride?"

At my hesitation, Justin cocked his head. "You don't have to. We can just wander around for a bit."

Rainbow petted Chip on the head. "I'm happy to watch her if you ride, if not, there are lots of places to go on the property where you won't run into anyone."

Except I sort of wanted to run into Dean. My counselling session had been intense. I need some lightheartedness—something Dean always provided. He took life, and my problems, seriously. But he could always come up with a quip or a joke on the fly. I pointed. "Those trees?"

"Yep. That part of the forest runs back to the property line. It's all fenced in."

Justin caught my gaze. We'd agreed to go riding as we had another fifteen minutes left in the session.

I gave a little shrug. "I'm certain you've got something to occupy your time."

"Sure. I have a report to send Dr. Marco. But I'm here for you." He scratched his trimmed beard. So different from Dean's bush.

"And I appreciate that. We said a week, right? Next Tuesday night?" That'd be ten days which, in my world, was just a long week. Everything sort of flowed together.

"Yes." He gave Rainbow a look, and she started to step away.

"No worries," I said, directed at both of them. "I'll take my pills and behave." On that note, I waved and headed out of the stable.

If Justin felt Rainbow was owed an explanation, he'd provide it. I'd basically just said I didn't care about confidentiality. I sort of figured Rainbow was part of the entire privacy thing around here. Even if she didn't know the specifics, she'd have some idea what was going on.

I headed in the direction Rainbow indicated. I might miss Dean entirely, in this semi-wilderness. Still, even as I headed deeper into the dense brush, Chip tugged and yanked on her harness. "Hey, slow down there."

She barked.

"Over here." Dean's accented voice rang out through the forest.

"Woof. Woof. Woof." Again, Chip strained.

"If you think she'll stick close to us, you can let her off-leash." Dean appeared from behind a tree. "The fence is good and solid. She's not getting through or over it."

I was looking forward to starting training Monday night with Torah. Feeling brave, I unclipped Chip's leash.

She barreled over to Dean, clearly trying to knock him over.

He tapped his chest.

She nearly climbed up it as he angled himself backward.

He caught her and hoisted her into his arms.

My breath stuck in my lungs. Slowly, I willed my heart to slow, even as he spun her around.

"You're such a good dog." He crooned as she licked his face.

"Are you okay?" I eyed him. Chip might only be nine months, but she was on the big side for a golden retriever. Almost sixty-five pounds. The reason I should've put her in training sooner.

"I'm fine." Dean laughed. "She's such a clever dog, Adam. I'll bet if Torah can train her properly...well, you and Torah" —he added, remembering Rainbow's comment—"then I bet she'd make a great therapy dog. She's super intuitive."

"Who's she going to see, Dean? When will I ever take her anywhere except here and Dr. Marco's office?"

"Things might change, Adam."

I met his stare. "The scars aren't going to get better, Dean. After ten years, they're as faded as they're going to get." The contours of my face would never be the way they were. I'd accepted that.

Most of the time.

He pursed his lips. "You don't have to live in your castle and be by yourself, you know. There are people out in the world who won't stare. Won't comment. Will just accept you for who you are. You're the one choosing to define yourself by looks, Adam."

"Everyone does." Rage bubbled within me. "You don't live

in this face. You haven't been there. All people see is the scars. That's never going to change."

"If you don't venture out from your hiding place, you'll never find anyone different. Hard to prove a negative." He shook his head. "Okay, baby girl, you've got to get down. I can wield an axe for hours, but you're way too heavy for me." As gently as anything, he put her down. "How did things go with Justin? Did you ride? Briar's a sweet—"

"I came looking for you."

"Yeah, okay." He scratched his beard. "And you've found me."

"I don't..." I faltered. "I don't want to argue, Dean. I just... want you to take me home."

He walked toward me even as Chip headed in the opposite direction. He whistled. "Hey, get back here."

To my surprise—although maybe I shouldn't have been— she pivoted and came right back.

When he was in front of me, he held out his hand.

I handed him the leash.

He clipped Chip, then held out his hand again.

After a moment, I took it. "They think we're just friends."

"You tell yourself that, mate. Does it matter? I mean, if you only want to be friends, I'm fine—"

I squeezed his hand. "Take me home, Dean."

When we emerged from the path into the clearing with the riding ring, stable, barn, and ranch house, no one was around. We made our way to the parking lot where I handed Dean the keys.

He nodded and rounded to the driver's door as I secured Chip into her harness.

Within moments, we were headed back toward the castle.

I drew in a deep breath. "You said you wanted to go to Fifties."

"Yeah. I mean, I didn't really enjoy the ambiance or the

food the last time I was there. The milkshake was amazing. Being dumped by my future landlady...not so much." He cut me a glance as he turned right. "But I met you, so I guess I should be thanking Mrs. Thistle."

"And you want to go to the bookstore."

"Well, yeah, but these are all things I can do by myself, Adam. I know you're uncomfortable—"

"Maybe with you..." I drew in a sharp breath. "Maybe they won't be so bad."

He slapped his thigh. "I'll just tower over folks and glare if they get out of line."

That made me smile. After the intensity of the session, I didn't want to be alone. And yeah, Dean might stick close to me at the house, if I asked, but he might also think I needed space. Perhaps I did—to absorb everything I'd discussed with Justin. But I also just needed some lightheartedness...and Dean could give that to me. Mind made up, I grinned. "Okay...so let's go." The curving of my lips upward was, I hoped, enough to show him I was okay with this.

So we went. We ran Chip home, to her annoyance, then we first went to Fifties for delicious milkshakes and burgers. Not great for my sugar intake—and therefore my kidneys—but I figured Dr. Marco would be okay with this.

Dean introduced me to our server, Sarabeth, and she didn't bat an eyelash as she took our orders and then returned shortly thereafter with food. We'd nabbed a booth in the back, and I kept the left side of my face away from the restaurant, toward the wall, but I still felt self-conscious.

At the booth across from us sat a young couple who were cuddled next to each other and completely wrapped up in each other.

Leaving the restaurant, though, a young child pointed at my face. His mother offered me a clearly apologetic smile. As they walked into the dining area, I heard her admonish her child to *not point out people who are different*. Given the words she could've chosen, those felt...almost okay. I *was* different. And that hurt in so damn many ways.

Dean had placed his hand on my lower back and guided me out of the diner. Although the gesture felt incredibly intimate, I welcomed the contact. He grounded me. Helped me find my center. Gave me hope where, moments before, I'd had none.

By the time we got to the SUV, though, I was shaking. Only when I was in the SUV and secure, did Dean walk around to the driver's side and hop in.

He looked like he wanted to take my hand, even inching his toward mine, but my left side faced him, and so he didn't make the move.

Boldly, I did. I gently touched his fingers with mine.

After a moment, he turned his palm upward.

I wasn't ready to hold hands—or even to have him grip me —but I managed to rest my fingers on his palm.

"Do you want to go home?"

I couldn't remember his accent ever being so pronounced. "We were..." I cleared my throat. "You wanted to go to the bookstore."

"Yeah. But I can go any day after work. Taking care of you will always take precedence. Always."

He said the word with such emphasis that it brought tears to my eyes. His sincerity shone through at every moment. He meant those words. If I said I wanted to go home to the safety of the castle, Chip, and Maurice, he'd point the SUV north and we'd be on our way.

Be brave. Justin hadn't said those words, but he'd implied I already was. I got up every morning. I got dressed every morning. I took care of Chip and Maurice every day. Well, Maurice took care of himself—I just fed him and cleaned the litter. "Let's go. I haven't been there before." I hadn't been anywhere, really, but I wasn't going to point that out. "If I need to leave, I'll give you a signal."

Slowly, as if taking my measure, he gazed at me with those intense amber eyes. Eyes I'd miss when he left. Until then, though, I'd take every moment I could get.

"Yeah. Just tap my hand twice, okay? Or give me a look. I'll know."

He would know. Of that I had no doubt.

Dean, as casually as could be, turned on the engine, put the SUV in drive, and drove us to the downtown area of Mission City. All eight blocks of it. "The library's the next street up," he pointed. "Ever been there?"

I shook my head. "Why would I need a library?" Belatedly, I realized he didn't know everything I did. "I have an e-reader. What else could I need that I can't get through that?"

He pulled into a spot that had just opened up in front of The Owl's Nest. "Well then, I guess this visit to the bookstore is superfluous." He put the SUV back into gear.

I stilled his hand and slipped it back to park. "You've made your point. Plus, we've got some kind of weird Dixon sister bingo going on. I'm ahead because I've met Zephyra."

"The vet." He drawled the word. "I'll have to find a way to sneak into the Mission City Gazette to find the elusive Spring." He patted my knee. "She's a damn talented writer."

"Huh?"

"She posts a piece every Monday on the website. I've been reading them for months."

I blinked. "You read the Gazette?"

"I have a subscription." He puffed out his chest.

"Well, I'll be damned. You take this seriously, don't you?"

He pointed to the store. "I hear Dickens has a good Canadiana section. Shall we go check it out?"

"Sure...?" Doubts still assailed me...but I had to do this sometime. Today felt like a good day.

We exited the SUV and headed inside. Little bells tinkled above the door as we entered and, after Dean pulled the door closed, he snagged my right hand again.

"Hello." A blond-haired man poked his head out from behind one of the shelves. "Hey, Ari, leave the new people alone."

I gazed down to find a fat white-and-black cat twining between my legs. We'd dropped Chip off at home, much to her annoyance, but—as always—my clothes were covered in dog fur.

Dean knelt, holding out the hand that wasn't still gripping mine. "Hello, Ari."

The cat headbutted the hand, and its purr reached me.

The attractive man approached. "Aristotle has her moments. I'm Dickens. Is there anything I can help you with today?"

Dean straightened, still holding my hand. "We're looking for your Canadiana section and hoping to spot a Dixon sister?"

If Dickens thought that was weird, he showed no signs as he grinned. "Sunshine's just run out to grab food. I was planning to eat mine with my husband over at his motorcycle repair shop. That will leave you alone with Ms. Dixon. May I trust your intentions are noble?"

The laughter coming from Dean warmed me from the tip of my hairline to the bottom of my toes. "Oh, Ms. Dixon's virtue is safe with us. We're seeing how many of the sisters we can spot."

"And here comes one..." Dickens squinted. "Nope, two, now." He leaned over. "I think that's Autumn. I'll try to help you out since I sometimes mix up the twins." He headed over to the door and held it open as the two women entered.

"Oh, good timing." The taller of the women smiled at Dickens. "You always know just when the food's about to arrive." She held out a tray of to-go cups and a bag from Tim Horton's. "Say *hi* to Spike from me."

Dickens grinned. "Will do. Thanks, Sunshine." He indicated over his shoulder. "They're trying to see how many Dixon sisters they can spot."

The other woman winced.

He nudged her. "All in fun, Autumn, I promise."

She noticed our interlocked hands and seemed to relax a fraction. I felt badly because this was supposed to be fun. As another oddity in town, I could see how she might not want to be infamous in this way. I said, "Rainbow suggested we stop by. Or maybe it was Kennedy." Her expression eased at her sisters' names.

Dean stepped forward, releasing my hand. "Can I take that from you?" He indicated the drink tray Autumn held.

Slowly, she smiled. "You're not British. And I'm going to say not Irish either. I met a professor over at the university—where I'll be studying next year. He's Irish."

Sunshine whistled. "And so hot. Professor Declan Byrne is as hunky as they get."

"You know I don't think of him like that. Ew." Autumn wrinkled her nose.

Something about the gesture struck me. Sure, she might be saying she wasn't interested in her professor. She held herself aloof from Dean as well, even though he radiated positive energy. I didn't want to stereotype her as a lesbian, or even bi, but I got that vibe.

When she noticed me, she offered a smile that didn't seem fake and met my eyes instead of looking away. "Yes, I'm Autumn. Not to be mistaken for my wild-child twin sister, Summer." She handed Dean the drink tray. "I'm going to head into the back. Nice meeting you."

The smile she bestowed upon me lasted just a fraction

longer than the one she gave Dean. But not in a bad way. I couldn't figure out how she felt about all this.

"Surely you didn't come all this way just to meet us." Sunshine grinned as she put the bag of food she carried on the counter.

"Canadiana," Dean said.

Her eyes lit. "Let me lead the way."

Chapter Nineteen

DEAN

Sunshine Dixon proved to be as charming as her sisters and, despite her sandwich growing cold, she gave us the full tour. Somehow, I left with seven books—way more than my budget could allow—but I couldn't identify a single one I was willing to leave behind. I noticed she gave me a bulk discount. I wasn't certain that was a thing, but the savings helped soften the blow. Adam and I had split lunch, even though I would've been happy to pay.

As I pointed the SUV north toward home, and ascended the first steep hill, I cast a quick look at him. He had the cloth book bag on his lap. Which also contained three books he'd selected for himself. Damn, that woman proved persuasive. Once she'd ferreted out the books Adam enjoyed, she'd located a collection of young-adult fantasy novels he'd never heard of. The Zaragoza Trilogy by local author R.D. Watts. He'd been a bit shy about admitting he enjoyed YA books, but Sunshine quickly confided she adored the books and recommended them to everyone.

Wanting to support local authors, I'd contemplated buying copies myself. I didn't read much fantasy, though, and

Adam assured me I could read his. Once he was finished with them, of course.

"Are you up for a movie tonight?" I grinned. "I was hoping for a repeat of last weekend." I pretended to contemplate. "Or just hanging out and reading? Do you think you could concentrate on the story while I give you a blow job?"

"Keep your eyes on the road."

Yet I detected no malice behind his words. More...amusement. "Is that a *yes*?"

"Dean."

"Yes?"

He sighed. "I'm your landlord."

"Well, or sort of like a roommate. A RILF."

"What the fuck is a RILF?"

"Roommate I'd like to fuck."

He sputtered. "Jesus, you really believe in laying things out plainly."

"What's the point of beating around the bush?" I slowed as we approached a red light but before I could stop completely, the light turned green and, as no one was in front of us, I accelerated through the intersection.

"You're an excellent driver."

"You mean I remember which side of the road to drive on?" Helped that the steering wheel was on the opposite side of the car—kept me honest.

"I mean..." He sighed. "I'm super sensitive about other people driving me places. I hate it. I always..."

"Need to be in control?"

"Yeah."

"But earlier you needed time to...regroup?"

"Something like that." He sighed. "I don't always know what's going to set me off. My session with Justin was intense."

"And yet you suggested we go out. You even survived with leaving Chip home alone."

"Well, you were the one who took her inside."

Yeah, it hadn't been lost on me that he hadn't been capable of being the one to lock Chip away in her crate. "She's fine, Adam. She needs to learn to be on her own."

"Why?"

"Because you might need to go somewhere she can't be. She also needs to learn to self-soothe. To be independent of you. She's bonded to you, which is great, but there need to be boundaries as well." I knew I was overstepping, but I'd done some reading and yeah, I wasn't an expert. But I foresaw issues if Adam finally ventured into the world and Chip reacted badly.

"I need her."

"And you're her person. But is it not okay that she wants to sometimes spend time with me?" Several times, she'd tromped up to my room. I always kept the door open, which she'd quickly figured out.

"Life's hard." He said the words on a sigh. "And what I was trying to say about your driving...some people, they ride the bumper of the person before them. They slam on the brakes. They accelerate super-fast. You're...smooth."

"Smooth enough to talk you into a—"

"Yes. Blow job." He laughed. "You really have a one-track mind."

And if he hadn't been laughing, I might've wondered if I was pushing too hard. I'd waited a week. Despite his intense session with Justin, his spirits were much higher today, and I was damn well going to take advantage of that. He could always say *no*. Consent was a thing. An important thing. "Am I pushing too hard?" So much for being confident.

He pressed his left hand to my thigh. "I would tell you, Dean. Honestly, am I not blunt about everything?"

"You haven't really talked to me this week. I mean, you don't have to tell me about the stuff you discuss with Justin, or listen to my work, which is super boring." I winced. "I just...want to get to know you."

"I'm an open book."

Bullshit. Still, I wouldn't say that out loud. "I consider you more like an onion."

"You don't like onions."

I squeezed his hand gently with mine before gripping the wheel again. "Metaphors, my dear."

He snickered. "Peeling back the layers? That's so..."

"Cheesy?"

"Yes."

"But perhaps accurate?"

He made some noncommittal noise in his throat.

"What food would you compare me to?"

Another snicker. "A banana."

"See, peeling back layers—"

"A peeled banana."

"Uh."

"Phallic-shaped, of course. Everything I see is what I get." He waved his hand. "I'm not saying you don't have depth— you do. I'm just saying that you live your life very honestly. I admire that about you."

"Thank you. I think."

He squeezed my thigh again.

I glanced over, getting a good look at his scars. Usually, he worked hard for me not to sit on his left side. Today, though, he'd appeared less upset by me seeing him. Or at least that was my perception. He was still struggling, for sure, but he'd loosened up a bit. I'd nearly fallen over from the shock when he suggested we go out. Aside from pointing out that we needed to leave Chip at home, I'd done nothing to suggest this hadn't always been the plan. My job sometimes required that I be nimble. I strove to be the same way in my private life.

At the driveway, I entered the code, and the gate swung open.

Adam sighed. Like he'd been holding his breath, and now he was safe again, he could fully relax.

"What movie do you want to watch?" I had no idea what was available, but given the sheer volume of stuff on the streaming platforms, I was confident we could settle on something we both agreed with. I parked the car in the garage, shut off the engine, then turned to face Adam.

"Will you come to my bed, Dean? Is it too soon to ask that?"

I nearly swallowed my tongue. I didn't know what his intentions were. Well, likely not *honorable*—which was completely fine with me. "Are you sure? You've had a big day—"

"Shut the fuck up."

My jaw snapped shut.

He held up his hand. "Sorry, that was rude of me. Just... would you like it if I was always questioning you? Treating you like I couldn't trust you to make your own decisions?"

Deciding silence was a good option, I didn't point out how many times he'd asked me if I was sure last weekend.

"Sorry."

"You don't have to be." I pulled the keys out of the ignition. "I'll hook up the SUV. You take care of Chip. If you're still willing after that, then we'll have a talk."

"I don't want to talk." He pounded his fist against his thigh.

"Adam." I used my persuasive tone and, after a moment, he met my gaze. "You set out some ground rules. I'm happy to follow them, but I need more details if we're going to be

GABBI GREY

naked. What you can and can't tolerate. What the boundaries are. What makes you feel good. And I'll tell you mine."

"And how do you know what'll make you feel good if you haven't…you know…"

"Between my dildo, my imagination, and porn? I figure I've got a good grasp of what I'll be okay with. I want to experience all of it. With you. That's the key, though. I don't want anyone else. I'm hoping you feel the same way."

He opened his mouth to speak, then shut it again.

"This only works if you're honest with me."

After a moment, he offered a rueful smile. "I was going to say I was attracted to Maddox, but that sounded weird in my head."

"Are you attracted to Justin? Because they're similar—"

He shook his head vehemently. "Justin's my counselor. Even if that weren't totally inappropriate…he doesn't have the lumberjack vibe." His cheeks reddened.

I scratched my beard. "Now the truth comes out. You want me for my forestry-management skills."

"I want you because you make me laugh. Because you make me feel again. And yeah, some of it hurts. A lot. But that's not all bad…" He swallowed. "I miss intimacy. I'm surprised to say that, as I was more of a fuck-and-run than a touchy-feely guy before—"

To reassure him, I slowly took his left hand in my right. "What came before doesn't matter."

His eyes darkened. "You wouldn't say that if you knew everything."

Careful. "If you want to share more, I'll listen. If you need to maintain privacy, I'm okay with that as well. I just…I assume we're going to be using condoms…"

He winced.

"Right. Should I be driving back to town? Because I sure

as shit didn't bring any with me." An admission—in case he needed one—that this wasn't the norm for me.

"I'm negative, Dean. Dr. Marco reminded me a few years back, when he was encouraging me to get myself out there. That I'd been screened for everything while in the hospital. And come up neg." He offered a sheepish smile. "I've never gone bareback. I might've been young and impulsive, but I was also careful."

"It's pretty safe to say I'm negative as well." I squeezed his hand. "I wasn't lying when I said I've never been with anyone. But if it's too soon for you to trust, or if you need me to be tested—"

He shook his head.

"Right-o. You take care of Chip, I'll run back to town for condoms—"

He shook his head. "I'm okay with bareback." He held my gaze. "But that means we're exclusive. I might've been suicidal in the past, but I don't have a death wish now. Or a desire for any of the other nasty things that are out there. And...in ten years, I've never found anyone else who made it worth stepping out of my safe space. I need you to tell me, if you decide I'm not enough. I mean, now you're trying sex, maybe you'll want more variety, but I..." His voice trailed off.

I knew. In that moment, I knew. That I could come to care deeply for this man. That I could love him. Hell, I was halfway there. This prickly, picky, obstinate man. Who'd started counselling. Who was taking his meds. I wouldn't say that I'd found the pill trays or that I'd noticed them getting progressively emptier. "I would never cheat on you, Adam. That's not who I am."

"Wait till you've had sex," he protested. "You might find you like it and want to see what it's like with other people. Or you don't like it with me and want to move on."

For just an instant, I imagined pressing my index finger to his lips. But he'd specifically said I couldn't touch his face or most of the left side of his body. I could respect that. Would respect that. He was asking for so little, I could at least do this. "Learning all about sex from a guy like you. Such a sacrifice." I tried a gentle tease. "Exclusive means you can't cheat on me either, you know."

That brought a shadowed smile. "I never leave this place."

I almost—almost—pointed he'd gone out today. That he'd met two gay men. Admittedly both were married, but I'd gotten the sense from Rainbow that, despite the town's religious underpinnings, plenty of gay men either came from here or had made the town their home. The downtown's rainbow crosswalks aside—a point of great contention, according to Spring's writings—this was a relatively safe place to be. "Let's go to bed, Adam."

He blinked. "Yeah, okay."

Chapter Twenty

ADAM

WHETHER THERE HAD BEEN AN INEVITABILITY TO this—really from the moment he stepped into my castle—a forward momentum carried me. I gave Chip a long walk along the line of the yard up to the forest, but not into it. I contemplated letting her run free again—she had come on command, after all—but I wanted Dean in my bed, and that meant moving getting us naked pronto. For once, Chip obliged my rush, and we were able to head back soon.

We were close to dinnertime, so I gave her a good meal. I wasn't hungry, though, and I hoped Dean wasn't either. We'd eaten enormous lunches at Fifties and, for me, the anticipation knotted my gut and food didn't appeal.

I expected to find him in the kitchen, but he wasn't. I gave Chip her favorite chew toy and tried to settle her on her bed.

Having been left alone, apparently, hadn't suited her, and she now showed zero interest in being abandoned again. She followed me upstairs, and I sort of shrugged as she made her way into my room. She made a beeline for her bed in the corner and was settled before I was even fully in the room.

I followed behind her, and my breath caught.

My bed was turned down, with the comforter removed—folded and sitting on the hope chest at the end of the four-poster bed. The sheet was also pulled down, inviting me to join the amazing specimen of male who lay naked on my bed. He gave me a wicked grin as he palmed his semi-erect cock. A light fuzz of burnished gold hair covered his legs and arms. On his chest, though, a thick pelt across his pecs arrowed down across a flat stomach and continued downward still.

Happy trail indeed.

"You're free to watch," he chirped. "But I'd prefer if you joined me."

I hesitated.

His movements slowed.

Wincing, I tried to speak.

"You're a top, right?" He cocked his head. "I mean, if I'm wrong—"

"You're not wrong."

"Is that why you're hesitating?"

"A bit."

"Well, since I love pegging my prostate with toys, I think we're in good shape. But if you just want to wank and suck again, I'm totally down with that." He pointed to my crotch. "I want to bring you pleasure. Unless you were lying last weekend, I know I'm good at something."

The blow job. The epic blow job.

"Yeah, I'd bet you're good at more than that." Slowly, I unbuttoned my shirt. Part of me wanted to keep it on, but that didn't make sense. I craved touch—even if only on my right side—so that meant clothes had to come off.

Dean's gaze held mine as I removed my shirt. Then I unbuttoned my jeans, slipped down the zipper, and shucked them, tossing them to the side. As they clunked, I gave a thought for my phone and wallet, decided neither was important, and yanked off my socks.

A light breeze carried from where Dean had opened the window. It touched me that he realized how much I prized fresh air. The last owner had wanted a hermetically sealed fortress. I worked to let in both fresh air and the sun whenever possible. So maybe not so much of a recluse.

"Adam—"

"I'm coming." I advanced toward the bed. "We're really going to do this."

He held out his hand to me. "As much as you're willing."

I held back asking him if he was sure. If he'd had doubts, he wouldn't be in my bed. I might not know everything about Dean Hargrave, but I knew that much. He didn't do anything he didn't want to. I took his left hand with my right, holding tight.

Giving me a slight nod, he shifted a fraction so he no longer sat in the center of the mattress, leaving me space. This massive bed felt almost miniscule as I contemplated sharing it for the first time. I knelt on the mattress and advanced toward him. He was perfection while...I was not.

He doesn't care. He's looking you in the eyes with desire, not sympathy. He doesn't feel sorry for you. I believed that. Because he'd stroked himself into full hardness, with a drop of precum on his tip. Surely if I repulsed him, if he saw me as less than human, he wouldn't have managed that.

I licked my lips.

He grinned.

I scooted until I positioned myself between his spread thighs. Then I took him in my good hand.

He whimpered.

Grinning, I continued with leisurely strokes, mimicking what he'd done before. What he clearly liked. "You ready for my mouth?"

"Fuck yes." He gritted his teeth. "Been waiting forever."

Forever was a big word, but I was happy to lick his crown.

He bucked.

I sucked, ignoring the way the stretch pulled my bad cheek, turning my head so he'd mostly see my good side. I hoped he liked the sight of my lips around his cock as I rose up and down. Except when he moaned and told me how amazing it felt, what he could see mattered less than how he felt. I lined up straighter, took him deeper, giving him my best.

Somehow, something that was so familiar also felt so new. I'd done this hundreds of times, with hundreds of guys, but it had never felt so...precious. Important. Like something monumental was shifting in my life.

I was vaguely aware of Chip dropping onto her bed with a huff.

Dean let out a little laugh. "Well, she's in for a show."

I'd jerked off a few times with her in the room and she'd never freaked out. Intellectually, I understood she had no idea what we were doing. That miniscule prudish part of me felt I should be locking her out.

Cupping my head, Dean refocused me.

"Right." I resumed my task, licking him from root to tip along the vein on the underside. Then, without warning, I took him all the way in. Having no real gag reflex was a blessing, and I swallowed him down.

"Oh God."

Humming my approval, I swirled him around in my mouth. With my left hand, I gently gripped his balls. My stupid fingers didn't have as much strength but for this, for rolling and tugging with a light touch, my bad hand could still give my partner pleasure.

He dug his heels into the mattress.

I sucked harder.

"I'm coming, Adam. Please, God, if you want to pull off..."

His words were far more coherent than I'd been a week ago. Still, I sucked harder.

He pulsed, then shot cum into my mouth.

Diligently, I swallowed, managing to keep going as I nursed him through aftershocks. Little tremors swept over him as I gently stroked his thighs. Finally, with a little pop, I pulled off his cock. The desire to kiss him was so strong that I nearly yielded and broke that rule. Kissing with the taste of a guy's cum in my mouth used to be an incredible turn-on for me.

Not that I needed help. My cock strained, demanding attention.

In good time. First, I needed to prep my eager partner.

I glanced at the nightstand. Good, he found the bottle of lube in the top drawer and had placed it strategically. I supposed I should've been vaguely concerned about him going through my things, but I trusted he'd sought lube and hadn't snooped. Going where he wasn't welcome was, luckily, not his style.

You still haven't shown him that room.

Shut up.

Fortunately, my inner voice was willing to be silenced—this time. I snagged the bottle of lube. "Do you want...?"

He pulled his knees up and out of the way, exposing himself completely to me. The trust involved staggered me. And obviously he wanted me to fuck him while we were face to face. I would've thought he'd want to turn away. To not stare into the ugliness.

And yet, I should've also known better. Dean didn't shy away from the tough. Even just coming to Canada showed courage. Picking up the pieces after his mother died was an example of resiliency.

I coated my fingers with lube. After I positioned myself

between his thighs again, I slowly slid one finger in, studying his expression.

He grinned.

I slid a second finger in, scissoring him, trying to open him up. I twisted my wrist and hit his prostate.

If possible, the smile grew wider. "Yeah, I love that."

"It's possible I could make you come again." Even as I said the words, his cock twitched with interest.

"Entirely possible." His amber eyes held my gaze. "But I want you inside of me when I do, okay?"

I blinked. "Yeah, okay." I tapped that spongy spot one last time before withdrawing my hand. "And you're sure?"

He cocked an eyebrow.

Breathe. "I don't have condoms, Dean. I've never gone bare before."

"We can stop. I can get you off, and—"

"No." That might've come out more strident than I'd anticipated. I snagged the bottle of lube, slathered my cock, then dropped the bottle back onto the nightstand. I'd used a fair amount while prepping him, so I figured we were covered.

Again, he pulled his knees up and out of the way. "I trust you, Adam."

But should he? I hadn't done this in ten years. Riding a bicycle and all that...except I didn't know how to ride a bike, and I wasn't certain things would come back to me. Still, I positioned myself over him, lined up, and slowly slid in.

I wasn't huge, but I wasn't small either. Certainly, more than a couple of fingers. Discomfort crossed his face as he furrowed his brow. I was about to pull out, but he grasped my right hip.

"Keep going. I can take it."

Sure. Maybe. But knowing I was causing pain affected me in a way it never had previously. I'd never been so attuned to my partner's pleasure. I hadn't hurt any of the guys who'd come before, but I also had never felt...this emotionally invested. Like if I hurt him, I'd be hurting myself as well.

"Honestly, Adam." His voice held a note of admonishment. "You're not much bigger than my dildo."

I laughed, grateful he'd said I was bigger. Given the size of some of the ones out there. Or he was flattering me now? *Does it matter?* Gauging his reaction, I slid in slowly, pushing against the initial resistance that morphed into acceptance.

As I bottomed out, he sighed.

The intensity of the tightness and heat around my cock surprised me. I'd always figured there wasn't much difference between rubber or bare. Yeah, I'd misjudged that one big time. "I'm going to move."

"Please do." More amusement.

I also couldn't remember the last time I'd had fun in bed. Or fun anywhere, for that matter. Well, the night we'd watched the movie. That memory had kept me going the past week.

"Seriously, Adam, just fuck me already."

Despite myself, I laughed. "Uh, okay."

Experimentally, I thrust in and out—taking it slow and steady.

Having none of that, Dean wrapped his legs around my hips and pressed down on my ass, urging me closer.

I went to work in earnest. I'd withdraw almost to the tip, then push back in.

He'd arch his hips to match that.

I sought to find a challenging rhythm.

He grunted his pleasure.

"Jerk yourself." He'd perked right back up as I nailed his prostate repeatedly. Even as I chased my orgasm, I wanted him to have pleasure as well.

As he moved his hand between our bodies, his hand grazed my left side. The touch stuttered across my scars.

My pace faltered as our gazes locked. Even as I saw the apology on the tip of his tongue, I gritted my teeth. "Wank off, as you would say. Now, mate."

He obeyed my command, his hand working frantically to keep up with my renewed thrusts. We fell into a rhythm together with our breaths synching. Connecting in a way I'd never done with someone before.

Even as my vision narrowed with approaching orgasm, and I tried to hang onto the edge, he shouted his release, and cum hit my chest.

Thank fuck. On the next thrust, I joined him. As I sank into the abyss—and the bliss—I marveled how something I used to take for granted could have come to mean so much tonight. This wasn't just a meeting of bodies, although that had been part of it. No, this had been a meeting of the minds. A connection I couldn't describe. Something that both terrified and energized at the same time.

I collapsed on him, as my body released all its tension. As I did, I slid from him with a little pop.

He giggled.

That sound resonated within me and, for the first time in years, my heart lightened.

Chapter Twenty-One

DEAN

OKAY, AS FIRST TIMES WENT, THAT'D BEEN FUCKING amazing. Whatever pain I'd started out with had quickly passed. And although I'd played with my dildo many times, having Adam nail me to the mattress had been more intense on so many levels I hadn't anticipated.

Emotional being the overwhelming one.

I'd believed sex would be sex. Because I was *not* going to fall in love with the first guy who fucked me.

Except...what we'd done was way more than sex. At least for me. He might try to come off as uncaring, but he'd taken great pains to ensure I had lots of pleasure. Hell, two orgasms plus the intimacy of him inside me. I might've waited a lifetime for this, but he'd also been celibate for ten years and changed that only for me. He'd said so. And I believed him. Because, for all his faults, he never lied to me.

As he lay heavy on me, I resisted the urge to wrap my arms around him and hold him close. We hadn't discussed aftercare, cuddling, or anything else that might push his boundaries. And he had boundaries. Walls so high I didn't have a chance in hell of scaling them. Yet even as I thought about the gate to his property and the impressive walls of the castle, I realized—to some extent—that I had a key. A literal key, for certain, but also a metaphorical one. He was, despite his best efforts to the contrary, letting me in. Showing me his sensitive side. Letting me see the pain. Twice I'd gone with him to his counselling sessions. I hadn't been party to them, but I'd met his therapist and the team taking care of him.

That had to mean something...right?

Slowly, I ran my left hand up and down his right flank, including squeezing his ass.

He groaned. "I am not up for more."

Desperately, I wanted to draw him into my arms. To prove I didn't care about the scars or the isolation or his past or whatever issues he still struggled with. To show him just how much I was coming to care for him. To show him there might be life beyond these walls. We'd done it earlier—with Fifties and the bookstore—but did I have a right to keep pushing outward?

Slowly, he rolled off of me, mindful of the cum between us, which had started to dry and stick. He winced. "Gross."

I hesitated. Did that mean we weren't showering together? After we'd shared such intimacy, I'd sort of assumed we'd just keep going. That now, given everything, things would have changed.

He rolled right off the bed into a standing position. Without looking back, he headed toward where I assumed his shower was.

And shut the door.

My heart seized. My chest squeezed. This *shouldn't* hurt. I shouldn't have given him the power to hurt me. Because I knew better. Everyone I loved died.

That's not true...just your mother. Which is sad, but don't catastrophize.

Adam stuck his head out of the bathroom. "Meet me

downstairs and look at the books after?" Then he closed the door.

"Uh...sure..." Great, I wasn't being tossed over. But that meant I needed to get my ass in gear. I scooted off the bed, petted a dozing Chip on her head, and made a beeline to the narrow staircase that would lead me up to my room.

I was almost there when I remembered I'd left my clothes in Adam's room. So I scurried back there to pick up all my stuff. Taking just a moment, I gazed at the gigantic bed. We'd enjoyed ourselves, right? He'd come. I'd come twice. Orgasms generally meant...what? That he might one day love me? That I could admit I was falling for him? I tore out of there, back up the stairs and into the shower. I scrubbed everywhere—everywhere—then donned fresh clothes, combed my beard, and headed downstairs.

To find Adam at the fridge. "Would you like a sugar-free iced tea? Or there's cola?" He'd offered me a lot over the past two weeks, and I felt vague guilt since the rent didn't include food. Still, I'd take the olive branch. "I love iced tea. One of my favorites. Can I help?"

He shook his head.

I grabbed the cloth bag, and we moved into the living room. He sat on the couch and I, wanting to be close, did as well. Close, but not touching. If he wanted more, though, I was all in for that.

We sorted our books. I winced when I checked my receipt, but I didn't want to give back a single book. I'd even bought a Canadian nature book, featuring flowers, fauna, and forests, for Sam. *Not sure he'll appreciate it quite the way I would, but he's a good friend.* Someone I should talk to about this situation. Adam sat before me, with his hair slicked back and a distant expression on his face. Like he wasn't quite certain what to say.

Join the club.

We settled down to read our books and drink our iced teas.

That night, we ate chicken teriyaki and vegetables for dinner and later enjoyed popcorn and diet sodas while watching *The Adventures of Priscilla, Queen of the Desert*. I wasn't certain how Adam felt about the drag parts of the movie, but he laughed in all the right places, so that meant something. I then encouraged him to watch *To Wong Foo, Thanks for Everything! Julie Newmar*. His only comment was he was sad Patrick Swayze was dead. I tried to remember how long it had been—I didn't have a memory of the actual death —but I couldn't put a date on it. That sort of put a pall on the evening in a way I hadn't anticipated, and as much as I tried to get some joviality back, Adam wasn't feeling it.

Again, no invitation to spend the night in his bed.

Clearly, he wasn't one for cuddling.

And I was too chickenshit to offer.

Sunday, we hung out in the family room on the big leather couches and read. Chip alternated between sleeping at my feet, and keeping Adam company.

I had yet to meet the elusive Maurice. I'd witnessed Adam taking the used litter to the garbage—and putting out food that subsequently disappeared—so I knew there had to be a cat somewhere.

Adam declared, after a dinner of burgers on the barbeque, that he wanted an early night.

So much for a repeat. My ass wasn't even sore, so I would've been happy to go another round. Monday morning, I didn't even see him.

At least Roxie was in a cheery mood when I got to work. "Hey, can you do me a favor?" She asked the question with a brilliant smile. Almost too bright.

I eyed her across the desk in her tiny office. We were reviewing some maps before we headed out. "Of course."

"Great. I have a doctor's appointment. Quick in and out.

But I also need to run by the library to pick up a book they've got on hold for me. If I give you my card, can you do that?"

"The library on Second Avenue?"

"That's the one."

"Won't the librarian question me?"

"You can go to the self-service terminal and they'll never know. But Loriana, Marnie, Johanna, and just about everyone else there recognizes me. You're wearing a uniform, so they'll give you a pass."

I wasn't convinced of this, but twenty minutes later, I stood in the holds section, trying to find this elusive book Roxie told me to find.

"May I help you? You look lost."

Turning, I found a striking shorter woman with shiny, raven-black hair, deep-green eyes, and a smile. She stood well back from me, but she met my gaze with a grin.

"I'm Roxie's coworker." Shit, I didn't even know her last name. "She asked me to pick up a book..."

"And they're sorted by last name." Without hesitation, she pulled one out with *Windig* written on the paper attached to the spine with an elastic. Offering it, she gave me a tentative smile. "We generally prefer the patron pick up their own book, but I know Roxie's always so busy and you've got her card. Reading brings her pleasure."

"That, in turn, makes us happy." Another woman happened upon us and her smile wasn't tentative at all. "I'm Loriana, the head librarian. I see you've met Marnie."

I glanced over to see a light blush creep into the other woman's cheeks.

"Lovely to meet both you folks. I'm Dean. From Australia." Just in case they couldn't place the accent.

"Fantastic. You seem to be happy in our little town." Loriana smiled, which seemed to brighten her light-brown eyes. She pushed her auburn hair back from her face. Auburn that quite resembled my own. I'd never met so many redheads. She met my gaze. "I don't suppose you'd be willing to do a *meet a stranger* session here at the library? Tell us about Australia?"

"Uh..."

"Oh yes." Marnie's lips curled up. "I know we have patrons who would love to learn about the land down under. Heck, I would."

This hadn't been on my agenda, but part of my role was to expand community knowledge and appreciation for the forests surrounding the area. If I were to attend, this...thing... and discuss the differences between Australian bush and Canadian forests, that was a win.

Right?

Have to ask Roxie's permission. "I'll, uh, have to talk to Roxie."

Loriana waved a dismissive hand. "I'm quite certain she'll approve it. Why don't I get your phone number so we can coordinate?"

We three, en masse, exited the narrow stacks to find a very amused-looking Maddox standing nearby. Violet rested on one of his hips while Victor sat on the floor, playing with a book. Maddox raised an eyebrow. "Couldn't help but overhearing. They're roping you in, eh?"

Loriana gently smacked his arm. "You do biannual safety talks. I'm just..."

"Recruiting," I added helpfully. "And I'll be happy to do it, should Roxie agree."

Marnie pointed toward a row of computers. "I need to help. I'll be back in time for Toddlers and Books." She headed off.

"And I'm going to get a pen and paper to take down your contact info." Loriana took off in the opposite direction— toward the circulation desk. Or so the sign above it indicated.

I turned back to Maddox.

"Yeah, they like to keep things moving forward around here." He grinned.

"Papa." Violet patted his beard. "Man." She pointed to Dean.

"Dean." I pressed a hand to my chest. "We met a couple of weeks ago. Lovely to see you again."

"Speaking of..." Maddox lowered Violet, but kept an eye on both the children. He spared me a quick glance. "How goes it?"

"Well."

His head snapped up and his blue eyes narrowed. "Really?"

I chuckled. "You thought I'd be locked away forever and held prisoner? Or completely ignored?"

"Perhaps." He crouched down to his children's level.

Following a compulsion I didn't understand, I did the same. "I'm enjoying myself, Maddox. And wanted to thank you. I don't just have a roof over my head..." I considered. "I'd say I have a friend."

His eyes held my gaze.

A slow heat crept into my cheeks.

"Oh, really. I have to say I didn't see that coming, but I couldn't be more pleased." He snagged Violet before she bolted. "How is Chip these days?"

"On a short leash. And you? How is..." I sought for the name of his dog.

"Princess Sofia? A little scamp."

"Doggie." Victor grinned, so much like Ravi.

"Yes, doggie." Maddox ruffled his son's hair. "We'd like to extend an invitation. To both of you, of course. Just a quiet affair. I have a couple of friends who are coming as well. We'd be six adults and two toddlers." He winced. "That's a lot, isn't it?"

He wasn't wrong. Coaxing Adam out to deal with such a large group of people, even if it was *just a quiet* affair would be a challenge. But he'd withstood the bookstore. He'd managed at Fifties. Most importantly, I'd be there. To help him cope. To make excuses if he was overwhelmed. Not to take charge, though. He had to make the decision himself.

Maddox snagged Violet by the waist and dropped her into his lap. "Loriana is going to start reading soon." He shrugged. "I've been bringing them since the day they were old enough to sit still. Doesn't always mean they do."

"This sounds like a great idea."

"So you'll come to dinner?"

"Oh." My eyes widened. "I meant Toddler and Books sounded like a great idea. Get them in early."

"Yep. We always leave with a stack of books. And often go to The Owl's Nest. A couple of local authors have children's books there, and we want to support them as well."

"I might've spent a bit of cash there myself."

"Ah, Dickens can be persuasive."

"Actually, he was eating lunch with his husband."

Maddox laughed. "Oh, left you alone with Sunshine, did he? I'm amazed you didn't buy the entire store."

"I kind of feel like I did." I nodded. "Let me talk to Adam about dinner. I'll happily be there. I can't commit for him."

"Well, it's Friday night."

I nodded slowly. "I'll check."

"Great. Got your phone handy? I can't remember if I gave you my number."

He hadn't. I entered it into my phone and then shot him a quick text so he'd have mine.

As Loriana returned, I rose. She handed me a pencil and paper. I dutifully wrote out my contact information.

I waved goodbye to Maddox, then accompanied Loriana to the desk, where she checked out Roxie's book for me.

"You qualify for a visitor card." She gave me a cute grin. "I'm assuming you have a local address."

In that instant, I hesitated. She didn't appear to be someone who gossiped, but Adam didn't want his business known around town—of that, I was certain. "Yes. But I'm in a hurry. Maybe another time?"

"Ask Roxie about doing a presentation."

"I will, I promise." Waving as I left, I headed back into the bright early June sunshine.

Refocus. You can talk to Adam tonight.

And so I went on my way.

Chapter Twenty-Two

ADAM

"I CAN'T BELIEVE YOU TALKED ME INTO THIS." I groused at Dean, careful to keep my voice low as we waited for someone to open the door.

"Stop whining."

"I'm not whining."

He cut me a look.

"I'm grousing."

"You sound like a toddler—"

He was cut off by the door swinging open.

A harried-looking Ravi offered us a smile. "I had an emergency at work that kept me late, and—"

"We can come another time," I quickly offered.

Dean propelled me forward. "We're happy to help if you need it. We're assuming you would've canceled if that's what you wanted." He mock-glared at me. Then he turned on the charm, handing Ravi a bottle of Okanagan's best red wine.

I didn't bother to offer up the tray of hors d'oeuvres Dean insisted on preparing. He'd dogged Maddox until the man had finally agreed to let us bring something. Since apparently no one was vegetarian, he'd made tuna and chickpea patties as well as beef curry puffs. A taste of home, he'd said. I'd tried one of each and thought he'd done a really good job.

Ravi indicated the tin foil covered plate in my hands. "You guys go ahead, set that on the coffee table. Simeon is here and we're expecting Everett any minute now."

Again, I gave Dean the evil eye.

He blinked, all innocent. "Oh, did I forget to mention it's a dinner party of six?" He grinned. "And two toddlers."

He was teasing. He'd told me that, of course, when he was sneakily coercing me into agreeing to this madness. And a second time on the way here, making sure I really was onboard while in my right mind. *If you can call this my right mind.* A big part of me wanted to run back to the car and go home.

"Speaking of which, perhaps you can assist Simeon? He's been in the living room with the twos and Princess Sofia." He cocked his head. "I'm surprised she didn't bark when you arrived." He shrugged. "Our guest does have the magic touch."

He headed toward where I assumed the kitchen was while Dean and I shucked off our shoes and headed into what I would term the *great room*. From the outside, this home appeared to be just a large wood cabin. The inside, however, charmed me. The soaring two stories reminded me of the living room at Healing Horses ranch. A staircase along the back wall led upstairs, presumably the bedrooms.

Even as I took in the large-screen television and fascinating art on the walls—some of it clearly Indigenous—Dean made a beeline for the pile of bodies on the couch, managing to scoop Violet into his arms before she tumbled to the floor. He swung her around, making her giggle.

"Fly, fly, fly." She screeched her order.

Dean positioned her on his shoulder and *flew* her around the room as if he'd done this before.

I seemed to recall him saying, at some point, that he didn't have much experience with kids. Maybe a bit, at least? Certainly more than me. I worried Victor might want that as well, but he was cuddled against a large man on the couch who held a picture book.

The man, upon spotting me, closed the book. He offered his hand. "S-Simeon."

Finding courage I wasn't certain I had, I offered my right hand back. "Adam. And that's Dean."

Dean who continued to hold Violet high above him as he gently spun her.

"Your b-boyfriend is c-cute."

Empathy washed through me for this man who had a clear stutter. His gaze didn't linger on my face, much to my relief. Instead, he turned his attention back to Victor. His blond hair caught the light pouring in from the massive windows, and when he flashed me another look, his hazel eyes settled on me for just a second. With his head, he indicated I should look down.

At my feet sat the cutest white canine furball who was clearly salivating over whatever was on the tray. I'd planned to put it down on the coffee table, but now I questioned that decision. Still, I removed the foil and stepped toward Simeon, offering.

His eyes lit with pleasure as he took one of each.

Victor reached out to grab the beef curry puff. For a moment, I worried. But between Simeon smiling and my remembering Ravi's Indian heritage, I figured we were probably okay.

Simeon tentatively nibbled the puff, but then demolished the tuna chickpea concoction in just a couple of inelegant bites.

I wasn't normally a fan of watching other people eat—but the clear pleasure in his expression and his wide smile made me a little less wary.

Dean held Violet just above the tray, and she nabbed a puff as well. He set her down on the other side of Simeon and indicated the book. "They love their reading, eh? I met them at the library the other day." He nudged me. "That's how I wound up with the invite." He snagged a tuna and indicated Simeon should speak up, if he wanted, to explain how he wound up here tonight.

"I f-fixed the kitchen f-floor."

"After my dishwasher broke." Maddox strode into the room. "Damn thing wasn't even that old. Stupidly, I'd left it to run and had taken the kids out for a walk with the dog. I ran into Stanley, we got to talking..." He shrugged. "I came back to water everywhere, and some of it warped the hardwood floor. My fault for having gone with traditional hardwood instead of laminate."

"Not anymore." Simeon smiled, gripping Victor's shoulder.

"Right." Maddox nodded. "Vinyl in the kitchen from now on." He met my gaze. "I have a bad knee, so doing it myself wasn't possible. Ravi's been working extra shifts because one of his fellow pediatric nurses went into labor almost two months early. Mom and baby are okay, but she'd planned to work right up to delivery. Which I think is nuts...but I've never been a pregnant woman."

"Oh yeah. You have maternity leave here too, right? We have twenty weeks of paid leave."

Maddox's eyebrows shot up. "That sucks. We offer a year. Some Scandinavian countries offer even more than that. Twenty weeks? Many women are still breastfeeding." He shook his head. "That's a shame."

"I shall take that news back home with me and lobby parliament. Anyhow, I heard the US sucks worse." Dean snagged another puff and grinned. "Maddox, I'll eat all of these myself."

Our host held up a little plate. "I'm snagging some for Ravi."

"Why don't I go help him?" Dean piled several of the items onto a plate and headed toward the kitchen.

Maddox shrugged, then snagged a tuna and chickpea for himself. "I'm not going to complain. First, my knee's hurting. Second, Ravi's a little tired of me right now." He dropped into the recliner, although he didn't raise his legs.

I took the tray over to him. "You have to try the beef curry puffs."

"Yes, so g-good." Simeon winced.

Telling him not to worry about his stutter would only, I was certain, make things worse. Just like when someone insisted that my scars didn't bother them. Which...I might've —just for a moment—forgotten about them. Or, at the very least, hadn't been focused on them. I swung the tray back to Simeon.

He grinned and snagged another one of each.

Victor grabbed another puff.

Violet opted for the tuna.

Honestly, I was impressed both were so happy to eat the food. I was pretty sure Dean had been thinking only of the adults.

A knock came from the front door.

I handed Maddox the tray of food so he wouldn't get up and aggravate his knee. "Shall I go?"

"Sure."

As I made my way to the front door, apprehension spiked. What if this newcomer didn't know about me? What if he judged me? After a split-second of hesitation, I opened the door, my head turned to the left in automatic reflex.

I beheld a handsome Black man with short, curly hair, a muscular body under his button-down shirt and smart trousers, and his dark-brown eyes alight with what I assumed was amusement. "You're not Ravi or Maddox."

"Uh, no. But this is their house. Ravi's in the kitchen with my—" Jesus, was I about to say boyfriend? Ugh. "The friend I came with. Dean," I quickly supplied.

"The Aussie." The man grinned. "That makes you Adam and I'm Everett."

"Simeon is here as well."

Everett cocked an eyebrow. "Fair enough. I don't know Simeon."

"Neither do I. But he seems really nice. He's great with the kids. And I should let you come in." I stepped aside to let him pass.

He was barely in the door when Violet charged at him. He tried to cower behind me.

I stood my ground and nudged him forward.

"Uh..." He shot me a panicked look with eyes wide.

Violet, apparently reading her target wasn't interested, barreled toward me.

Remembering how Dean held her, I scooped her into my arms. "Let's go find your dad." I rearranged her, so I held her on my right hip as I carried her into the great room. Then, to my shock, she touched my face. The scars, no less.

Just as she did, Ravi entered the room. "Oh dear, Vi, what are you—"

"It's fine." I maintained eye contact with the child as she contoured my face with her tiny fingers. "She's not hurting anyone." Anyone meaning me. Her deep-brown eyes were a laser focus on me as she brushed upward until she grasped my hair. "Ouch. Now that hurts."

Ravi scrambled over to us, gently pulling her out of my arms. "No grabbing hair, sweetheart." He met my gaze. "I'm sorry—"

"Really, it's fine." I even pressed my hand to Ravi's arm. "She didn't mean anything."

He appeared undecided.

"Yeah, well, we're here to say dinner's served." Dean met my gaze, correctly reading my discomfort. Then he glanced over at the empty tray. "You didn't leave any for me?"

"Or me." Everett offered a mock pout, even as he grinned.

"The k-kids." Simeon met Ravi's gaze. "I think we spoiled their appetite."

Ravi glanced over at Maddox, who simply smiled. "Oh, I'm sure you think you might have. You haven't met my kids, though. Nothing stops them from consuming their corn and peas."

Vi clapped her hands. "Peas, peas, peas."

Not to be outdone, Victor grinned. "Corn."

As a group, we moved into the dining room. Ravi had Violet in his arms. Simeon held tight to a toddling Victor's hand. Dean moved beside me as Everett and Maddox brought up the rear.

"I'm impressed by you." Dean leaned in close.

"Nothing to be impressed at." I gave the response dismissively, but his words meant more than he'd ever know. I'd stepped out of my comfort zone. That had to mean something, right?

It either meant something momentous, or it meant I had one night of courage in me but nothing had changed and tomorrow I'd be right back to the hermit in the castle. As my nerves jittered at the thought of sitting at a full table, I had no clue which.

Chapter Twenty-Three

DEAN

PART OF ME WAS SAD I WASN'T SITTING NEXT TO Adam. Instead, we were across the table from each other. The other part was pleased because I got to sit next to Simeon and look at Adam. A glass of wine—only one, because he was driving home—loosened Simeon's tongue a little. He still stuttered, but he shared a bit about his work. As a handyman, he took a large variety of projects and had seen the inside of many homes in Mission City. Clearly, he thought highly of Maddox and Ravi, adored their children, and saw neither marriage nor children in his future.

That might've been a bit of me reading between the lines. I was enjoying my second glass of wine. Adam said he couldn't drink and was therefore happy to play driver. We probably could've walked home, we were so close, but he kept talking about raccoons. He didn't like them, just like I wasn't a fan of bears.

As I refocused on Simeon, I tried to put heading home with Adam out of my mind. We hadn't made love again. I'd tried some easy affection, and although he hadn't rebuffed me, he hadn't welcomed it either. He could be as prickly as a scarlet sprite when he wanted to be.

"You're in town for six months?" Simeon offered a small smile. "T-that's great."

"Maybe we can get together sometime?" As much as I enjoyed spending time with Adam, I wanted to make more friends. I was enjoying myself so much tonight that I wanted to repeat—

"Oh, I'm not..." Simeon blushed.

"Wanting to have fun? We can go to the Springs Pub—I've heard about it. Right next to the police station so we have to behave, right?"

Slowly, Simeon nodded. "I d-don't go there often."

"The police station? I should hope not. You seem like a law-abiding citizen."

After a moment, he chuckled. "I like you."

I believed him. He had that vibe—someone very genuine. Very down to earth. "We can just hang out."

The flush turned crimson. "I, uh, live with my parents."

"Okay, first, I'd never throw shade on living with parents. Plenty of good reasons to do that." I considered. "Okay, and a few that might be questionable." I offered a smile. "I don't know if I could've lived with my mum after uni, but I sure would've been willing to try if it meant having her back."

Compassion filled Simeon's eyes as he blinked.

"Oh no, sorry, mate. I'm okay." I pressed a hand to my chest. "It's been eight years. And she'd suffered, so letting her go, although tough, was the right thing to do."

Still Simeon winced.

Clearly, I'd underestimated the big man. I knew better than to judge someone by their looks. I might be a big, burly guy, but I also could feel things acutely. Like my missing my mum. Like my empathy for Adam. I glanced across the table.

He glared back, even as Everett asked him, "So what do you like to read?"

After a long moment, he refocused on the man next to him. "Fantasy. Big surprise." No missing the cutting edge.

"Why not? It's not my cup of tea, but my friend August loves reading fantasy. His boyfriend, Julian, is more into SciFi romance. Give me a good old law journal any day."

Everyone at the table laughed, even the twins.

Well, except Adam.

"Julian and August?" I cocked my head.

Everett nodded. "Yeah, August and I went to undergrad together. He's an arborist. Oh." He pivoted his attention to me. "You should meet him. He's into trees too. Julian jokes that he just fells them, but he knows a lot as well. They've worked together for years, but only recently hooked up. Cute couple."

"What about you?" Ravi grinned. "Anyone to tempt you?"

Everett chuckled. "I haven't met the right man." He passed a speculative glance over all the men at the table who weren't named Baker—Ravi haven chosen to take Maddox's name. "I suspect you're trying to set us up."

Maddox chuckled. "My husband is not subtle. But no, this is just a gathering of friends. We've got Ravi's sister and her wife Meg coming to town next week."

"Balancing testosterone with estrogen?" Everett smiled.

Ravi burst out laughing. "Uh, we're not. A month from now, my ex-wife, her husband, and their two children are visiting. Two daughters. One is two years older than the twins and one is their age."

I turned to Maddox. "That sounds like chaos."

"Hence the reason we couldn't offer you the spare room." He pointed toward the back of the cabin. "We're seriously considering a renovation." Then, as if tonight wasn't totally orchestrated. "Simeon, could we hire you to do it?"

Simeon blinked. "I don't design—"

"Oh, we have the plans all drawn up. We can show you after dinner."

"Why do I feel m-manipulated?"

I tried not to feel sorry for Simeon, but he struggled with that one. Casting Maddox a glance, I attempted to convey Simeon's evident discomfort, setting a hand on the back of his chair to show my support. Then, as if commanded, I glanced over at Adam.

Apparently, my solicitude hadn't gone unnoticed because Adam glared.

Oh, for Pete's sake.

Except I didn't know a Pete, and this was getting really out-of-hand.

"We can talk about the renovation later." Ravi rose. "Pie?"

I pushed back my chair and stood, gesturing Simeon to join me. "We can clear the table. Do you need the pie heated?"

"It's in the oven. I'll get it." Maddox eyed Victor.

"I can watch him," Everett offered. "He can't really do anything, can he?"

Victor, secure in his highchair, eyed the man as if to say, *just watch me.*

Maddox handed Everett a sippy cup. "He needs a couple more sips. Good luck." He made a beeline for the kitchen.

Adam attempted to rise while Ravi continued to clear up the mashed mess Violet had made of her place.

I waved Adam off. "We've got this." And, within moments, Simeon and I had all the plates and used cutlery gathered, and we headed off to the kitchen.

To find Maddox pulling the most heavenly smelling pie from the oven. "Cherry. Hope that's okay. No one said they had allergies."

"Cherry's my favorite." I preferred Pavlova as a dessert, but occasionally my mom made cherry pie. "Next time, I'll prepare Pavlova." My appetizers had gone over well, after all.

"N-next time?" Simeon glanced up from where he stacked the plates into the dishwasher.

"Of course." Maddox sliced the pie into six large pieces and two tiny ones. "Ravi and I love company." He eyed me. "Okay, I used to be a hermit until I met Ravi. We're pleased... well...that you also seem to make a difference."

I chuckled and murmured, "He's here. Reluctantly, but here."

"Adam?" Simeon finished with the cutlery and raised the door.

"Uh, yeah." How much to say? Clearly Simeon didn't know Adam. "I'm pushing him out of his comfort zone."

"Tonight is out of m-my comfort zone," Simeon said.

Almost to himself, but enough so Maddox and I exchanged a glance. I tried to interpret Simeon's meaning, but I couldn't tell if he was pleased about this or hesitant. "You'll come back next time for my Pavlova, mate, right?"

Another flush crept up his cheeks. "If I'm invited."

Maddox handed him two plates. "Standing invitation. As soon as our friends take off, you're all invited over again. Or before, but I think it'll be quieter with just two kids."

"I think you're right." I grabbed the two plates he offered. "About to burst your cherry, Simeon."

I hadn't known cheeks could go that scarlet.

Which answered about three questions I had. None were my business, but I liked knowing. Could Adam and Simeon make a relationship work someday, when I was halfway across the globe? Or Adam and Everett? Clearly tonight was about matchmaking and, although I was here now, I'd be going home in just under six months. Which was either a really long time or the blink of an eye—depending on one's perspective.

Maddox cocked his head.

Yeah, or I could admit I was head over heels for Adam and fuck the idea of matching him with someone else.

Best to keep my mouth shut on that count.

Chapter Twenty-Four

ADAM

I saw red.

No, wait. Red was anger.

I saw green.

Green was jealousy, right?

I grunted as I got into the SUV. I'd never wanted to drink again so much as I had tonight. The other men clearly enjoyed their chardonnay with dinner. No one, except Dean, had drunk more than one glass, so we didn't have to worry about anyone driving home. As Everett and I cleared the dessert plates, and the kids played on the great room floor, Ravi and Maddox pulled out the plans for their addition.

Despite his earlier discomfort, Simeon eagerly looked them over, made a few suggestions, then clearly got onboard.

Figuring out how Everett fit into this evening hadn't been quite as easy. The lawyer had an amiable nature, but very little in common with the rest of us. Well, except being gay. I hadn't been certain about Simeon, at first, but his closeness to Dean —along with their conversation—made it clear, to me anyway, that he was gay. Or bi or at least bi-curious.

Or maybe I read the signals all wrong.

Dean and Simeon.

Simeon and Dean.

Ugh, no way could they go together. Aesthetically, although I found both attractive, I couldn't see them as a couple.

Except...Dean had been as interested in the drawing of the extension as Simeon. Even offering to lend a hand. If he wouldn't be in the way, of course.

Simeon assured him, in his sweet way, that he wouldn't.

Now, as we drove home in silence, I contemplated my words carefully. Should I tell him about how I felt? That I'd wanted to be the man he comforted? That the kindness he'd shown Simeon had nearly broken my heart. Because he treated me the same way. And I'd believed I was special. Clearly, I was just another pathetic soul in need of tending.

Not fair. Simeon's not pathetic.

For that matter, neither are you.

I pursed my lips as I entered the code.

The gate swung open, and I drove through. As always, out of sheer habit, I waited for it to close behind me. Someone could scale the fence, if they wanted to. But I just liked the routine of watching the gate close and feeling, even if ridiculously, like I could keep the outside world, well, outside.

"Do you want me to walk Chip?"

"I want you naked on my bed, prepped, and ready to be fucked." I didn't look at Dean, but his sharp intake of breath intrigued me. Was he going to turn me down? Acquiesce? Fight back?

"You want to root me?"

I shot him a glance. "Root?"

"Yeah. Fuck. Or shag as the Brits say. We had a British guy in my class, and he carried on all the time about all the women he shagged—"

I pressed my finger to his lips. "Less talking, more action. On your hands and knees. Waiting for me."

He swallowed. "Yeah, I can do that." He grinned. "Right-o. I'll be off." With that, he hopped out of the SUV, slammed the door a little harder than necessary, waved, and headed toward the castle.

Normally I took comfort in the strength of the walls. No edifice could withstand an earthquake of a massive magnitude, but it would still be standing under most conditions. And we didn't get hurricanes up here, but gales and vicious windstorms were common. Even when they knocked over trees, downed power lines, and took off roofs, my castle withstood it all.

But one Aussie bloke threatened it unlike anything that had come before.

Dean could easily be the ruin of me. I kept counting down the days until he'd leave. Kept telling myself this was just a fling. A *friend with benefits* thing. The lie only soothed so much. Even I understood I was deluding myself. Justin, my counsellor, saw through the façade. I admitted I had feelings for Dean—all the while maintaining the attraction was just physical.

I exited my vehicle, set the alarm, and headed toward the house. *Keep telling yourself that. Delusional is the right word. Because he's way more than a fling.* For all my jealousy tonight, his solicitousness toward Simeon warmed me. And as much as I found Everett attractive—and clearly brilliant—he didn't move the needle for me.

Not the way a certain Aussie dude with a shaggy beard and stunning amber eyes did for me. Even Maddox paled in comparison.

Chip greeted me with great enthusiasm when I stepped through the door. I snapped on her leash, and we began our ritual evening walk. Tonight, though, I wanted her to hurry.

Will he do what I asked? Is he naked right now, prepping himself? Will I be able to bring him pleasure, even as I chase my own?

My cock certainly enjoyed the direction of these musings. I grew thicker in my jeans, anticipating another night of bliss.

Maybe this time you'll find the courage to invite him to stay the night.

That thought brought dread. He might stretch in his sleep. He might touch me...

I shook my head. Would it really be so awful? *A child touched you tonight and the world didn't end.*

He wouldn't judge any more than Violet had. He wouldn't be repulsed. He'd be the same gentle man who'd tried several times over the past week to coax me into more intimacy. Truthfully, I wasn't accustomed to such kindness. *Wham, bam, thank you, sir* was my normal. This touching and joking and gentle teasing weren't what I was used to.

Chip did all her business and, as if sensing my impatience, directed us home. Once inside, I unclipped the leash, gave her a thorough rubbing, and tossed her a couple of baby carrots. "You're going to be good tonight, right?"

She stared at me.

"Of course you don't understand. Still, just be on your best behavior, okay?"

She quirked an eyebrow, as if to say *when am I not perfect?* And she just might've had a point. Having her in the bedroom while I drilled Dean might not have been ideal, but leaving her outside the bedroom would, I was quite certain, lead to whining and feelings of guilt—on my side, anyway. Especially since we'd left her at home tonight.

Maddox commented that he'd expected us to bring her and that, assuming she was good with kids, she was always welcome. That invitation warmed me, and I assured him she was good with kids. Perhaps a little overenthusiastic, but no more than Princess Sofia who'd almost knocked Violet over when they played on the floor. And I realized I was looking forward to going over again and bringing Chip because she needed the socialization.

Or maybe I'd invite them here. Not certain I'd extend the invitation to Simeon—

That's mean.

Right.

I'd leave that up to Dean. This place wasn't childproofed, but surely Maddox and Ravi knew how to deal with that, right? And I could read some books. Do some research. Although I didn't plan to have kids of my own, being careful wasn't a bad thing. I'd puppy proofed the house. How much harder could it be to be careful of toddlers?

All thoughts of children fled when I stepped into my room. The ambient temperature might not have increased, but heat rushed through me at the sight before me. Dean, on his hands and knees, that ass up, a wicked grin angled back at me...

With my last working brain cell, I indicated Chip should lie on her own bed.

She huffed but, after a long moment, complied.

Dean jiggled his ass. A silent invitation? Plea?

Slowly, I stripped off my clothes, taking an extra-long time. Because as much as I wanted inside him, I also wanted to savor. So I'd have the memory of him. Once I was naked, I snagged my phone and strode over to attach it to the charger on the nightstand.

After a moment, Dean glanced over at me. "Uh, anytime now..."

I glanced at his impressive erection. "In a hurry?"

With his chin, he indicated his cock. "Uh, yes. Definitely. My ass is full of lube, and I'm hoping soon it'll be full of you."

"You prepped yourself?"

He rolled his eyes. "Yeah. Even found my prostate. Sorry, leaked a bit of precum on your clean sheet."

Since I planned to make him come several times tonight, that was hardly an issue.

And he knew it.

We both did.

I snagged the bottle of lube from the nightstand, put some of the liquid on my palm, and then stroked my already very interested cock.

Dean licked his lips. "I'd offer to blow you..."

"But you want me inside you."

"Yeah. Like yesterday. Or the day before. But I'll take the next thirty seconds."

I chuckled. "Needy?"

"Desperate." He released his right hand, which—along with his left—had gripped the headboard. He gave himself a couple of good tugs.

Another chuckle escaped me. "Point made." I smacked his ass, then crawled onto the bed behind him. I momentarily mourned that we wouldn't be face-to-face, but he needed a good *rooting*—and so did I.

Odd word, but still a synonym for fucking...which works.

I positioned myself and slowly slid in, mindful of my size.

"Oh God, mate, please go harder."

"Dean, I'm barely in you, and—"

He pushed back, trying to seat me. His tight heat enveloped me as I took in every nuance of his body. The slight slick of sweat on his back. The hitched breath. The slight tremble as his knees held both his weight and mine.

I scratched down his back and grasped his ass with my fingers, squeezing hard.

"Right-o." He chuckled. "You've made your point quite effectively."

Cocking my head, I asked, "What point?"

"That you're in charge. And have way better self-control than me." He squeezed me tight. "I'm about to come, and you've barely grazed my prostate."

Yet another chuckle escaped me. I shifted experimentally, pulling out a bit, then fully seating myself. "How hard do you want it?"

"Well, I'm not working for three days and would be quite happy if I could still feel you tomorrow. To remind me of what you've been up to."

I pulled back, then pushed back in. With more force.

He grunted and gripped the headboard so tight his knuckles turned white. "Any time now."

Acknowledging that, for me, premature ejaculation was becoming a real possibility, I started to move in earnest. I gripped his hips as I thrust into him again and again. His grunts, and my panting, filled the normally silent room. So much of this house was like a mausoleum, but with him in the space, it came to life. Chip and Maurice helped, but the true vibrancy came from this beautiful man.

"My cock." He gritted the words out.

Given how precariously he clutched the headboard, in no way could he let go to take care of himself. I reached around to grasp his shaft and began tugging to the rhythm I set as I continued to thrust in and out. Part of me chased the orgasm, and part of me knew I needed to hold out. "Need. You. Come. Please." I made that thrust extra-hard and yanked just as powerfully.

Under me, he stiffened.

I held my breath.

He tightened around me as he spurted over my hand.

I thrust a couple more times, even as I tried to help milk him through his orgasm. Stuttering, I flew over the cliff and soared as my body shook with the power of my climax. My vision narrowed as I sank into the pleasure. "Thank fuck."

"Mate, you can say that again." Tremulously, the words came from him.

"Thank fuck." Slowly, gently, I pulled out of him, vaguely amused at the squelch and the abundance of both lube and cum. "Good God."

"Yeah, you can say that again." Then, as if all the tension fled him in that instant, he collapsed onto the bed, releasing his grasp on the headboard.

And, since I'd been leaning on him, I sort of tumbled with him. At the last moment, I angled myself so I landed on the bed next to him and not on him. Instinctively, my arm wrapped around his waist and I drew him close.

"Mess," he muttered.

"Sleep," I responded.

Within moments, he was gone.

Shortly thereafter, so was I.

Chapter Twenty-Five

DEAN

As morning dawned, the ache in my ass reminded me of just where I'd been last night. Or, more precisely, where Adam had been.

At some point in the night, he'd yanked a sheet over us. Still, one of my feet stuck out as if I just needed that bit of reprieve. Adam was like a furnace against my back. And I loved it.

Still, as I shifted, our skin stuck together in awkward places.

Really should have cleaned up last night.

"Are you going to keep shifting around or actually get up?" Amusement rang through his words.

He didn't kick me out. That has to mean something.

Right?

"I'm thinking shower, mate."

"Go ahead."

Gently, I turned in his arms. He lay on his left side, so the scarred part of his face was hidden in the pillow. But as he turned to look at me, and the red edges of his scar appeared, I didn't want him any less.

As always, he took my breath away. Those intense gray eyes. The adorable slightly floppy hair that I desperately wanted to run my hands through. The stubble that had increased in the almost three weeks since my arrival.

Three weeks that had alternately dragged and sped by, depending on my mood.

"What?" He blinked. "It's really early."

Having no idea the time, but knowing this was later than I usually rose, I grinned. "Let's have a shower."

"I said to go ahead."

"No, let's do it together." *Please say* yes. *Please trust me with this.*

He held my gaze. "Chip needs to go out."

I purposely gazed over his shoulder to find Chip sleeping on her back at an odd angle with all four paws going in different directions. "Chip will last twenty minutes more."

"You think a shower will take that long?"

Boldly, I snagged his cock—pleased to find morning wood. "I think I can give a blow job in less time…"

Slowly, he removed my hand. Disappointment had nearly set in before he snagged me instead. Instantly, my dick hardened in his palm. "Oh, I think I need to turn the tables on you. And I'd do it right now, but I need to piss, brush my teeth, and hydrate."

"Right-o." And I wouldn't try to dissuade him. The hydration thing likely had something to do with his numbers being out of whack, and I'd never interfere with that. "I can borrow your toothbrush, we can alternate pissing, each drink water, and then…"

"You're insatiable."

I grinned. "I went twenty-eight years without touching another human being sexually. You think I'm not going to dive in and take as much as I can?"

"Greedily." Amusement was clearly writ across his face as he grinned.

"Absolutely. I'll piss and you can drink." Without waiting for a response, I rolled away from him and out of bed. I jiggled my ass, and he chuckled again as I headed to the bathroom. Pissing in another guy's company was incredibly intimate. So was sharing a toothbrush and, uh, fucking.

Rooting.

I grinned as I emptied my bladder. My ass was just the right amount of sore. I might've only done this twice, but I knew enough. Was comfortable in my own skin. Was also incredibly glad I'd waited for the right man. However things ended, I couldn't regret him.

He joined me as I was washing my hands. He placed a glass of ice water next to me and then chugged his own.

I sucked down half the glass, enjoying the cool glide of the liquid. When working outside, I focused a tremendous amount on hydration. Not so much while indoors. I resolved to do better—if only so Adam would be more likely to do better as well. I was curious about his health, but that level of intimacy would have to come from him wanting to share, not me asking.

"What are you thinking?"

"About morning breath." I pointed to his toothbrush.

He winced, opened a cabinet under the sink, and pulled out a fresh one.

I spotted three identical ones, all still in their wrappers. "Boy Scout?"

An eye roll was the only response I received. Still, I happily used a generous amount of mint toothpaste and brushed vigorously. Perhaps harder than my dentist might've liked, but I really wanted fresh breath. Temporarily fresh.

Adam pissed and then, while he brushed, I turned on the

water. "This is amazing." The multiple showerheads turned on, soon blasting hot water. The overhead rainfall one didn't. I pointed.

"I use that at the end. I don't like getting water in my eyes."

"Right." I stepped into the pulsing spray. "This is so cool. Like getting a massage."

He joined me, keeping a bit of distance. "Yes, although I'm more of a bath person."

"I bet you like to read in the bath."

"On occasion, yes. When Chip was a puppy, I couldn't because she liked to splash."

"Did you run her out yet?"

"I put her in the dog run, yes. A bit of fresh air will do her good." He stood in the spray and the water dampened his hair. "I think a bit of fresh air will do me good as well."

"Oh, great." I grinned. "Let's do a picnic, with beans and chook and rolls and coleslaw." I stepped toward the spray and wet my beard. Grateful cum hadn't landed in it last night, I snagged a bit of shower gel and scrubbed under my chin.

"Dare I ask what *chook* is?"

"Well, let me loose in your kitchen, and you'll find out. I have the ingredients..." I nearly swallowed my tongue as Adam raised his arms and soaped his hair. The scars marked one side of his chest, but the sleekness of his lean body as he arched and twisted got my libido revving in all the right ways. I used more shower gel to soap my chest, groin and legs. Finally, I grabbed a handful and angled to clean my ass.

"Let me do that."

Our eyes met. He hadn't turned on the overhead light, but a pebbled window lay in the shower wall, part of the outer façade of the house. We couldn't see clearly, but the diffuse light perfectly illuminated the space. His gray eyes glinted as he put some shower gel in his palm, then coated his fingers.

I grinned, turned away, then braced myself against the wall.

The first touch was his hand skirting nimbly down my spine. Feather-light. Just the slightest trail of fingernails.

Then he dipped his hand between my crack.

My hole tightened when he ran his finger around the pucker. "Right-o. Please get on with it."

He chuckled. "You're always in a hurry."

"Mate, I waited twenty-eight years for you. Now that I have you, I want you all the time. However I can get you." I flexed my pelvis back, pressing against his finger.

"You weren't waiting for *me* for twenty-eight years."

I swallowed. "Well, I sort of was. For a man who would understand me. Who wouldn't judge. Who would accept I wasn't...experienced."

"Dean—"

"No, lemme finish. I might have book smarts—and I might know trees—but I'm not great with intimacy. I wouldn't say it was fear of the unknown...although that was part of it. Trust doesn't come easy for me. Not in a situation like this. I needed to be with someone who would understand."

He sighed. "Well, that I do."

He snagged a bottle I hadn't noticed before and I grinned. *Ah, lube.*

He coated his fingers, then, gently, he pushed one in.

I sucked in a breath as I tried to absorb the sensation. This wasn't the first time he'd done this, but somehow it felt different. Like we'd breached some barrier. Like he was showing me a side he kept hidden from everyone.

He added a second finger, then began scissoring, probing, twisting and...

Nailed it. My cock pulsed as he stroked over my prostate again and again. "I'm going to come."

Instantly, he withdrew his fingers.

A feeling of profound emptiness filled me.

"Turn around, lean against the wall."

I complied, and my shoulders were barely touching the cold stone before Adam dropped to his knees.

Without a moment's hesitation, he took me in. No preliminaries, just deep.

I worried he might choke, but he was already sucking me off. He swirled his tongue around my crown, speared my slit with his tip, and then swallowed me down again. I didn't even have time to warn him. I should've said something. Given him some indication. Instead, my balls drew up, and I shot into his mouth. Waves of pleasure washed over me as I marveled at just how quickly that happened. I had nothing to compare it to, of course, but my suspicion was I wouldn't encounter better. Anywhere.

And I didn't want to.

Gripping the stone of the shower wall, I resisted the urge to run my hands through his hair. To tug his chin up to mine so we could kiss. To hold him tight and take away all the worries that, at times, consumed him.

Slowly he rose. Clearly catching my expression, he cocked his head. "What?"

"I...it doesn't matter."

He arched an eyebrow. "I just had you down my throat. If I did something wrong, I need to know." He held my gaze. "Whatever it is, it does matter."

Slowly, clearly telegraphing my movements, I grazed my hand down his right arm. Finally, I took his hand, raised it to my lips, kissed his fingers like I wanted to kiss him, my eyes on his.

He winced. "Not that, Dean. I'm sorry."

"I appreciate the honesty." I looked down at his straining erection. Even if he wouldn't let me touch his face, or his scars, he'd let me give him pleasure before. I met his gaze. And winked. "Fancy a wank?"

Guiding our hands to his cock, he grinned. "You bet."

And so we wound up getting dirty again before we washed ourselves clean.

Chapter Twenty-Six

ADAM

"THIS CHOOK IS DELICIOUS." I LICKED MY FINGERS after having consumed more chicken than should have been possible. We'd each had a small bowl of cereal for breakfast, and then I'd sat, enraptured, as Dean prepared and then cooked the chicken. Rotisserie style. The entire castle smelled heavenly, and of course Chip wanted some. I'd let Dean give her a slice, then she'd wandered off in pursuit of a rabbit or some other creature.

Torah said as long as I could keep her coming back, a bit of time off leash was okay. Only in the fenced yard, of course. And, despite my lack of formal experience, the trainer had been impressed by much of my work with Chip. A few lessons to tighten things up, and she felt we'd be good. She'd also mentioned the pet-therapy training program she ran.

Dean nudged me to try it.

I resisted. Classes, strangers, contacts. *Not yet.*

We were at an impasse, but here, just the two of us together, that was irrelevant.

"Ah, this sun." He stretched out on the tartan blanket I'd located.

"Why don't you put your head in my lap?"

He gazed up at me, over the rim of his sunglasses. "Yeah?"

"Sure." I offered a cheeky grin. "Seems like a very romantic thing to do. We should've brought our books." We'd both applied sunscreen but hadn't discussed how long we'd stay outside.

Despite having just positioned his head in my lap, he grinned and sat up. "Why don't I run and get them? Yours is on your nightstand, right?"

"Yep. While you're doing that, I'll get Chip engaged with some recall exercises. Meet you back here in ten?" I gathered our plates.

"Sure. I'll run these in and put the chicken in the fridge. Back in a few." With that, he took off.

Slowly, as if in a dream-like trance, I pushed myself up. I whistled, and Chip darted from the forest. "Come."

She bolted to me and halted when I held my hand up.

I indicated she should sit, and she did. "What a good girl you are." I dug in my pocket for a treat. First, though, I took her through down, shake a paw, and heel.

She did each flawlessly.

I was grateful for her eagerness to please. Also happy to dole out the praise and rewards. As we practiced walking off leash, I again thought about Torah's suggestion that Chip would make a great therapy dog. Not just a personal support animal for me, but a dog who went out in the world and helped people. Not a service dog either.

After his visit to the library the other day, Dean spoke of a program where kids read to therapy dogs. A way to practice the skill without the stress of doing it in front of people. I didn't doubt Chip's temperament or ability to sit still when commanded to do so. I hadn't planned on getting her.

But Dr. Marco knew Froufrou had died, and Torah just

happened to have a puppy who needed to be re-homed immediately.

I didn't doubt, not for one second, that I'd been tricked. But if that meant I got Chip, then what was a little manipulation between friends?

Even as I was wondering what was taking Dean so long, he came out of the castle. He carried his rucksack over one shoulder and my book in his hand.

Chip trotted over to him.

He petted her, but then headed directly to me. He handed me the book. "Shit, Adam, I'm so sorry. I have to go. The university has a team heading up to Fort Nelson. There's a zombie-peat-bog fire they want to study. It's probably the only chance I'll get, and Roxie's given me a couple of weeks off to go—"

"Weeks?" I blinked. "You're going to be gone for several weeks? I thought your job was here—"

"It is." He waved his hand. "But a spot on the survey team opened up, and Roxie wants me to have the chance to see this up close. We don't have anything like it back home, and I'm so sorry, but I have to go right now. She's meeting me at the yard so I can leave the truck and then driving me over to the airport in Abbotsford. The plane leaves in just over an hour."

Which meant he'd barely make it. "Go. Is there anything you need me to do?"

"Yeah. Tell Ingrid I'm sorry the room's a mess." Even as he said the words, he jogged toward the garage.

Chip started to follow.

"No. Halt."

She obeyed.

"Come."

Like the reliable dog she was becoming, she obeyed, quickly putting herself in the heel position by my right leg.

Helplessly, we watched as Dean drove away.

I let out a long sigh. Wearily, I headed over to the blanket. After folding it over my arm, I headed toward the house.

Chip stayed by my side.

Inside, I tossed the blanket into the washing machine. I turned to Chip. "I can go clean his room."

Her tongue lolled.

"And I could, you know, change my sheets." Because cum-covered sheets weren't the most hygienic thing in the world.

But they smelled like Dean.

Which was why, an hour later, I was still cuddled with his pillow against my nose and wondering, one, when he'd return, and two—more importantly—if I'd ever have the courage to let him touch me in the way I knew he wanted to.

Not having answers to either of those questions, I eventually drifted into a nightmare-riddled sleep.

Six days later, on Friday night, I sat in a chair in Dr. Marco's exam room. He eyed me. "When did this shortness of breath start?"

When Dean left me?

Not fair—he went for work. He didn't actually leave you.

No, but he will...eventually.

"Uh...mid-week."

"Let me see your hands."

I held them out, but struggled a bit.

"Have you been drinking enough fluids?"

"Uh, yes?"

"Have you been urinating regularly?"

"Um...sure?"

"Adam."

My gaze snapped to his, but I had trouble focusing.

"I'm going to check your pulse."

"Okay."

He put that little thing on my finger as I gently stroked Chip. She'd been unusually restless over the past three days, but she'd settled now we were here, with Dr. Marco. He grimaced. "I'm calling an ambulance."

I blinked. "Okay. For who?"

"For you."

Another blink. "I'm fine. I—"

"Have all the signs of acute kidney failure. I need to run a bunch of tests, and on a Friday night, the easiest way to do that is at the hospital. Mission City's hospital is too small. I'm sending you over to Abbotsford. I know the nephrologist over there. Whip-smart woman who's not going to take any bullshit."

I blinked yet again. "You don't *know* there's anything wrong." Yet even as I said the words, I knew he was right. I hadn't felt good for days. I'd assumed this was yearning for Dean. Not once had it occurred to me that it might be physiological. "And besides...you know..." I indicated the dog.

"Hortense will take care of her."

That sounded at once logical and impractical.

Dr. Marco was already dialing.

I managed to still his hand. "No ambulances. I can drive myself."

"Like hell you can. You shouldn't have even driven here." He eyed me. "I'll drive you myself. That will cut some of the red tape. Let me tell Hortense."

Before I could react, he was off his stool and out the door.

Chip whined.

I gazed down at my hands. Okay, so they were a bit swollen.

Well, maybe a lot swollen.

But I'd been taking my meds.

Mostly

Well, sometimes.

Better than before.

Sort of.

Hortense bustled into the room, holding out her hand for Chip's leash.

"But her food," I protested.

"Text me while Dr. Marco drives you."

"Can you take her? Honestly?"

She blinked. "I'll work it out."

No missing the concern. For me or for Chip? I couldn't sort it out. "Let me call Maddox."

"Well, that's a great idea."

I struggled a bit with the phone, but managed to dial him.

"Hello, Adam."

"They're taking me to the hospital."

"What do you need?" So like Maddox—very succinct.

"Chip and my SUV are down at Dr. Marco's clinic."

"I'll get someone to watch the twins, and I'll make my way there right now. Are they taking you to Abby? In an ambulance?"

"This is Hortense, Maddox. Dr. Marco's taking him. I'll wait with Chip, so no rush. I've got all the time in the world."

"I'll call Justin and Stanley. Ravi's working right now."

"If it's too much—" I tried.

"It's not too much trouble, Adam. No worries, okay? You just let me know what food she eats and we'll take care of the rest. Do I need to worry about Dean?"

"Fort Nelson." I squinted. That's what he'd said, right? Somewhere up in the northern part of the province.

"Well, I'll text him—"

"No." I snapped the word. "Don't."

"Okay."

Dr. Marco bustled in.

"Maddox Baker is going to take Chip and organize to drive Adam's SUV home." Hortense held out her hand.

After a moment, realizing what she wanted, I dropped my keys into them.

"Take care, Adam. Everything will be okay." Maddox's voice sounded kind of far away. Or maybe that was because Hortense now held the phone.

"Thanks Maddox. See you when you get here." She cut the call and handed me back my phone.

I couldn't get it back into my pocket.

Dr. Marco scooped it up and put it into his doctor's coat. "Let's go."

The rest was just a blur.

Chapter Twenty-Seven

DEAN

In my country, north meant closer to the equator—and therefore hotter.

Theoretically, in Canada, north meant closer to the Arctic circle—and therefore cooler.

After a week dealing with an out-of-control wildfire several hours north of Fort Nelson, I was beginning to wonder if I wasn't in the seventh circle of Hell. I vividly remembered the bush fires in my country almost half a dozen years ago. The really devastating ones. The heat had been unrelenting.

As we hosed down on Friday night, I vaguely mused this might be just as bad.

Some sort of heat dome had settled over British Columbia. Not as severe as the one that killed almost a thousand people a couple of years ago, according to the crew, but pretty bad nonetheless.

My mate Craig handed me a bottle of water.

I drank greedily.

"And just think...we're not fighting the fire." He grinned.

I managed a snicker that resulted in a bit of a dribble down my chin.

No one in our little group noticed nor cared.

Craig wiped his forehead with a handkerchief. "I think you've likely seen enough peat bog to last a lifetime."

"No." I grinned, but then faltered. "I'm really sad the fire reignited and has been so destructive—but I was so glad to be here."

Sandy waved her radio. "Fire service is pulling back. We need to go. Right now."

We all grabbed our gear, jumped into the Jeep, and were on the road within just a couple of minutes. The vehicle reminded me of my mate's Ute back home—really sturdy and really fucking dirty. Still as we clocked out of there, Sandy gasped.

Craig and I shot glances over our shoulders from our places in the back seat.

The winds had shifted again and now the inferno was heading our way.

As Sandy floored the gas, I watched, mesmerized, as the trees caught fire.

The smoke was intense, and the embers blew around us, landing on grass, trees, and our vehicle.

I glanced at Craig. "I don't think I signed up for this."

"Fucking hell." Sandy swerved around something.

Craig knocked into me.

We kept right on going.

I was unclear how everything had gone so sideways so quickly, but given that fire could travel at almost twenty-three kilometers an hour, we needed to put some serious distance between us and the flames.

Soon, though, we hit the main road. Sandy swerved us onto it and floored the gas.

A very tense fifteen minutes later, and we were out of immediate danger.

Craig handed Sandy a bottle of water as she eased off the

accelerator just a bit. He clapped her on the shoulder. "Good job." He winked at me. "Mate."

Melba, the researcher in the front passenger seat groaned. "Okay, that's enough. No making fun of the Aussie."

"Hey," I protested. "I insist you make fun of me."

As we rounded a bend in the road, back toward camp, all our phones started buzzing.

"Ah, to be back in the world of cell signals." Craig had his screen unlocked even as I scavenged in my back pocket for mine. "Oh, a warning about the winds changing. How lovely."

I found my phone, unlocked the screen, and my chest seized.

—Don't panic. Adam's been taken to the hospital. We have Chip and she's fine. Be safe wherever you are. Maddox—

Don't panic? Don't panic? Jesus, my heart kicked up about ten times the normal rate. "I have to make a call, guys."

They all waved me off.

Maddox answered on the second ring. "I take it this is you panicking?"

"Maddox." My voice, raw from the smoke over the past week, strained. "How is he?"

"I haven't spoken to Dr. Marco. The office manager, Hortense, told me that Dr. Marco was concerned. He drove Adam over to the hospital in Abbotsford. I just didn't want you arriving back at the house and finding everyone gone."

"What about Maurice?" My panic hadn't abated, but I was vaguely concerned about the cat whose existence I questioned.

"The cat?" Maddox chuckled. "I put out fresh food and water. He's got one of those automatic litter boxes. Justin's going to go over again on Sunday. He's better with cats than I am."

"Justin...Adam's counsellor?"

"Yeah. He also lives between our place and yours. He helped me collect Adam's SUV while Stanley watched all the kids. We're having a big party while we wait for Ravi to get off shift." He sighed. "He'll be okay, Dean. I didn't want you to panic—I just wanted you to know."

"I'm going to try to fly out."

Melba grabbed her phone. "I'll check the airport."

"Dean, that might not be necessary—"

"Maddox, Adam is in the hospital."

"Yes."

"Then that's where I need to be."

He sighed. "Okay. But don't kill yourself trying to get home. I heard the fires are getting pretty intense up there."

"Yeah. This was supposed to be research, but at this point we're more likely to get in the way. We've got plenty of data to work with. I think we were planning to leave in the next day or so anyway." I glanced at Craig, who nodded.

"If you're not back by tomorrow, I promise I'll go and visit Adam. Make sure he knows he's not alone."

"He...I think he hates hospitals."

Maddox chuckled. "That's a hatred I completely understand. Look, Ravi's going to check in on him before heading home tonight, so I might have news. I'll text you if I do."

"Okay. And, uh, thanks."

"Be safe, Dean. Promise me. If something happened to you because you were rushing home, that would devastate Adam."

I knew he was right—but that didn't alleviate the burning in my gut that said to get back to Cedar Valley as quickly as possible.

Chapter Twenty-Eight

ADAM

I HATED HOSPITALS.

Not that most people liked them. But I had an actual reason to hate them. Even if this wasn't the hospital I'd recuperated in after my accident, that didn't make it any less... awful.

Quinton, today's nurse, did his best to make things more tolerable. South Asian, twinkish, wearing a rainbow pin, and a matching grin. He admitted nephrology wasn't where he normally worked, but he seemed competent. He definitely brought a smile to my face. I appreciated that probably more than he knew.

As I watched the dialysis machine filter the toxins out of my blood, I believed I might actually get better. Acute kidney failure, my nephrologist, Dr. Lucia Maroni, had said last night. Treatable. In my case, likely reversible. I'd developed a blockage in my urethra—with kidney stones—and my decreased urine output... At that point, I'd checked out. I'd expected kidney stones to hurt much more than the dull ache I'd had. Believing it to be some form of melancholy—or even a mild depression —I'd ignored the symptoms. Hell, if I hadn't had my regular appointment with Dr. Marco last night, I'd likely still be ignoring the symptoms. And apparently, I was within days, if not hours, of irreversible damage. Like kidney-transplant territory.

Instead, I was having dialysis. Overnight—to both my annoyance and relief—the rather large stone passed harmlessly. That *had* hurt. All was well now, though. Or would be after several days of dialysis, fluids, and rebalancing. I had high potassium and low blood calcium. I probably should've given a shit, but I kept wondering what was the point? I'd beat the post-burn infection. I'd defied so many odds. But, at times, I wondered if I was really living.

Rescuing Chip, in a moment of weakness, ensured I had to stick around for another ten to twelve years minimum. Maurice wasn't likely to live that long, but one could never tell with felines. They truly had a mind of their own.

To my shock, when Ravi showed up for his shift this morning, he had my book—snagged from my nightstand—as well as my favorite pajamas, slippers, and his phone with plenty of photos. Chip playing with the twins. Chip having an apparently earnest conversation with Justin's son, Angus. What an eleven-year-old might say to a dog had me curious. Oh, and Chip flaked out on the couch with Princess Sofia after a long night of adventure.

By my calculations, Ravi'd had barely any sleep, but the pediatric nurse appeared chipper and ready to head to that part of the hospital.

After he left, Quinton let it slip that Ravi specialized in helping to treat kids with cancer.

Which properly schooled me on just how selfish I could be sometimes. When my money came through, I'd make a donation to that department. Healthcare might be universal in Canada, but hospitals were chronically underfunded. A bit of a boost from my soon-to-be replenished coffers would be appreciated.

"Oh, thank God."

I turned as Dean barreled into the room. He was disheveled, dirty, and...beautiful. His haggard face told of a long night. Or a long week. I'd followed the news diligently, and apparently things weren't going well up north. Given we were only in late June and another drought was predicted, things weren't looking good.

Why are you thinking about forest fires when you've got an incredible man in front of you? So what did I do? I scowled. "What are you doing here? Your text on..." The last week was a little fuzzy.

"Tuesday," he prompted. He dropped his rucksack on the ground and ventured over to the bed. "You don't look well." He winced. "Right, not a great thing to say to a hospital patient. Maddox couldn't—or wouldn't—tell me anything."

"You spoke to Maddox?" I rolled my eyes. "Of course you did. Otherwise, you wouldn't be here."

He approached until he was within reaching distance. He glanced down at his hands. "Oh, crap. Let me wash up."

Before I could suggest he use my bathroom, he darted out to the hall.

Likely to find a public washroom. *He'll be back. He left his bag.* I tried to do some calculations in my mind. I had no idea how easily, or not, he'd been able to secure a flight. If he'd paid a lot of money, I couldn't reimburse him for a couple of weeks.

Quinton breezed in, eyed the rucksack, and arched an eyebrow.

"Friend."

"Fair." He indicated the machine. "We're done for now. We'll see what the doctor says about doing it again. More blood and urine tests to come shortly."

"Whatever." I met his gaze. "Whatever it takes to get better."

He grinned. "I'm liking this friend. A mood elevator, to be sure."

I'd no idea he'd perceived me as having a dark mood.

Don't bullshit yourself. Ten minutes ago, you didn't care.

True. But Dean was here.

Speaking of the man, he strode back into the room with beard glistening, damp, clean hands, and a brilliant smile. His amber eyes sparkled.

Quinton gave Dean the once-over as he unhooked me from the machine. "So you're the friend." No missing the emphasis.

Dean cocked his head.

"The one who's brought a smile to my patient's face."

Heat might've flooded my cheeks.

Dean grinned. "Mate, whatever it takes." Carefully, he moved toward me. "I'd do anything for him."

Quinton sighed. "Oh, Lordy, hang on to this one or I might try to snag him."

"He's only here for a short time." I might've groused that.

"Almost five more months." Dean tilted his head at Quinton.

Who scrutinized his hands. "You can hold hands. Just don't climb on the bed or some crap like that."

Dean chuckled. "But it's such a romantic thing to do."

Quinton mock-glared. "Jostle him the wrong way, and it won't be so romantic."

"That bad?" Dean stilled, his hand still not touching mine.

"He's on the mend," Quinton pointed out. "But being gentle with a patient is always a good idea. Dr. Maroni is the only one who can give him the all-clear to resume...activities."

This time, Dean was the one to turn an interesting shade of pink. He sputtered. "I wasn't."

"Well, with a guy this handsome, I would be." Quinton winked at me. "Be good to the person drawing your blood." He checked the IV. "I've left a sample jar in the bathroom. Hit the buzzer when you've gone."

Again, a bit of heat rose in my cheeks. "I, uh…"

"Great." He grinned. "Let's get you up and moving. Someone will come to take the dialysis machine."

Dean moved to my side. "Can I help?"

Quinton organized the IV stand which had way too many things attached to it. "Sure."

"Okay, mate, grab on to me." Dean positioned himself to support me as I scooted off the bed. I appreciated that Quinton didn't just hand me a urinal as he had several times already today. Plus, Dr. Maroni said I needed to get off the bed to increase circulation. After almost twenty-four hours, I was ready to move.

As I grabbed on—and Dean helped me out of bed— Quinton giggled. "Oh, that accent is so swoon-worthy."

I rolled my eyes.

Dean grinned and turned to me. "Did you tell him about our meal of hot chook, rolls, and coleslaw?"

"He's waiting for you to make him Pavlova." My tone was as dry as the Sahara.

"Oh, that's a great idea. I'll make it tonight." We moved toward the bathroom. "I assume I'm not allowed to stay."

"You're assuming correctly." Quinton nodded.

I sighed. "And you look like you need rest."

"Oy, yeah, that." He blinked a couple of times. "I don't even know what time it is."

"Time for me to pee. In peace."

"Well, I'm staying." Quinton snagged the sample jar.

"I've seen you piss before." Dean grinned.

Oh my God, he did not just say that.

"Wow, you guys are really in deep." Quinton grinned. "I have to say I've never done that with a guy I've been with."

"But I bet you've done more than I have. Or at least before I met this guy." Dean leaned over conspiratorially. "I was a virgin when I met him."

"Okay, now I really want details. But scoot."

Dean finally did, closing the door behind him.

Quinton handed me the sample jar.

Within a few minutes, I'd emptied my bladder—much to my relief.

"I think you're lucky." Quinton and I both washed our hands. "I'd love to meet a man who cared for me that much."

Our gazes met in the mirror.

"And don't point out that it's only for another five months. Maybe just enjoy the time you have?"

"Easier said than done."

We moved back toward the door. When we re-entered the room, I noted it was nearly five o'clock already.

Even as Dean guided me back to my bed, a young man arrived with a tray of food. He put it on the side table and headed out.

Once I was settled, and vaguely comfortable, Quinton wheeled the stand so it was directly before me.

He lifted the lid.

I sighed.

"Well, it's not so bad. You have to avoid high-salt foods—which I'm certain you know. We're also aiming for lower potassium foods. At least for now." He pointed to the apples, strawberries, and cooked cauliflower.

"No cheese sauce?"

"Too high in salt." Quinton indicated the tray. "I expect all that to be gone when I come back."

"Well, he can eat it." I tilted my head toward Dean.

To everyone's amusement, his stomach rumbled. Yet he

shook his head. "Nice try, mate. Maddox is bringing me a burger and fries. And I'm not sharing, so eat what's on your plate. Make the man happy."

"Man...?" I frowned. "Oh, this is Quinton. The boss of me."

Quinton grinned and stuck out his hand. "Nice to meet you."

Dean shook it. "I'm certain you have to other people to help."

"And a sample to send to the lab. It's looking better than before."

"Oh my God. Just go."

Quinton grinned and headed out of the room.

Dean laughed. Then as if the wind was knocked right out of him, he dropped to the chair beside the bed. "Please eat, Adam. If they want this, then it's the right thing to do. You need to get healthy so you can come home."

I tried not to think about how absurdly giddy I got when he said the word *home*. I poked at the apple. "You do look exhausted. When was the last time you ate?"

He rubbed his face. "We stopped for a bagel at Tim Horton's in 100 Mile House."

"Wait...you drove?"

"Uh..." He rubbed his face. "I hitchhiked. I couldn't get a flight and, obviously, I needed to be here. I caught a ride with a trucker from Fort Nelson to Prince George. Then I hooked up with a guy in a pickup truck. He was heading to Vancouver and in a bit of a hurry. So we took turns driving and made pretty good time."

I blinked. "Okay, how long?"

He yawned. "I left Fort Nelson at eight last night."

"You need sleep."

"I got a good eight hours in the truck. The guy prefers

driving at night. Although you have to watch out for the caribou."

"Of course." I shook my head as I speared a piece of strawberry. I didn't remember ever getting such great food when I was recovering. Then, to my amazement, two things dawned on me at the same time. First, I hadn't worried about my scars since I'd gotten into Dr. Marco's SUV and he'd driven me here. Not a single time. Secondly, with Dean here, I didn't hate the hospital so much. Still wanted to leave as soon as possible but, for these precious few minutes, I hadn't felt... alone. Isolated.

"Hey, what's up?" Dean grasped my hand. "Are you tired? Do you want me to feed you?"

That absurdly generous offer brought tears to my eyes. "You're here."

"Of course I am." He blinked. He so rarely wore his glasses, but tonight he did. "There's nowhere else I want to be." He shrugged. "And we'd finished most of our research and were headed home in a few days. I've got a lot of writing to do."

"Can you do it here? Oh, you'll need a car."

"Maddox will drive me home tonight. He says your SUV is in the garage. Is it okay for me to drive it?"

"Of course."

"Great. So Roxie's given me the week off—"

"You can't take a week off." I tried to cross my arms over my chest, but his gripping my right hand prevented me.

"I just worked seven straight days. Roxie would've ordered me to take some downtime anyway. Plus, if I'm writing my paper, then I'm working. I want—need—to be home with you."

"I don't have a say in this, do I?"

He cocked his head. "No, mate, you really don't."

I smiled inwardly and ate my strawberries.

Chapter Twenty-Nine

DEAN

WHEN I ARRIVED HOME THAT NIGHT, I HAD virtually nothing left in me.

Gracious and generous, Ravi and Maddox offered to keep Chip with them until Adam came home from the hospital.

Quinton had let it slip that might happen in just a few days if Adam continued on the trajectory he appeared to be taking.

Relief flooded me—both for not having to manage Chip and visiting the hospital, as well as just knowing Adam was on the mend. That had been the most harrowing nineteen hours of my life.

Maddox sent a few updates, but he hadn't had much to share.

Medical stuff was still private, but Quinton said enough things to Adam that I was able to pick up on much of it. I had a list of things to research.

In the morning.

The burger, onion rings, and root beer, although appreciated, sat heavy in my belly. I still stank—which nicely no one had commented on—so a shower came first. I put out some wet food for the cat I was quite convinced didn't exist.

Okay, except his food disappeared, I'd hear the litter box, and there didn't appear to be mice in the house, so...Maurice must be here somewhere.

Part of me wanted to wash in Adam's extraordinary shower, but that felt just a touch too invasive. Yes, I'd stayed the night. More than a week ago. And although I didn't regret going up north, I could see the timing couldn't have been worse.

I stepped into my turret room, and then dropped my bag.

The room was still pretty fucking cool.

Removing my clothes, I realized I didn't want them in my room. So, naked, I sauntered downstairs, threw everything into the washing machine, added as much soap as I dared, hoped Ingrid wouldn't be mad, and started the load.

Then I trudged back upstairs—aching in places I'd never ached before. I was accustomed to long days. Sometimes heavy work. But all that sitting for such a long period of time plumb wore me out.

After waiting for the hot water to flow, I stepped into the shower. As I washed away the grime, grit, and smoke, I contemplated my life. Well, first I thought about Melba's text.

There'd been a lightning strike not far from where we'd been. Dry lightning, as there hadn't been any rain. The strike ignited the fire. Wind had pushed that fire toward us, and that's why we hadn't been prepared. Much longer and we'd have been cut off. Since I'd been the one to push us to go farther into the bog, I felt responsible. We'd had permission, but with the caveat that we better never need rescuing. I'd thought I understood fire, but I'd acquired so much knowledge in the past week that I could now admit I had so much more to learn.

I washed my beard twice, deciding that although I was

exhausted, I needed a trim. The rest of the grossness washed away, and soon I shut off the water and stepped onto the cold tile. I could've switched on the heated floor, but that felt a touch too decadent. Plus, I dried off quickly and headed into my room.

Although I didn't want to take the time, I sorted through my bag. I pulled out my netbook and set it to charge. My phone had two percent left, so I set it to charge as well. Oh, a text from Maddox. Attached was a photo of Princess Sofia cuddling against Chip.

Fleetingly, I wondered if Chip needed a companion. I dismissed the idea. Although she'd enjoy another dog, Adam likely didn't have the bandwidth to take on more. I'd found it hard to miss how sometimes he tired quicker than me. Or how he struggled. I wanted to be here to help him. Sometimes, though, I didn't know how.

Finally, I yanked back the duvet and the fresh top sheet. Ingrid had asked, just after I arrived, if I minded a little lavender scent. She claimed it helped Adam sleep and, if I didn't mind it, her life would be simpler if she could do it with my sheets as well. Since I'd slept like a rock every night since she'd started doing it, I figured she was on to something.

I pulled the sheet over me, settled onto my side, and was out as soon as my head hit the pillow.

Hours later, I awoke to sun streaming into the room.

And illuminating the tabby cat asleep on the pillow next to me.

As I shifted, he cracked open an eye.

"Hello, Maurice." I feared he'd leave, but he merely closed his eyes. Gently, ever so slowly, I reached out to touch him.

His eyes popped open, but he didn't move.

I stroked him.

He purred.

All was right in the world.

Except I needed to get up, grab a bowl of cereal, and head to the hospital. I'd take my netbook as well as a book I'd picked up from the university library a couple of weeks ago. I still needed to prepare a lecture for the University of British Columbia students in a few days, and that had me a little freaked out.

I would be delivering the same lecture to the university students here, in the valley. For reasons I couldn't explain, that panicked me a lot less. Something about heading into Vancouver and addressing students at one of the top universities in the world turned my stomach into knots.

After I'd dressed and trimmed my beard, I headed downstairs, Maurice hard on my heels. I put out some wet cat food for him, and he pounced like he was starving.

"Ah, so that's the real reason you came to keep me company last night. Well, thank you for not waking me. I was exhausted."

He purruped.

"So we're friends now?"

He eyed me, then slowly wound his way around my legs.

"I promise I'll be home every night, and soon Adam'll come with me, and then Chip will come, and you'll never have to be alone again."

More purrs.

As I ate oat bran cereal, I ran through everything that might happen today and the next week. Truthfully, the only thing that mattered was getting Adam better and home. I hated the antiseptic smell of the hospital. It reminded me of my mother's last few days before she passed.

She'd hoped to die at home, but her medical needs had been too complex for me to handle. I'd been with her at the end, fortunately. But that smell—as well as the constant fluorescent lights and beeps—just got to be a little much.

Especially when the beeps stopped.

I blinked. I hadn't revisited that part of my past for a long time. I'd arranged to have flowers left at Mum's grave before heading to Canada. I hadn't made it back to Perth since her death and doubted I ever would. Canberra was my home. Although, more and more, I wondered if the pull to Canada hadn't been prescient. I hadn't foreseen Adam...and I sure wasn't going to regret finding him.

Which meant getting into his SUV, pointing it south toward Abbotsford, and doing my best to put on a cheerful face.

Chapter Thirty

ADAM

FIVE DAYS.

I was nearly out of my mind.

Dean being by my side for hours on end was the only thing keeping me sane. I tried to encourage him to work either at the university library or at home. Somewhere with a proper desk, an ergonomic chair, and quiet. I didn't know much about Dean, but I was aware he worked best when he had silence.

The hospital was never quiet.

Still, he used the little table Quinton had located, and he typed away. He had stopped in at the university library to grab some more reference textbooks, and he'd also nabbed the rest of the Zaragoza trilogy from home for me. Casually, he mentioned R.D. Watts was actually Raven Duhamel, and that she taught creative writing at the university. Through Dickens, at The Owl's Nest, he hoped to get my copies signed. He said he'd wanted to do it in secret, but then admitted he was the worst secret keeper ever.

I didn't necessarily agree. He had something up his sleeve now, but he wouldn't divulge it. Instead, he asked me to read a passage from some massive book on British Columbia trees so he could quote—and credit—it in his paper. I'd also commented on how good he looked. Not as a come-on, but as a general observation. He shot back that lavender sheets and tabby cats made for good rest.

Of course I laughed. Trust Maurice to pick the perfect time to make an appearance. I worried about his fur, but Dean assured me he didn't have allergies.

He'd also visited Maddox and Ravi several times to give Chip some extra love.

Apparently my baby was being completely spoiled. Big surprise. Given how much leeway Maddox gave Princess Sofia, I couldn't see him being a disciplinarian with Chip.

This morning, though, Dean was at the University of British Columbia giving a lecture about Australian forestry-management programs for the bush that covered much of the continent.

He'd explained some of it to me, but I didn't always understand him. I didn't want to fall back on the *I'm just a retired fashion model with no meaningful education*, because he didn't need to hear that. He'd spend his time arguing, and that would eat up what we had left. So I just nodded and pretended I understood. Come to think of it... I snagged my tablet, intending to research that thing he'd mentioned...

Quinton appeared before I had the chance. "You're looking good."

Normally I glared when someone said that. But I knew he wasn't making a sarcastic comment about my scars. More likely commenting that some of my color had returned. And it had. So, in response, I offered a smile. "Feeling better too. Can I go home?"

He checked my IV. "We're running more tests in the morning. I'm not going to jump ahead of Dr. Maroni, but she's a big proponent of convalescing at home—if the patient has the right support structure and will follow instructions."

At this, I rolled my eyes. "First, lesson learned."

He cocked his head. "Yes, I believe you have."

"Second...do you honestly think Dean's going to let me do a single thing that won't be to the betterment of my health? That I'll somehow be able to misbehave?"

A narrowing of eyes. "I believe you capable of deviousness."

I might've resembled that comment.

"And Dean's not going to be around all the time. He's not here now—"

"He's giving a guest lecture." I tilted my chin. "He's really important."

"I know he is." Quinton moved to the side of the bed. "Which is why he shouldn't have to be following you around like a hawk."

Appropriately chastened, I ducked my head. A few moments passed before, finally, I met his gaze. "Okay, I get it."

"Great." He left the room and was back a moment later with a wheelchair. "There's someone I want you to meet."

"I already have a therapist. A tough one at that. Justin? Cute guy? Ginger? Beard? Blue eyes—"

Quinton rolled his own dark-brown ones. "You'll understand why I'm asking you to do this."

His phrasing caught me off guard. Intrigued, I let him guide me, gently, out of bed. I already wore pajamas, thick socks, and a housecoat. He added a goddamn blanket to my lap. "What am I, a hundred?"

"Live that long and you'll be grateful for the consideration of others."

He wheeled me down the hall and toward the elevators.

"Where are we going?"

"Pediatrics."

My first instinct was to hold out my hand to stop him. Kids? Seriously? I so did *not* do kids. Victor and Violet had been nearly beyond my capacity—and they'd had two parental units right there with three other adults hovering. Plus, a yappy dog. Well, maybe not yappy. Just...intrusive. Very little respect for personal space.

Yeah, like Chip doesn't try to jump all over strangers. Likely because she didn't meet many strangers. Something I needed to rectify.

When we arrived at the pediatric department, Quinton used his ID to get us past the nursing station.

"Are you going to tell me anything?"

"Don't be an asshole."

Then he pushed me into a room with bright-yellow walls. Glorious sunshine poured in from the south-facing windows which, if one looked out of them, overlooked the highway. At least the hospital was insulated from the noise.

"Sydney?"

The figure in the bed, with long, blonde hair, faced away.

I worked off the assumption Sydney was a girl, but I had little else to go off.

Quinton repeated, "Sydney, this is Adam Granger.

I glanced up at him. Who the hell would care—

Yet the young girl peeked toward me.

And my heart sank. She had a nasty burn right across her face. The skin grafts didn't appear to be holding well. That could happen if the person didn't take care of them.

Like I hadn't. My scars were more noticeable than they should have been—because I hadn't followed what I'd been told to do. I'd barely cared about myself, let alone what I was going to look like in the future. I hadn't believed I had a future. Current me sometimes wanted to go back in time and slap sense into that younger man. Admittedly, I'd been depressed. But that hadn't been an excuse.

"Are you really Adam Granger?"

I glanced uneasily back at Quinton.

He smiled. "I might've told Sydney you used to be a fashion model."

I glared.

He steadily met my gaze. "But that you've made a good life beyond your accident."

This time, I didn't roll my eyes—but it was a near thing. "Yeah?"

I glanced over at the young woman before me and offered my best smile. "Quinton's not wrong."

"Quinton's never wrong." Apparently unconcerned about referring to himself in the third person, said nurse pushed me over to the far side of Sydney's bed, planting me between her and the window.

After an endless moment, she met my gaze.

I foresaw a brutal next hour or two. Possibly the most consequential of my life. I took a deep breath. "I'm Adam. And yeah, if you're willing, I think we could, you know, talk."

Slowly, she nodded. "Yeah, okay."

Chapter Thirty-One

DEAN

I BARELY CAUGHT THE TRAIN, HOPPING ON JUST AS the conductor was doing a last sweep of Waterfront Station in downtown Vancouver. The buses from the university were so packed that I hadn't made it onto the first one. By the time the second one arrived, I was near panic. I shouldn't have been, given there would be two trains after the one I hoped to take, but I was so exhausted that I just wanted to get home. I'd promised to visit Adam tonight—although he'd been adamant I'd be too exhausted.

He wasn't wrong.

The train was pretty packed, but when I moved to the upper level, I found an empty seat facing forward. Well, I thought it was forward and, in fact, when the train lurched, I received confirmation. I tucked myself into the aisle seat and gazed out the window. The Port of Vancouver with the huge cranes to remove freight from the massive ships lay just ahead, and as the train curved, I was able to get a sense of just how long this thing was. Just under a dozen stops between the metropolis and the tiny town of Mission City which was, conveniently, the end of the line.

Inadvertently, I glanced at the laptop of the gentleman beside me.

And did a double take.

I'd assumed everyone on the train would be, I don't know...businesspeople.

As I angled my head, I reasoned that surely there'd be students as well. So I gave the guy the once-over.

Dark-brown, slightly mussed curly hair. Dark-brown eyes behind glasses, and a youthful face.

Then I gazed down at his left hand. And a wedding ring.

Suddenly, he turned to me. "You seem very curious."

"I...uh...I mean, I'm sorry—"

"And you're Australian?" He nearly vibrated out of his seat. "Oh, this is so cool. I've always wanted to see the Southern Cross. My husband, Tex, says we should plan to go. But I'm working on a big new project. I work in quantum physics, which really has little to do with astronomy, but I'm fascinated.

"Tex likes to take me up in his helicopter at night so I can feel like I'm closer to the stars. Well, not *his* helicopter. My dad's. That his business owns. But Tex used to fly for him. Now he flies an air ambulance out of Abbotsford. Which is why we live in Mission City. I mean, it's kind of far for me to come to do my research and teaching at UBC, but I love small-town living. So, three days a week, I come into the city. On the West Coast Express. Isn't the train awesome? No stress of driving."

He drew a breath. Before I could speak, though, he continued.

"Tex taught me how to drive when we first met. Imagine, twenty-two years old and I didn't know. But my mom died in a crash when I was young. And then I did my undergrad at MIT in Boston, and who wants to drive in a big American city? Although I suppose a big Canadian city is much the same, right? But I lived on campus and therefore didn't need to know how to drive. Do you know it?"

"Boston?"

"Yes. And MIT."

"Massachusetts Institute of Technology. Yeah, even we Aussies have heard of that. Well, especially those of us in academic circles—"

"You're in academia?" More vibrating. "What's your area of expertise? Like I said, mine is quantum physics..."

"Right, mate. Uh..." I blinked. "I'm in forestry-management services. I'm here working for the municipality of Mission City, but also doing lectures at the University of British Columbia as well as the university out in Abbotsford."

His eyes widened. "Oh, you were at UBC today?"

I nodded.

"Lecturing?"

I nodded.

He grinned. "You'll have to give me the heads-up next time. I'd love to hear you lecture."

"It's..." I waved at his computer. "It's trees. Only a little bit of physics involved."

"Oh, I know." Another smile. "Tex calls me a renaissance man because I'm interested in so much. I wasn't as much, before I met him. I was hyper-focused on my studies. Now, though, that I'm nearly finished my PhD, I'm ready to expand my horizons. See how quantum physics interacts with the world."

"Well, okay." I held out my hand. "Dean Hargrave."

He returned the shake vigorously. "Randall Davis Jefferson the Third."

My eyes widened.

"Oh, right. I go by Davey. I just figured, you know, formal introductions and all."

"Right." I gazed out for a moment, catching the pinkening sky with wispy clouds. "And this water?"

"Burrard Inlet. Pretty soon we'll be mostly inland. Well, until we get to Port Haney and then the Fraser River will be on the other side." He offered me an impish grin. "I always switch over. I just...water's so neat, you know?"

"I come from Perth, a coastal city. So yeah, I know."

Davey shut his laptop. "Tell me everything."

An hour later, as we pulled into Mission City's train station, I was glad I'd tossed a water bottle into my bag. Early in our encounter, I'd believed Davey would be doing most of the talking.

I'd been wrong. Once he'd gotten over his initial nerves and excitement at meeting someone new, he'd settled into the role of interrogator. As promised, we'd switched over to the other side of the train for the last leg of the journey. Davey shared a few odd bits of trivia about the area, but he mostly asked me questions. About my studies, my life, and my loves. I'd tried to be circumspect about my love life, but somehow, with this odd stranger, I'd shared everything.

Everything.

He hadn't let me leave anything on the table. And, by the end, he declared that obviously I was in love. And how he and Tex had been thrown together in unusual circumstances and now they were husbands and crazy in love, and it took someone in love to recognize another person beleaguered in that state and, obviously, I needed to do something about it.

I didn't have a chance to ask what before the train pulled into the station.

We thanked the conductor and hopped off. Even before I could blink, a tall man grabbed Davey and spun him around. Well, the guy was my height, although a bit less bulky. More slender. Just...Davey was on the smaller side—about five eight —so the difference was noticeable.

"Put me down." Davey laughed.

The man, obviously Tex, obliged him. Then planted a huge kiss on his lips. When he pulled away, he grinned. "We helped save two lives today. Well, I mean they're still sick and, you know..."

"I know." Davey brushed a lock of Tex's hair from his eyes. "But you did good."

"I did." The blond man had the biggest smile and the brightest blue shiny eyes. "I'm Tex."

"I'm Dean. I think..." I eyed Davey. "I'm going to venture to say I'm your husband's new...friend...?" I left the space open for Davey to comment, but he merely grabbed my arm.

"And I'd invite him home for dinner. Or we could go to Stavros's. But he's got to get over to the hospital. His boyfriend's over there. Nothing too serious anymore, although it was. But the guy's on the mend, and when he's feeling better, you two absolutely have to come for dinner." He dug into his back pocket, yanked out his wallet, and pulled out a business card, holding it out to me. "Please email me tonight. Or text. Oh, even better, do both. Then I can remind you to tell me about your next lecture, and we can set a time for dinner, and—"

Tex cut him off with a kiss. When it finally ended, he winked at me. "I think we're going to be good friends."

Something told me I'd have little say in the matter.

And I didn't care.

ADAM

"How are we feeling today?" Dr. Maroni swept into the room, midday on Thursday morning.

"Great." Dean rose, offering a grin. "Hospitality around here is the best."

My doctor grinned. "Glad to hear it." She eyed me and raised an eyebrow.

I nodded. Yeah, Dean could stay.

"Well, I'm pleased with your results. I'd like to do a couple more dialysis treatments, but we can do that with you as an outpatient. If the labs continue to improve, I can see us discontinuing them in the next few weeks." She eyed me before gazing over to Dean, then back to me. "That means eating properly, getting the right amount of exercise, and keeping your stress level down."

I wasn't certain what stress had to do with kidney health, but I'd do whatever she wanted. "I'll laze about and read a book. Except when I'm walking my dog."

"Well, that's perfect. I'll sign your discharge papers and get you out of here as soon as possible."

Although I was ready to leap—well, okay roll—out of bed,

I listened carefully to all her commands. She said Quinton would bring my discharge papers along with instructions for when I got home.

"We'll do all of it, Doc." Dean grinned. "Trust me."

Dr. Maroni had met him every day this week, and she appeared just as charmed with him as she was the first time. She fluttered her hand a bit. "Yes, well see that he does. Nice to meet you both." She met my gaze. "We're going to have a long-term relationship. Keep seeing Dr. Marco, but know he's forwarding your test results to me." Then she looked back and forth between the two of us. "No reason not to resume...everything...once you have more energy. Have a great day."

Dean coughed his thanks as his cheeks pinkened. Then he faced me with a big grin on his face. "We're going to do everything to increase your energy." Then he faltered. "Well, that is...if you want—"

"I want. I definitely want. Help me off the bed?"

He did and helped me dress, and we impatiently waited for Quinton to bring the paperwork.

The nurse did, and I forced myself to pay attention while he went over everything carefully.

Fifteen minutes later, Dean drove my SUV to the hospital door and helped me into the passenger seat. I'd known the past week, or more, had taken a lot out of me—but I hadn't realized just how much.

He buckled me in, waved to Quinton, then rounded the hood and hopped into his seat. "This is a truly lovely machine." He buckled his seatbelt, then slowly headed out of the parking lot. He made a right and headed for McCallum Road. "Nothing like the Utes I'm used to. Oh, but I did kind of like the Jeep we had up north. Sandy let me drive it. Took a bit of work as it was a stick. North American stick."

I chuckled. "And yet you managed."

He jutted his chin. "Of course I did." He took the left, heading us north and back to Mission City.

"You don't even need the GPS."

His grin lit his face.

Lit my life.

"I only need to do something once and I'm good. I admit that weird intersection had me fooled once, but I figured it out. Most important thing is that I get you home. Ingrid's filled the fridge with foods that are good for you. We're going to ensure you don't wind up back at the hospital."

"So no stopping for burgers."

"No." He grinned. "But we can stop at Starbucks to get a right-proper coffee." He'd brought me one every morning, as the hospital had a shop in the lobby. Still, something about going through the drive-thru felt decadent.

"And those egg things."

"Yeah, yeah, those egg things."

As the SUV ate up the miles as we drove up Highway 11, my eyes drifted shut. I'd been safe at the hospital. But now that I had Dean to myself, I truly began to relax. To feel like maybe the possibility of a happy few months lay ahead of us. It wasn't the forever future I wanted—

My eyes popped open.

Forever future? What the actual fuck? You don't do relationships. You don't even do people.

I've done Dean. Twice, in fact.

My inner voice didn't have a snippy comeback for that. And I knew this thought was nuts. Just because we'd shared a couple nights of incredible sex—as well as some wanks, jerks, and sucks, as he liked to say—didn't mean he'd want to stay. Or that I could go to Australia. Or that he could even come to visit several times a year. We didn't have a future.

And yet...

"You just want a plain coffee and the egg things?"

Startled, I realized we were pulling up to the drive-thru in Mission City. I'd missed the trip over the Mission-Abby bridge. "Yes, thanks. I think my wallet—"

"It's on me." Dean pulled out a Starbucks card. With a moose on it.

"Very Canadian."

"Yeah, I thought so. And I registered it and will, eventually, get free stuff. I like free stuff."

So did I...which was why I also had a card.

Still, I settled back as Dean ordered. Some flowers bloomed in the garden on the right side of the drive-thru. I squinted. Yep, those were roses. I fought this irrational desire to leap out of the car, grab one, then present it to Dean.

In that moment, I realized what I could do for him. What I should have done weeks ago but had, thus far resisted.

We inched along in the busy lineup and I sat quietly with the idea of what I could give him. Something so simple. And yet, to me—and hopefully to him—something truly profound.

"You all right, mate? I mean, you're not normally much of a talker—"

I punched his biceps.

Lightly.

He chuckled as he pulled up to the window.

A young man swiped his card and offered a broad grin. "Hello, Dean."

"Hey Tristan! How's it hanging, mate?"

"Too many classes, not enough graduating."

"You're in the upper-level ecology class, right?" Dean accepted a bag, which he handed to me.

"Yeah, excellent memory." Tristan handed him the two cups of coffee.

Which Dean handed to me.

"Well, we'll see you on Wednesday then."

"Looking forward to it." Tristan offered a wave, then shut the window

Dean slowly pulled away. "Got everything?"

"Yeah, we're good." I put his drink in the cup holder. "You know Tristan?"

"He's fantastic. Great guy. Very chatty. Roxie introduced us."

"Oh." I tried to keep my voice neutral.

"Yes." Dean turned right and narrowly avoided the lineup for Tim Horton's drive-thru. "And his girlfriend Olivia. Lovely woman. I found out she's basically Marnie McGrath's niece. Through marriage or something."

"Marnie?" I sipped my coffee.

"The assistant librarian. She's married to a reporter from Vancouver. Well, originally from Toronto...? Loriana explained it, but I kind of lost the thread."

"How many people do you know?"

"Well, Miss Edna was the top of the *must know* list in this town. She knows everyone and everything. She hangs out at the library and The Owl's Nest. Gets into all kinds of mischief. Matchmaking and stuff."

"Oh, well, you better avoid her." I sipped my coffee again as Dean rejoined Highway 11 so we could get onto the Cedar Connector.

"Right-o." He grinned. "Because I've met my match." At the red light, he turned to me. "And I don't want anyone else."

Chapter Thirty-Three

DEAN

AND I DON'T WANT ANYONE ELSE.

Those words echoed in my mind as I drove us up Cedar Street then toward the hills of north Mission City. I meant them. For whatever time we had, I only wanted Adam. Quinton was adorable. Tristan was charming. I'd encountered a couple of other men as I'd been introduced to this beautiful country.

None ticked every box the way Adam did.

None made me want to run home every night to them.

None touched my heart the way he did.

Goddamnit. You're not supposed to be looking for love. This is temporary. Temp-o-rary. Get that through your thick skull.

I told my inner monologue to shut the fuck up. It wasn't like I was telling Adam that I loved him. Not like I expected reciprocity. Hell, I'd only been invited to his bedroom twice. And only once did I get to stay. I wanted more. I wanted it all. Now I'd discovered sex—and intimacy—I wanted to sink into the pleasure of oblivion until the day came when I had to fly home.

And I was *not* going to think about that. The thought of

flying back to Australia made me sad. I didn't want to be sad. Hence, I'd only look for the positive.

Like the fact Adam was out of danger, on the mend, and on his way home. Like we were picking up Chip. Like we'd basically been given the green light to resume things when his strength returned. Like I still had five months in my contract.

"How did your lecture go yesterday?" Adam sighed. "I'm sorry, I forgot to ask. Seeing Tristan reminded me." He forked his egg into his mouth.

"Yeah, yesterday was the University of British Columbia." I slowed as the light ahead of us turned amber. Oh, yellow. Right. "I think it went well. We ran overtime because the students had so many questions about Australia's bush." I'd been reticent to leave Adam, but he'd truly been on the mend. That being said, the fact he was coming home with someone—as opposed to being left to his own devices—might be the reason he was discharged today. Rather than being left to, as he put it, *languish* in the hospital. In truth, as he regained his strength, he needed to be home. Just not alone.

For now, anyway.

But what would happen when I left? Could I ask Maddox and Ravi to check in on him? Justin was his counsellor, so maybe asking Stanley to drop by might be breaking some rule. Surely I could find other people, though. Right? If Ingrid knew what to look out for...

Truthfully, I didn't trust any of them to truly care for Adam the way he deserved. Not coddled—because that would never work—but he was one of those people who reacted best to a smattering of tough love mixed with some sweet love as well as someone who was willing to kick his ass.

Somehow I doubted he could find that person on a hook-up app.

Maybe I was overthinking this. Both Everett and Simeon

were amiable guys. No reason Adam couldn't hook up with one of them.

Even as I had the thought, I dismissed it. Yes, they were both great guys. But they weren't Adam's type. If he even had a type. Well, he'd admitted being attracted to Maddox. He was clearly attracted to me. Or so I supposed. I might also just be a convenient lay, and—

"Turn here." Adam pointed.

I slammed on the brakes and quickly checked the rearview mirror. Relieved to find no one behind us, I took the turn a little more sharply than would have been advisable. "You didn't spill coffee on yourself, did you?" I would've looked, but I really was an *eyes on the road* kind of driver.

"Nah. I was almost done anyway." He sipped. "You're really far into your head today, my friend. What's up?"

My friend. Not *my boyfriend, lover, confidante...*

I was reading too much into that. Friends was a great place to start.

"Just excited about picking Chip up. You're certain you've got the strength? I mean, I'm off work for a couple more days, and you can put her in the dog pen—"

"Breathe, Dean. Chip and I will be fine. Sure, she's got jelly beans and zoomies and all those other things, but she can also be calm when she needs to be." He might've muttered *I hope* under his breath.

Hard to hear. "Maurice will be pleased to see you."

Adam snorted. "He rarely deigns to give me his presence. I am just another servant, in his mind."

I couldn't argue with that. Except the cat continued to sleep on my spare pillow every night. And speaking of sleeping arrangements...where would I be spending the night? Adam didn't have a physical injury—nothing that precluded us sharing a bed together. I was completely respectful of the fact he needed some good, solid sleep. Hospitals were never quiet.

That being said, I really, really, really wanted to hold him in my arms tonight. The couple of weeks without him had been torture. In truth, I'd slept with a man, as in just sleeping, one whole time. And I was already hooked.

I took the left turn into Maddox and Ravi's driveway carefully, mindful of jostling Adam. And of any wayward canines. I wanted to trust Chip, for sure. Princess Sofia also had, I'd learned, a propensity to declare her territory on occasion. And since these occasions were never predictable, I drove with caution.

"I'm not breakable."

I snickered. "No, but the pooches are...and speaking of..." I barely had the SUV in park before the front door opened. Two dogs, two toddlers, two men, and a young boy poured out of the house. Although I didn't recognize the boy, I remembered Stanley and Justin saying they had a boy of about ten. "Is that Angus?" I unbuckled my seatbelt.

"Entirely possible." Adam struggled with his.

"Why don't you stay here? Chip might jump up, and—"

"I can fucking handle my dog, Dean."

I winced.

He winced.

Maddox waved uncertainly.

Ravi, though, was quickest to react. The nurse was around to Adam's side and opened his door while shielding him from two chaotically barking pooches. "You're welcome to come in, but the place is a mess. Maddox had a meeting in Vancouver with a client, and I've been here by myself. I swear I don't know how he maintains control over the brood. I never seem to be able to."

"Maybe because you're so tired after working three days of night shifts?" Maddox looped his arm around Ravi's waist as Victor and Violet plopped onto the ground and started pushing a ball back and forth between the two of them.

The young boy I assumed to be Angus supervised.

"Must be nice to have a playmate." My own childhood, although not desperately lonely, had wanted for a companion.

Maddox snickered. "Half the time, they're trying to rip each other's hair out." He met my gaze through the open door.

Subtly, I shook my head. Adam had lost all color, and I knew him well enough to know he was fast losing whatever strength he had.

Ravi must've caught my signal as well. "Come here, Chip." He opened the backdoor of the SUV and encouraged the golden retriever in.

Who promptly began licking Adam and myself in alternate bursts.

Everyone chuckled.

Adam snagged her snout, looked her in the eyes, and gently shook his head.

Her vibrations calmed.

Somewhat.

"Okay, guys, we thank you again." I gave them a salute.

Princess Sofia launched herself into Adam's open door, sprinted across his lap, and landed in my arms. She proceeded to give me an immense pile of doggy kisses.

Adam gave me a look.

I shrugged sheepishly. "I might've given her, you know, the last time I was here."

"The *T* word?"

Apparently both dogs knew what the phrase meant because a chorus of barks erupted in the small confines of the vehicle.

Maddox rounded the hood, strode over to my door, gently opened it, then yanked a protesting Princess Sofia off my lap. "Good God, dog."

She started licking his face.

Ravi chuckled. "She might love me and the kids, but she'll always have my husband wrapped around her little paw." He patted Adam on the shoulder. "Please take it easy. Do what they say so I don't wind up seeing you at my workplace again."

"He might want to see Quinton again, though." I winked at Ravi.

Who groaned. "Yes, he's cute." He gave us both an assessing look. "I think you might find what you're looking for closer to home." Gently, he closed Adam's door.

Maddox, still clutching his white little furball, closed mine as well.

Ravi joined the kids and Angus on the ground while Maddox waved goodbye as I backed down the driveway. I paused before we reached the road, to hook Chip into her harness for the five-minute drive home. The roads were clear, we weren't going to see another soul, and the sun was shining, but I didn't want Adam worrying about anything.

The world felt full of possibilities in a way it hadn't since I'd gotten that phone call a week ago.

Chapter Thirty-Four

ADAM

HOME SWEET HOME.

Even if my home was an imposing castle.

Dean parked us in the garage. He opened the back door of the SUV and coaxed Chip out. As she stayed by his heels, he rounded to my side.

I'd managed to unbuckle my seatbelt, but that was about it.

He grinned as he opened the door. "How about you handle the coffees and the garbage and I take the dog and your bag? Glad to see you ate the eggs."

My *bag* was far heavier than I'd thought. Dean brought another set of clothes and the second book in the trilogy—which got added to the pajamas and the first book which Maddox brought me. I'd been well-cared for and thoroughly entertained. "Sure." I grabbed the coffees while he snagged the bag. He clipped Chip's leash onto her collar, and they were off.

I was a little slower getting to the house. I couldn't remember ever being this tired. Probably because I did my best to forget the horrors of ten years ago. The reconstructive surgeries, the infections, the hospital stays, the convalescing. All that, I could barely remember. The hospital this week had been a grim reminder. Except Quinton, Dr. Lucia, Maddox, Ravi, and—most especially—Dean had endeavored to make my stay as pleasant as possible. To find productive ways to pass the time.

Once inside the house, I found Maurice ready to twine between my legs, purring like I'd never heard before. I almost scooped him up, but between my fatigue and the fear of frightening him, I opted not to. Instead, I moved to the kitchen where I could reheat our coffees. I was surprised to see how much of mine I'd consumed, and was debating making another one when Dean and Chip bounded in.

Instead of bolting, Maurice started crawling up Dean's jean-clad leg.

"Hey, buddy, that's not a good idea." He gently removed the cat's claws, then swung him into a hug. "You're just the cutest thing."

My cat licked Dean's nose. Well, okay then. I held out his coffee, newly reheated.

"Thanks, mate." Still holding the cat, he sipped the coffee. "Man, did I need that."

"Too many long hours at the hospital." My admonishment was half-hearted at best—I'd appreciated every moment he'd spent with me. So different from my previous stays when, after my agent dropped by once, took a fast look, and dropped me as a client, no one had come to see me.

Dean moved to my side and nudged me. "Anytime, Adam. In all seriousness—anytime."

"You're leaving soon."

He snorted. "Not for another five months. And you're not going to wind up back in the hospital while I'm here—and you're certainly going to take care of yourself when I leave so you don't wind up back there again either." He said the words so matter of fact.

As if I wouldn't do everything in my power to not disobey him. "I want you to see how hard I'm trying. I want..." My voice nearly broke. "I want you to be proud of me."

He set the cup on the counter, gently put Maurice on the floor, and moved swiftly to me.

I had a fraction of a second to pull back as he wrapped his arms around me. I didn't try. Instead, I leaned into the hug. Took all the comfort offered by the embrace and soaked up all the emotion that his grip conveyed. Stress, pain, and...dare I say...love?

At least, for me, there was love on my end. Just over a month, and my life had changed irrevocably. And I could mourn my loss when his time for departure came, or I could cling to each moment now and hope for the best. Believe that somehow it would all work out. "Thank you."

He chuckled. "Somehow this feels like the least I can do."

"Well, there's something I can do."

He pulled back. "Doctor said not until you're rested."

Heat raced up my cheeks. "That, uh, wasn't what I was referring to." I gazed into those dear amber eyes. "I have something to show you."

"Oh, I think that might get us into even more trouble."

I chuckled, withdrew from his embrace, then coaxed him into bringing his coffee.

"Are you going to reheat yours?"

"No." Little remained, so I poured it out and ran the water for a few seconds to chase away the lingering scent. Nerves jangled as my stomach contracted, threatening to bring all that coffee back up. *He'll love what you're about to show him.* Okay, possibly. He might also wonder—correctly—why I hadn't shared it before. And believe—accurately—that I hadn't trusted him. Still, I snagged his hand and led him through the dining room and into the living room. I brought him right up to the doors I never opened.

Removing a key, I unlocked the door.

He stilled my hand. "You don't have to do this."

I cocked my head. "Why not?"

He colored an adorable pink. "Well, like, if it's your dungeon or something, right? And I'm not into that kind of stuff. I don't think. Although maybe I would be, under the right circumstances. But I can't imagine what they would be. Except, of course, being with you and—"

I placed my index finger over his lips.

All blathering came to an abrupt end.

"I don't have a dungeon. *If* I had one, wouldn't you think it might be, I don't know, in the basement?"

He cocked his head. "Do you have a dungeon in the basement?"

"No." I eyed him. "If you decide you want to try...stuff... just let me know."

"You...?"

"Some. In my wilder days." I indicated the door. "You're ready?"

He drew in a deep breath. "Yeah, I'm ready."

I opened the door.

Chapter Thirty-Five

DEAN

WHATEVER I'D BEEN ANTICIPATING, WHAT I FOUND before me wasn't that.

A library.

And not just any library.

A massive, humongous, enormous, vast library.

This room lay beneath my turret bedroom, and so was essentially a circle. It soared to what I estimated to be nearly twenty feet of height as it took up two stories. The walls were crammed full of books. Most were clearly leather-bound tomes, but as I gazed upon the visual feast, I spotted a couple of shelves with colorful spines. I wanted to run and touch them all at the same time. As a child, given we didn't have money for luxuries such as books, the library had been my favorite place.

Adam had his own giant library right here. This place easily rivalled Dickens's The Owl's Nest. It truly stunned me. "Oh, Adam."

He gingerly stepped into my line of sight. "You like it?"

"Like it?" I clasped my hand to my chest. "It's truly stunning. How...?"

"That eccentric dude who built the house? Sent a book buyer across the world in one-hundred-and-eighty days to see just how many books he could find. I saw the receipts for that venture when I was organizing things on moving in. Honestly, he should've doubled the price of the house with what's in here. I got the sense the real estate agent assumed everything would be removed and had been startled when giving me the tour upon my taking possession. Silly woman offered to have the books removed…" He gestured around. "But I knew. I hadn't given much thought to literature growing up. Books were required reading to accomplish completing high school. I don't think I read a single book my entire first decade of adulthood. Every fashion magazine I could get ahold of? You bet. But books…" He gazed around. "Not so much."

"The accident?"

He blinked. "Yeah, the accident. I struggled to hold books, but a nurse introduced me to audiobooks. She started me on traditional novels, but when she discovered I enjoyed fantasy, she started finding those for me. I had an iPod for music. She would download books from the library for me. That year I was in the hospital, and then in rehab? I listened to nearly a book a day. I'd no notion such things existed. I still listen to audiobooks—mostly borrowed from the library. Just, now I read as well." He glanced around. "Uh, don't look too closely at the spines."

I arched an eyebrow.

"Many, many, many of them are in foreign languages. The previous guy wanted the prestige of owning the books without, apparently, any intention of reading them."

I burst out laughing. "Okay, that's hilarious. And you…?"

He moved toward a shelf with colorful spines. "I alternate between the classics and more modern stuff. I buy books from publishers, mostly. And, thanks to a certain pushy Australian who's recently come into my life, from bookstores."

We'd only gone to The Owl's Nest once, but obviously it'd had an impact. Clearly, he planned to go again.

"What's your favorite? Of all these books, Adam, which do you love the most?"

He held my gaze, then blinked several times. "This one." He pulled out a children's book and held it out. Robert Munsch's *Love You Forever*.

I wasn't familiar with it, so I gingerly took it from him. From the first page, I was captivated. Spellbound. By the end, thinking of my own mother, I wiped a tear from my eye. Slowly, I handed it back to him.

"My mom..." He cleared his throat. "This was my favorite book. I had her read it to me all the time. Really, I think it's my first memory. Or believe it is. After all this time, I just don't know."

"I'm sure she still loved you—"

"No." He shook his head violently. "The things I did, Dean." He gently reshelved the book.

Along with it, I spotted about another dozen Munsch books. I thought of Victor and Violet and how their fathers were already reading to them. Of how my mum had read all those library books to me. I gazed around the room. "I don't know what to say, Adam. Except shutting yourself away from the world isn't honoring your memory of your family."

"What would you have me do?" He closed his eyes. "Shutting myself away is all I have."

Gently, I took his left hand in mine, tracing the scars. "Keep seeing Justin. Keep going to Fifties and The Owl's Nest and other places that make you happy. Show the world you're stronger than they give you credit for."

He smiled sadly. "I don't think anyone gives me a second thought. I'm up here, they're down there. Why should I risk being stared at? Being mocked? Made fun of? Frightening children?"

"Were Victor and Violet afraid?"

"Well...no..."

"Because they just saw you as another human to manipulate." I struggled to find the right words. "I believe in you." *Am I making a mistake?* "I think you have more to give the world."

"What if the world rejects me again?"

Was he talking about people after his accident or his family after whatever horrible things he'd done? I couldn't absolve him of any of it. Absolution, for him, had to come from within.

He squeezed my hand. "I haven't told you about Sydney."

"The city in Australia? Because I know about it—"

He laughed. "Uh, no. Didn't see that coming, either. No, Sydney is a young woman who's had a profound impact on me, even though we only met for a couple of hours." He met my gaze, with his gray eyes solemn. "And I think, if you want —and if she wants—that you'll meet each other. Because she needs more people in her court."

And so, as we wandered around the library, me gazing at book spines, Adam told me about a young woman desperately in need of acceptance. Her parents could love her and tell her everything was going to be okay, but she needed to see that it really could be.

A grease fire had left her with third-degree burns on her face, and she wasn't taking care of herself—something my man clearly understood. With her parents' permission, he was going to try to be someone in her life who she could be honest with—about all of it. And since she lived locally, Adam recommended she see a therapist at Healing Horses.

Her parents readily agreed, as the harried social worker Sydney was seeing right now didn't specialize in trauma, and was clearly in over her head.

As Adam spoke, he became animated. He talked about

inviting Sydney and her parents over—people he'd spoken with and clearly held in high regard. He spoke of how enthusiastic Chip would be.

Chip who, apparently exhausted from her visit with Princess Sofia and the twins, had flaked out on her bed in the kitchen. She needed to eat.

As did we.

When Adam wound down, I took his hand in mine. "Let's do this."

Chapter Thirty-Six

ADAM

Ingrid had prepared all my favorites in anticipation of my return home and, despite the heat outside, I wanted lasagna.

Dean heated it up while I sat at the kitchen table with Chip's chin resting on my thigh.

She'd recovered a bit of her energy from her power nap, had gobbled up dinner, and now contented herself with being near me. She kept a close eye on Dean, though. In case he dropped something. One could never be too vigilant when near the kitchen.

Maurice had settled on one of the chairs, lazing and indolently licking his paw. He truly was a happy cat.

I'd always sensed that, the few times he'd deigned to be in my presence, but his pleasure in having me home really warmed my heart.

After a few minutes of microwaving the food, Dean placed a steaming plate of tomatoey-good pasta before me. He grinned. "I'd like to see you eat the entire thing."

Since I had my appetite back, I grinned in return. "I'll do my best."

Within just a couple of minutes, he had his own plate and settled next to me. He held out his right hand, and I placed my left in it with no hesitation at all. For an absurd moment, I thought we were going to pray. Instead, he squeezed my fingers gently. "It's so good to have you home."

"The place is too empty without me?" Given the sheer number of rooms, I could hide myself away and he'd never see me. As I'd intended when he moved in. As, thank God, had never happened.

After a moment of gazing into each other's eyes, Dean released my hand. Still, his amber eyes glinted as he picked up his fork. "I heard tomorrow is Canada Day."

I blinked at the change of topic. "Uh..." I ran through the calendar in my mind, but came up blank. "Well, if it's July first, then yes, it's Canada Day." I wracked my brain. "I think they're doing something down at Heritage Park. Did you want to go?"

"You won't have the strength for that."

"I wasn't suggesting I go. I was thinking you could, and—"

"I'm not going anywhere without you. Just in case that wasn't incredibly clear. I'm not letting you out of my sight."

"You have to go back to work on Monday."

He didn't look pleased with that—scowl and all. "Sure, but I don't have to like it."

"Dean, I'll be fine. How much trouble can I get up to in eight hours?"

He waved his fork in the air. "Knowing you? A whole bunch. Look, I know you're trying, mate, and I appreciate it. But I'll worry. Just accept that and we'll move on."

Chip whimpered.

After giving me a steady stare, Dean ducked his head under the table. "I'm reading him the riot act for your sake, Miss Chip. You need him around and healthy for a very long time, and if my nagging him contributes to his good ongoing health, that can only be a good thing."

Those deep-brown eyes held his gaze before she came over to him and licked his cheek.

He giggled.

I laughed.

The rest of the meal was consumed with the same lightness of spirit which we'd enjoyed before my hospital stay. Before he'd gone away. And sure, next time I'd react more aggressively with any kidney stones I might have, but that wasn't a guarantee it would be enough. I might still get sick again. Chip and Maurice might depend on me, but that wasn't enough to keep illness away. Still, I offered a genuine smile as we discussed possible movies to watch.

And while I'd thought we might head down to the basement and the recliners, Dean insisted we get into my bed. The last owner had installed a television in the bedroom, but I never used it. My companion figured out the controls, and soon we were watching another Canadian Indigenous film.

Guilt swamped me as I realized how many great films were out there that I hadn't seen. This one involved two younger men in a gay relationship. So much done through actions rather than words. With a happy ending, no less. Having read Margaret Laurence, Margaret Atwood, Robertson Davies, and Mordecai Richler in the past, I wasn't certain one could read a story by them and have a happy Canadian ending. I was pleased to have been proven incorrect on that score.

Dean selected an Australian Aboriginal film but, despite my best efforts, I couldn't keep my eyes open. "Can we do this tomorrow?" I might've yawned that question.

"Sure, mate." He powered down everything. "So you've got your phone. I mean, you can yell, but I doubt I'd hear you, even with my door open. You can send Chip—"

He was right about yelling—the main suite and the turret

room were on opposite ends of the house and on different floors to boot. Sending Chip might work, but... "You're not staying?"

"You need your rest."

"I *need* you." Damnit, I'd been without him for two entire weeks. I didn't want to wait another moment.

"Adam."

"Dean." I repeated the exaggerated and exasperated tone.

He winced.

I sensed capitulation. "We don't have to do anything. You can just hold me—the way you like to do." The whole one time we'd spent the night, if I recalled correctly. That memory was hazier than I would've liked. So much had happened since then.

Finally, he sighed. "Right-o, mate. Let me go upstairs, put on my pajamas—"

"No way." I waved my hand in the air. "I don't want to turn the air conditioner on. Tomorrow's going to be super-hot. We can just be naked tonight."

"Oh, yeah, like that won't tempt us." He frowned.

I shrugged. "Look, you're right. I'm exhausted. I haven't slept properly in two weeks—"

"One week."

He was thinking since I'd been in the hospital.

"Two weeks," I corrected.

His cocked eyebrow enamored him further to me. "I didn't sleep well while you were up north. Like, fighting fires. People die doing that."

"I wasn't *fighting* fires." He pursed his lips. "I was *studying* them."

"And you almost got caught when the winds shifted."

"Yeah, I knew I'd regret telling you that story."

In his defense, he'd been exhausted when I'd finagled it out of him. He'd been tired much of the past week.

I patted the bed beside me. "Take off your clothes and climb into bed with me."

He eyed Chip, fast asleep in her bed, with paws sticking out at odd angles.

"Like you said, I'm tired. You're tired. We'll just sleep."

"Right." He rubbed his red-rimmed eyes. "Okay." He grabbed the hem of his T-shirt and hauled it over his head.

I began unbuttoning my night shirt that I'd put on when we'd first come up here—at Dean's insistence. That I was still a *patient*.

"Hey, what're you doing?"

"What does it look like I'm doing? I'm undressing."

He scowled. "That wasn't part of the plan."

"Look, I've been sitting on the bed, pleasantly warm." *Especially with you sitting next to me.* "I know you prefer having a sheet over you, so if I don't want to overheat..."

"Why do I feel like I'm being manipulated?"

I blinked innocently at him. "I have no idea."

He growled.

The sound went straight to my neglected cock.

He pointed. "Don't get any ideas."

I finished unbuttoning my shirt and took it off. Whereas I'd felt self-conscious previously, a lot had changed in our dynamic since the first time we'd made love. Being in the hospital with lots of pokes and prods helped as well. Since the nurses and doctors weren't worried about whether skin grafts would hold, they treated the scarred skin the same as the rest. And talking to Sydney had really helped. So I scooted out of my pajama bottoms, tossed them over the side of the bed, and crawled under the sheet.

Dean was naked by that point—gloriously naked—and I observed him avidly as he tucked away his glasses, which he wore pretty much all the time these days, pulled down the comforter, and arranged the cotton sheet in *just that way*. He was an odd perfectionist, and I loved that about him.

His room was always a disaster, but he liked how things felt against his skin.

I related to that.

He shut the blackout blinds, petted Chip on the head, and came back to the bed, crawling in.

I hit the button to put the ceiling fan on low, then I killed the lights.

The sudden darkness felt oddly comforting. This close to the solstice, the sun came up early and stuck around until very late. I was going to bed while it was still light out and waking up after the sun crested the horizon. But, slowly, the days would shorten. Yes, we still had the summer left to enjoy, but eventually fall would come.

And then Dean would leave.

My breath caught.

He tugged me in toward him, encouraging me to lie on my side, then pulling me into his arms. "You're safe, baby. You're home and you're safe. I'll take care of you."

But for how long? I didn't voice the words. Simply resolved to do a better job of taking care of myself.

On that note, I let myself go.

Chapter Thirty-Seven

DEAN

I awoke to a nice, round, firm ass rubbing against my very interested cock.

Then the situation crashed down around me and I cursed my morning wood.

Adam grasped my thigh as I tried to pull back. "Please." He said the word in a hoarse whisper.

I relented.

A tad.

Okay, at least I halted my retreat.

He pressed his ass back against me.

"I'm just a man," I said through gritted teeth. "Flesh and blood and—" I sighed. "—horny as fuck."

He chuckled. "Good, so you can fuck me."

I stilled. *Did he just...?* "Okay, two things. One, you're recovering from a major illness. Two, I didn't think you bottomed."

After a long, still moment, he blew out a breath. "I don't... normally. Especially with guys I've just met."

I considered pointing out one month barely constituted much of an acquaintance, but even I saw the folly in that.

Without doubt, this past June had been the most intense month of my life. Even Mom's passing, because it had been expected, hadn't been this...nuts. "I'm not sure about this. You're still recovering."

"There's nothing wrong with either my heart or my cock. I'll drink a pile of water when we get up. Just a gentle, leisurely fuck. My heart rate will barely rise."

I might not have studied anatomy and physiology, but I was pretty sure he was bullshitting me. I had a choice to make —trust him and believe he knew what he was doing—or mollycoddle him for the rest of the weekend. And possibly beyond. Truthfully, I firmly believed the last week had been a wake-up call for him. That he hadn't intended to let things get as dire as they had. And that if he said he would take care of himself, he truly would. If only for me and to not scare me again. I drew my fingers lazily up and down his thigh.

He shuddered.

I kissed his shoulder.

He sighed and pressed back against me.

Teasingly, I slapped his hip. "Keep that up and I'll come before I'm even inside you."

"Wouldn't want that." No missing the pretend pout in that voice.

"Okay." I rolled over and then rummaged in the night-stand drawer, successfully locating the bottle of lube. Was I supposed to just open him up and fuck him? What about finesse? Seduction? Kissing?

He doesn't do kisses. He doesn't want you to touch his left side.

Fortunately, his right side was up, so I could manage to adhere to that rule. I really wanted to be face-to-face when we made love, though.

Maybe next time.

If there's a next time.

There would be, I decided with certainty. Because I hadn't had my fill of him. Not by a long shot.

Still, I had *this* moment—I intended to make the most of it. Snagging his hip, I gripped it, then gently slid my hand down to his inner thigh. "Lift up a bit." When he obeyed, I slid my thigh under his.

He shivered.

"Cold?"

"No. Opposite."

For just a flash, I wondered if he had a fever. Then I understood. I chuckled. "Patience, good man."

"I've never been a good man."

I stilled.

He kept right on going. "So just fuck me already, okay? I need you inside me, like, this instant. I need to feel alive, and the only way for that to happen is for you to sink inside me and then fuck me into oblivion."

"All right, baby, I'll do that." I didn't know where the endearment came from. Because he wasn't a baby...but something in him kicked my nurturing into gear. Sweetheart would've sufficed. Or something else. Just something other than *mate*. Because I used that term so liberally, it wouldn't have the same meaning. He needed to know how important he was to me, and that meant a name I would only ever use for him.

I coated my fingers in lube and began the slow process of opening him. Unless he used toys, he wouldn't have had anything stuck in his ass for over ten years—I had to be respectful of that.

"Jesus, could you take any longer? I'm going to die of old age."

Well, living that long's a good thing. I'd never seen him suicidal—but I'd rarely seen him embrace life either. I intended to change that.

I twisted my fingers and hit the spongy spot inside him.

"Oh, fucking Christ. Yes. Yes. Yes. More. It's been so long."

He elongated the *so* in a way that made me smile. Still, my cock was straining and leaking random drops of precum. I withdrew my hand, he whined, and I coated my cock with lube. "You have to tell me if this hurts."

"It's the good kind of hurt. The kind I can take."

His insistence had me smiling. I was about to fuck someone. Thus finishing the loss—or maybe surrender—of my virginity. Taking just a second to absorb that made me smile. *Too bad he can't see.* I lined myself up, took a deep breath, and started to ease my way in.

He was so damn tight.

I was so damn scared.

He reached behind to grab my thigh. "I can take it, Dean. Just push in already."

Unable to deny him, I did as told. I pushed the crown of my cock against him until finally it slid in.

The sigh coming from him vaguely concerned me, but then he started pushing back.

"I need this, Dean."

Taking in the surreal feeling of my shaft being squeezed so much, I slowly slid in farther. I'd go a centimeter or two, pull back, then push in farther.

Each time, he'd either sigh or grunt.

I worked off the assumption these were good noises of pleasure. Trusting him to be honest with me if I messed up was tough, but I had to let him speak for himself.

When I was fully seated, we both held still for just a moment. My body demanded more, but I just wanted to take in the sensations. I didn't know if he'd ever ask me to do this again. No doubt in my mind, though, that I'd say *fucking hell yes.* And I didn't know if there might be someone else in my future. Or if Adam would be my one and only. I was totally okay with that—right now, anyway. When I went home, and was alone again, I might eventually feel differently. *Don't want to think about that.*

"Now, Dean. I need you to move now. Don't hold back, okay?"

Uncertain of what *holding back* meant, I started to move. To give him what he so desperately needed. What I needed as well. I grasped his hip and held on tight as I pulled back, then thrust back in.

He pressed back against me, clearly seeking more.

I snapped my hips as I thrust harder. Deeper. Longer. I'd never felt this way, the overwhelming sensation of not only chasing my own pleasure but—more importantly—chasing his. "I...uh..." I continued to thrust.

He laughed. "I'm going to jack myself off. I might just come from you nailing my prostate, but I want to come so fucking bad—"

"Do it." I'd always wanted to be a generous lover. To have my partner come first. The way the orgasm was bearing down on me, I wasn't certain I'd make it. I increased the pace of my thrusts, willing him to come. To allow me to sink into the promised pleasure.

"I'm coming." Adam let the words hang as he frantically jerked. Then, in an instant, his body went rigid. His ass squeezed my cock as the orgasm washed through him.

In return, I thrusted several more times before coming myself. The cliff I threw myself over bore no resemblance to anything that had come before. I was flying high with no worries. I was floating in warm water with my skin tingling with pleasure. I was soaring to a height I almost didn't understand.

Then reality crashed down. Still pleasure-filled, but also a couple of realizations. First, I'd come inside him. Without a barrier. That kind of intimacy was beyond anything I could imagine. Even my mate Sam had never done it without a condom. He said the risks were just too great. And yet here, in this moment, I trusted my partner completely.

The second thought was that I never wanted this to end. I wanted to live like this for the rest of my life. Of our lives. To settle in this house with Chip, Maurice, Adam, and the entire town of Mission City. I wanted this to be my home.

With no way to make that dream come true.

"I'm going to pull out."

Adam's breath still came in ragged exhalations.

So much for no strain on him.

I didn't have any regrets. Well, as long as he didn't get sick again. Which was highly unlikely. If sex might cause something bad, Dr. Maroni would have said something—of that, I had no doubt. Slowly, I withdrew, laughing in my head at the little *pop* when I slid out entirely.

"Oh Jesus." Adam tried to turn his head.

I kissed the back of his neck. "No, just Dean."

He laughed. "Yeah, okay, I fell into that one."

"We should get cleaned up."

"No."

"Uh...okay." Personally, I thought a shower and changing the sheets was a good idea. We'd both come, and lube also made a mess. Just generally, we needed to fix this place up before Ingrid returned on Monday. Well, unless we made another mess. *I hope he owns plenty of sheets.* I held myself still as he started to shift onto his back.

He oriented himself so I lay flush against his right side. I longed to touch. To caress. To comfort. But he'd made it clear he didn't want those things.

"I want to kiss you."

Well, okay, maybe he wants some *of those things.* "I don't have a lot of experience." *And you told me you didn't want me touching you that way.* As I gazed into those deep-gray eyes, barely visible in the morning light, I knew I would never be able to deny him anything. I didn't understand the ache in my chest, but I could recognize it as a new feeling. Something I'd never felt before. Something special.

"Just press your lips to mine. We'll figure out the rest."

Chapter Thirty-Eight

ADAM

JUST PRESS YOUR LIPS TO MINE. WE'LL FIGURE OUT the rest.

Even as I said the words, I understood how complicated the request was. I'd spent the past month telling him to stay away from half my body. And he'd been so incredibly respectful of that demand. Yet he never looked at me with either disgust or pity. He saw me as a man. Just a man.

Not a monster.

And as he blinked those amber eyes several times, I couldn't miss...something. Love? Tenderness? Compassion? In all honesty, I'd never seen someone look at me like that before.

Slowly he lowered his lips to mine.

Slowly I angled my body, so we'd be closer.

His eyes drifted shut, but I kept mine open—I wanted to see him. All of him. And, as expected, his lips were super soft. Along with daily sunscreen, he'd mentioned he used some kind of SPF moisturizer product on his lips. He was so diligent about taking care of himself.

You should emulate that.

Okay...but after I've kissed him.

I wound my arm around his neck so I could press against the back of his naked head. So I could urge him toward me. So I could prove to him that I wanted that touch. I nibbled at his lower lip, and he opened his mouth. Immediately, I thrust my tongue inside.

He hesitated for a moment, before twining his tongue with mine. His movements were...unschooled. But he was a fast learner, and soon he parried, and then he tried to take control of the kiss by thrusting his tongue into my mouth.

Glorying in the sensations he elicited, I pressed myself against him, even as my cock stirred to life again. I'd have thought another erection impossible, as he'd fucked me sense-less mere moments ago, but his dominance in the kiss brought all kinds of wicked images to my mind. The truth was, I enjoyed ceding control once in a while. I enjoyed being a switch, but I never told people that. Instead, I exerted domi-nance—even if I was the smaller partner. Dean made me feel protected. Cherished. Even, dare I say, loved?

After a time, he tentatively moved his hand to my hair, grasping it. Giving an experimental tug.

I thrust my hardening cock against him.

He moaned.

I giggled.

He ended the kiss, pulled back, and arched his eyebrow. "Okay, what's so funny?"

"Not funny." I tried to unscramble my scrambled brains. His kiss was pretty damn potent. "Just..." I met his gaze and blinked. "You make me want things. Things I didn't think I could have."

"Baby, I'll give you everything."

I'd never had someone use an endearment with me before. And I would've thought I'd hate *baby*, but I understood what he meant to convey. That he was using the vocabulary he had to describe what I felt in return as well. Something special between the two of us. I took a deep breath. "Will you touch me? Everywhere?"

He held very still.

So still I wondered if I'd said the wrong thing.

He blinked. Then wet his lips. "I'll do anything you want, Adam. But I want to make certain you're doing this for the right reason."

I cocked my head.

"You set very clear boundaries. I'll always respect them—"

"That was before I really knew you." I took a deep breath. "Before I came to trust you."

"You trust me?"

"With my life."

He swallowed hard. "I want to be the man you think I can be."

"I know you're the man I think you can be. The man you are." I frowned. "Oh, fucking hell."

He grinned. "I know what you're trying to say."

"That's good, because I'm not sure anymore." I caressed his cheek and grasped his beard. "You're the only one who's ever made me feel cherished." I held his gaze. "Loved."

"That's because you are."

I felt it. Deep in my bones. So I grasped his right hand and tentatively placed it on the left side of my face.

Slowly, he traced along the ridges of my scars, then scratched my beard, which had grown since I'd been in the hospital.

"I need a trim."

He grinned. "You don't want to be burly like me? With a brawny body and a long beard?" He winked.

"Uh...no." I grasped his hand and held it against me, absorbing the warmth. "I just want you in my life. For now, anyway."

"I can do that, Adam. As long as you'll have me."

"As long as the contract runs," I corrected.

"Well, both." He shifted his gaze away, then settled it back on me. "Things are happening."

I cocked my head.

"Argh. It's too soon. Just...things are looking different."

His words didn't make sense, but I wasn't going to press. He'd tell me when he was ready. Or not at all. I didn't have a claim on him. I *wanted* one—but I didn't have it. Then, ever so gently, I drew his hand down my neck to my shoulder, than along my chest. No one except medical professionals had touched me there in ten years. Now, though, as I gazed into this man's eyes, I could forget the pain. The loneliness. The depression. I could look to moving forward in the world. To maybe even stepping outside the castle walls. To finding a purpose beyond existing and taking care of my pets.

Speaking of... "Is Maurice sleeping on the lounge chair?"

"Yes."

"And Chip is in her bed?"

He glanced over. "Yes, with that odd angle she loves so much. Truly, you have a weird dog."

I leaned over to kiss him. "And you love her."

"And I love her." He held my gaze. "And I might just love you too, baby. I know it's too soon. That I should be suave and sophisticated and distant about it."

"Says who?"

He cocked his head. "Well, my mate Sam—"

"Sam's an idiot."

"Uh...well, he's...a bit of a playboy. He enjoys sex."

"Don't you?"

He pressed his erect cock against my hip. "Very much. So why don't we head into that massive shower of yours so I can show you how much?"

"I like that idea."

"Right-o. Then I'll take Chip out, make you breakfast, and we can watch the Parliament Hill thingy."

"I'm not certain Canada Day celebrations have ever been called *thingies*, but I get your meaning. I can take Chip out, you know."

"I know you can. But you're going to let me because I promised Quinton I'd take care of you, and that means you staying in bed while I make you waffles."

"Can you make them blueberry waffles?"

"Are blueberries in season?"

I shook my head. "No, but Ingrid froze a massive number from last summer's bumper crop. Just throw some of those into the batter."

He grinned, then pressed our lips together. That gentle touch turned into a full-fledged tongues-clashing, teeth clacking, French kiss.

Only, much later, did everything sink in. By the time we finished our shower—with him grasping our cocks together in his massive fist and jerking us off—did reality crash down. Exhaustion overtook me and I dozed while he took care of my dog, my cat, and breakfast.

As I curled against him, and he watched our Canadian Prime Minister make a speech, I was able to admit how fucking lucky I was. For however long that might be.

And when we made love that night—very gently and languidly—he repeated his words of love.

I repeated mine. I drifted off to sleep in his arms, secure in the knowledge I'd found my person. That might only be for the next five months, but I pledged to enjoy every moment.

DEAN

FUCKING SNOW.

Roxie laughed as I recalled fishtailing my way down Adam's street.

Our street, as he insisted on calling it.

I'd never dealt with fishtailing before. Jesus.

"This is one of the earliest snowfalls we've ever had." She held out her mitt as the snow continued to fall. "Climate change."

I stomped my boots to bring feeling back to my feet. "Yeah, this is not *global warming*."

She scowled. "We just had the hottest summer on record. This year will be the hottest...again."

"I'm not arguing...just saying that this is not warm." I huddled in my coat. I'd steadfastly refused to buy an actual winter coat because winter started December twenty-first and I was scheduled to leave November thirtieth.

Adam, who looked wistful when I mentioned my departure date, also pointed out that Mother Nature didn't exactly follow the Julian calendar.

I grinned. "But you should see Chip in the snow. I

thought only huskies love snow, but apparently plenty of Canadian dogs do. But she comes in covered in little snowballs." That required warm water to melt them and then she needed a good blow dry. So very much fur. "Heck, even Maurice likes the stuff."

"Maurice is adorable." Roxie had joined us for an end-of-summer barbecue along with about thirty people we knew. Damn diffident cat had snuck out of the house, joined us at the fire pit, and curled into my boss's lap.

I'd been stunned, but Adam even more so. Quite a transformation from a cat who appeared biweekly to a companion we saw almost as often as Chip.

Adam, at first, had been incredibly nervous the night of the party. By the end of the night, he was joking around with my petite supervisor, sharing their love of cribbage and fresh apple cider made by some guy and his husband out on a farm across town.

Seriously.

Whatever made him happy.

Whatever made her happy.

About two dozen neighborhood kids showed up for Halloween—including Victor and Violet who were on their first trick-or-treat adventure, being led by Angus and his newly adopted sister Opal.

Maddox and Stanley snapped about a million photos while Ravi and Justin stood back and laughed. Both families were thriving.

We also had another gay couple move in down the street. Their story intrigued me, and I'd planned to invite them over, but Adam wanted us to hunker down in November. He didn't want to share me, knowing our time was scarce.

Now, on the fifth, I eyed my boss. "Can we get out of the snow?"

She grinned. "Yeah, but first I want to share the good

news." Her pink cheeks appeared even rosier than usual—likely due to the freaking cold.

"You can't tell me inside?"

"Well, you might...react."

I eyed the municipal office. "I can behave."

"Sure, but when I tell you they're offering you a permanent contract, and that they've worked out the paperwork to get you permanent residency because you're *irreplaceable,* and—"

I scooped her up and twirled her around.

She laughed. "Yeah, that's what I thought. Put me down, you big lug. People might get the wrong idea."

Normally, I wouldn't care what idea people got, but harassment was a thing. So I gently placed her down. I did, however, grasp her hands. "That sounds too simple."

"Dean, we've been trying to fill your job for two years. The economy's good. We're at near full employment. The government is trying to put in a real conservation effort. That means adequate surveillance and boots on the ground. Now, you've still got the leeway to work at the universities a couple of days a month if you want—"

"I want." I nearly jumped up and down. "Both asked me to do guest lectures in the winter semester. I had to say *no.* Hopefully it's not too late for me to go back to them."

"I'm sure it's not. Unlikely they found another Australian forester in the meantime." She eyed me. "Are you okay with leaving Australia? With becoming Canadian?"

"I'll miss my mate Sam, of course, but I don't see him often. Maybe I can convince him to visit Canada." Ideas swirled in my mind. November through May were peak tourist season for him. He might be able to swing a month or two in the winter when Sydney wasn't quite as packed. He didn't take enough vacations.

Roxie bumped my arm. "Payroll and human resources

have a ton of paperwork for you to fill out. You still have a few more hurdles, but you should hear for certain before you're due to go home." She narrowed her shrewd gaze. "Are you going to be looking for a place to stay?"

Shit. "I...I don't think so. I mean I can't imagine Adam's going to kick me out. We, uh...don't talk a lot about the end of the month."

She grinned. "I think you can tell him tonight. Unless you want to wait until it's permanent."

I shook my head. "If he wants me gone, I'll need to start looking for a place sooner rather than later. He's with Sydney at her doctor's in Vancouver today."

Roxie nodded. "Nice girl. She seemed to have fun at the party."

"Yeah, I think she did. Anyway, she wanted Adam to accompany her and her parents to an appointment today. Adam was hesitant, but I pointed out the courage it must've taken her to ask him. And that she likely had a purpose in mind. His experience will, undoubtedly, come in handy."

"Brave of both of them."

"Yep. So I'll make him a special dinner. Now can we go inside? My nuts are freezing."

She laughed. "Okay, watch who you say that to."

Heat rose in my cheeks.

"And it's barely freezing. Wait until the temperature goes down a whole bunch."

"Yay." I winced. And huddled further.

"Oh, work has a winter coat for you—with the city logo and your name on it. If you want it."

"I want, Roxie. I really want."

So we headed inside, where I officially began a new phase in my life.

For dinner that night, I cooked rosemary chicken,

GABBI GREY

seasoned baby potatoes, carrots in salt-free butter, and cheese-covered broccoli—all Adam's favorites.

When he walked in the door, both Maurice and Chip would come running to greet him. He'd taken some computer courses over the summer and now worked for a non-profit run by a brilliant woman, Emma-Jane Ward, in Mission City. Adam worked from home two days a week, but he also made regular appearances in her office.

And handled all that peopling just fine. Sometimes it drained him, some days after an office trip he came home muttering about a jerk who stared or someone who offered to pray for him, but he handled it. Sometimes he needed an extra session with Justin, or *accidentally* broke one of the hideous china plates, but he never quit. He was so fucking strong, it blew my mind.

Chip and Maurice didn't like being left alone when we were both out. When Adam casually mentioned that to EJ, as she preferred to be called, she insisted he bring Chip in with him. Maurice, poor dear, was not invited. Still, he'd sit in the turret window, waiting for vehicles to appear. And he might've been rewarded with extra treats for being such a good boy. And since Adam had started taking Chip, the number of broken plated had dropped way down.

I was just pouring the eggnog as the sound of Adam pounding his boots on the floor in the mudroom carried to me. It seemed this was a very traditional Canadian thing—stomping one's boots to get the snow off. I'd thought the snow down by the yard was bad. Adam's house, though, was at an even higher elevation and, apparently, that meant more snow. He was also on the lee side of Iron Mountain. Fortunately, that meant the wind usually wasn't as bad up here. On the occasions when the wind whipped up, though, I found that of little comfort. We'd had a couple of fall storms with gale-force winds. A few trees in Mission City had toppled, but fortunately, none up our way, so we hadn't lost power.

Chip barreled over to Adam, greeting him with the waggiest of tails when he entered the kitchen.

He crouched down. "Were you a good girl today?"

She held out her paw for him to shake. When he did, she leaned forward to lick his cheek.

"Ah, well-behaved, I can see." He rose, headed, my way, and planted a kiss on my lips when he arrived before me.

"Remember she was at Sofia's today?" Sometimes, when we were both doing long days, Chip would head over to her best buddy's house for a play date. I'd needed to do a run over to Abbotsford for an early morning class, and Adam had been in Vancouver most of the day. Hence Chip had enjoyed occupying the twins with plenty of doggie kisses—according to Maddox. "Oh, how's Sydney doing?"

Adam made his way to the fridge, put some ice in a glass, added water, and drank deeply. "Doing better every time I see her. The doctor in Vancouver was really pleased with her progress." He took another sip. "And Avery's talking about making their counseling sessions once a month." Although Adam still saw Justin for ongoing care—dealing with loss as well as what would happen should he backslide—Justin kept things a bit less formal. He, Stanley, and the kids had been over a couple of times this fall. Friendly, but not friends. At least not until the therapeutic relationship ended. Adam felt that might happen within the next few months or year.

"That's great."

"Yeah, she's working on a book. I mean, that young and she wants to be an author. To write about what she's been through." He moved to the kitchen table, placed his water by his cutlery, and snagged the eggnog. "Oh my God, heaven."

"Leave room for the food." I opened the oven and pulled

out the plates, then I placed them on the table with cozies underneath. "They're freaking hot."

"I freaking love you."

Chip woofed.

"Has she been fed?"

I shook my head. "I figured I'd leave that honor up to you."

"I'll do it quickly." And he did just that—portioning out her food and setting her up in her corner of the kitchen.

Maurice sat on a kitchen chair and indolently licked his paw. I'd given him some wet food—which he'd devoured.

Adam and I sat next to each other, him at the head of the table and me beside him. We both cut open our chicken and inhaled deeply as the meat cooled a bit.

He took the first, tentative bite. Moaning, his gaze caught mine.

Damn, I'd meant to light candles. We did that sometimes. Because I loved how his gray eyes shone in the low light.

He grasped my right hand in his left. "Thank you. For all of it. I might just keep you around for your cooking."

"You might just keep me around for more than that." I winked.

"Yeah, okay, the rooting's pretty good." He tried to mimic my accent—and did a terrible job.

"Well, I might be around longer than you think."

Slowly he laid his fork down. "You mean beyond November thirtieth?"

"Yep." I scrutinized him, trying to discern his true reaction. Shock—which I'd expected—with his wide eyes. Confusion—also anticipated—with his furrowing of brow. Then...a neutral expression. He pulled his hand back.

Well, that's not good.

"That's, uh, great."

I blinked. *Does he not want me to stay? Is this the kiss-off?* I cleared my throat. "Mrs. Thistle's daughter has met a new man and has moved out of the basement. The suite's mine...if I want it."

He poked at his potatoes, cutting them open and letting the steam escape. "Do you want to live in Mrs. Thistle's basement?" He wouldn't meet my eyes.

"Adam."

His gaze snapped to mine. "What?"

"Do you want me to stay here, or do you want me to move on? This is your call—I can't make the decision for you."

A long moment passed before he placed his cutlery on the table. "I'm not going to...talk you into staying. I can be difficult. I'm obstinate, particular, and annoying—"

"Jesus Christ, Adam, you're none of those things. You're prudent, caring, and generous. You've..." I swallowed. "You've come a long way since I met you. Maybe you don't see it, but I do. And I'm just thinking that now you're getting out into the world, maybe it's you who might find someone more...suitable."

"In what way?" He finally looked at me. "You're the one who might want a partner with more education, someone more like you."

I rolled my eyes. "Do you think Tex discusses quantum physics with Davey? Or that Davey understands the internal workings of a helicopter engine?"

"Well..."

"Or that Justin understands the ins and outs of venture capitalism while Stanley understands...psychological theories?"

"Maybe..."

"So I'll teach you about basal areas and all-aged stands. And then—"

He held up his hand. "I get your point."

I poked at my potatoes. "I...I asked at the university today.

You'd qualify for a discount in tuition...if you were my partner."

"Partner...?" He said the word as it trying it out.

"Well, in Canada, if you've lived together in a conjugal relationship for a year, then you're considered common-law married."

He frowned.

This is not going well.

Adam nodded, head tilted in thought. "So we're six months away from that."

"Well, yeah...if we want." *Don't you want it as much as I do?* This wasn't the celebration I'd imagined.

"Or we could have a Christmas wedding."

This time, I blinked. Hope rose inside me. "Yeah...if we want."

Slowly, he smiled. "I think on the grand staircase. With our closest friends. Do you think Sam could make it?"

"Uh...probably not. December is his busiest time." I bit my lip to keep from grinning like a fool.

"Well, we'll just have to do a renewal ceremony in the spring, when he can make it."

He cut his broccoli with a precision I found adorable.

"Because I spoke to my lawyer today. She said if I married, then she could release another tranche of money, instead of me having to wait until I'm forty."

"So you just want to marry me to get hold of your money?"

"No!" He kicked my ankle. "It's a side benefit, though."

"We don't need the money." I was adamant about this. I made a decent salary with excellent benefits. After a time, Adam had opened his books to me. He wasn't in dire straits, but his budget was tight. "We'll be fine."

"But I want to make a donation to the hospital. And I

want to hire Simeon to fix up the attic room upstairs. The way you suggested."

My brow furrowed. Slowly, I remembered the conversation we'd had in June, when he'd given me the full tour. How I'd suggested I'd fix up that room, if it were mine. "That's...an idea." I raised my fork. "Speaking of. I ran into Simeon in town the other day. I forgot to tell you. We were at the library at the same time, checking out books. He's been hired to do some project up at Healing Horses. Putting together some kind of modular home. I think..." I closed an eye, trying to remember his exact words. "For Kennedy's parents when they come to visit. They're moving up to 100 Mile House, I think. Her father's retiring from piloting. And her mother wants to commune with nature more."

Adam pointed out at our backyard. "There's plenty of nature in Mission City and the surrounding area."

"True. But there aren't eight daughters around the corner." I grinned. "I think the Dixon parents want a break."

"We have to invite Simeon to the wedding."

"And Everett." I grinned. "Because if either of us had found either of them attractive, then we wouldn't be getting married."

Could it really be that simple? Every day we said we loved each other—because we did—but marriage? Could I live in Adam's castle with him all the time? I blinked. "And...kids?"

Slowly, he shook his head. "I think babysitting for the twins, as well as Opal and Angus is enough. Dickens and Fritz don't have kids, and they're happy." Adam toyed with his food. "Loriana, the librarian, is trying to convince me to talk about fire safety. With Finn, one of the firefighters she knows."

My breath caught. The kind of vulnerability he'd have to show for that was breathtaking. "And you're thinking about it?"

"Yeah." He drew in another breath. "And my agent called.

She said she knows a photographer who's doing an exhibit. Not of the macabre, she maintains, but something artistic."

"That's..." I reached out to grasp his hand again—this time needing the connection for myself.

"Wrong?"

"No." I said the word abruptly. "If women who've had mastectomies can be brave and show their scars, how is this any different? You're not honoring Frederick, or your parents, if you continue to hide away. Have his death mean something. Share how a drunk driver took away your precious brother."

"I was drunk too, Dean. If not for me—"

"But you knew better than to drive. So the accident rests at the feet of the man who drove drunk. We had a parent come to our high school and talk to us about the son they'd lost to a drunk driver. That story impacted me. I've always been damn careful to never get drunk and get behind the wheel. There's nothing wrong with sharing your story. Of turning your pain into something that saves lives."

He poked his chicken. "This conversation...we've taken a dark turn. We should be celebrating our engagement. Because we are engaged, right...?"

I rose from my chair, then tugged him up into my arms. To my relief, he came willingly. "I love you. I'll always love you, okay? You're forever for me. And not just to hustle along my permanent-resident card."

"See, and here I thought this was all romantic and lovey-dovey." He nuzzled my neck. "You just want me so you can become a Canadian." He pulled back. "Are you going to miss your home? We can go back—"

"Yeah, we will. But for now, let's reheat our food. After dinner, I want to take a walk in the snow with you and Chip. I want to enjoy this cold weather." I placed a kiss to his lips. "I want to enjoy you."

He grinned. "Yeah, we can do that."

Later, as we snuggled under the comforter, we slowly came together in a way that was so familiar to both of us. Adam often claimed I'd *tamed the beast*. And perhaps he saw it that way—much to my annoyance.

To me, though, I'd shown the hurting man love. Taught him to love in return. And that, for us, was our happily ever after.

* * *

INTERESTED IN KNOWING MORE ABOUT SIMEON? HIS story is coming soon! Check out *Sleigh Bells and Second Chances* book 3 in the Love in Mission City series:

https://books2read.com/SleighBellsAndSecondChances

RYAN

The moment I landed in that war zone, I knew I'd made a big mistake. I wasn't a soldier, and my good intentions almost got me killed. Being wounded and shipped back home to Canada was both a blessing and a curse. I'm safe now, but I can't stop thinking of the men I left behind. My therapist claims Healing Horses Ranch will help heal my wounds— physical and mental—but I'm not sure how much tranquility and wholesome fresh air I can take. But then I meet a beautiful, shy man who makes moving forward seem almost possible. Can I let go of the past and reach for a future with Simeon?

SIMEON

I've made peace with being different from the folks around me. I love my home in Mission City, and if anyone needs something fixed, I'm the guy they call. When the owner of the therapy ranch hires me for a big project, I'm excited to get started. I always work alone, but one of the patients keeps hanging around, and I can't bear to send him on his way. I can see how much he's hurting. If helping me helps him, that's a win for us both. As we share the work, something about that wounded man draws me deeper and deeper in. I'm no therapist, and I have my own issues, so am I a fool to be thinking about a future with a guy who's likely to leave once he's healed?

Sleigh Bells and Second Chances is a slow-burn, age-gap, hurt/comfort, mid-angst, gay romance novel with a shy handyman, a reckless former gamer, a precocious borrowed kid, and a therapy dog named Tiffany.

Want more Gabbi Grey?

Check out her *Love in Mission City* series, set in beautiful British Columbia.
The first book is Maddox and Ravi's Story!
Ginger Snapping All the Way (Love in Mission City Book 1)
The second book is Justin and Stanley's Story!
Stanley's Christmas Redemption (Love in Mission City Book 2)
Davey and Tex's story (*Fly Guy Boyfriend*) is in:
Love in Mission City: The Boyfriends Duet
Dickens and Spike's story (*Page Against the Machine*) is in:
Love in Mission City: The Shorts

ALSO AVAILABLE

Ace's Place (free)
Axe to Grind
Grindstone's Edge
Hugh (Single Dads of Gaynor Beach)

Anthony (Single Dads of Gaynor Beach)
Xavier (Single Dads of Gaynor Beach)
Love Furever (Friends of Gaynor Beach Animal Rescue)
Husky Love (Friends of Gaynor Beach Animal Rescue)
My Past, Your Future
If Only for Today
Catch a Tiger by the Tail
Solstice Surprise (free)
Valentino in Vancouver
You See Me
Love Without Reservations
An Uncommon Gentleman
Caressa's Homecoming (Bound by Love Book 1)

AUDIOBOOKS

Ginger Snapping All the Way
Stanley's Christmas Redemption
Love in Mission City: The Shorts
Page Against the Machine
The Lightkeeper's Love Affair
Ace's Place
Marcus's Cadence
Not in it for the Money
My Past, Your Future
If Only for Today
Catch a Tiger by the Tail
Solstice Surprise
An Uncommon Gentleman

* * *

Want a free short story? The story is set in Gaynor Beach,

California where there are plenty of single dads and puppy rescues! You can sign up for my newsletter so you can keep up with all the great stuff I'm doing as well as pictures of my own pooches, Ally and Finnegan.

Hemingway's Happy Day

Interested in knowing more about Gabbi?

Sign up for her newsletter
Follow her on Bookbub
Follow her on Instagram

USA Today Bestselling author Gabbi Grey lives in beautiful British Columbia where her fur baby chin-poo keeps her safe from the nasty neighborhood squirrels. Working for the government by day, she spends her early mornings writing contemporary, gay, sweet, and dark erotic BDSM romances. While she firmly believes in happy endings, she also believes in making her characters suffer before finding their true love. She also writes m/f romances as Gabbi Black and Gabbi Powell.

www.ingramcontent.com/pod-product-compliance
Lightning Source LLC
Chambersburg PA
CBHW031549240626
47153CB00002B/444